21.95

A SAGA OF TEXAS:

UNTIL SHADOWS FALL

A Western Story

Other Five Star Titles by Will Cook:

The Rain Tree
A Saga of Texas: Until Day Breaks

A SAGA OF TEXAS:
UNTIL SHADOWS FALL

Will Cook

Five Star
Unity, Maine

Five Star Western

Published in conjunction with Golden West Literary Agency.

Cover photograph by Johnny D. Boggs

March, 2000
First Edition

Five Star Standard Print Western Series.

The text of this edition is unabridged.

Set in 11 pt. Plantin by Rick Gundberg.

Printed in the United States on permanent paper.

Library of Congress Cataloging-in-Publication Data

Cook, Will.
    Until shadows fall / by Will Cook. — 1st ed.
    p.   cm. — (Five Star standard print western series) (A saga of Texas ; 2)
    "Published in conjunction with Golden West Literary Agency" — T.p. verso.
    A saga of Texas was originally published as a number of separate works which included Comanche captives, later reprinted as Two rode together.
    ISBN 0-7862-1847-9 (hc : alk. paper)
    1. Frontier and pioneer life — Texas — Fiction. I. Title.
II. Series.
PS3553.O5547 U55   2000
    813′.54—dc21   99-055127

*Resting here until day breaks and shadows fall
and darkness disappears.*
from the gravestone of Quanah Parker

Editor's Note

A serial version of part of this historical saga appeared in *The Saturday Evening Post* under the title "Comanche Captives." A motion picture version derived from this magazine serial was produced by Columbia Pictures in 1961 under the title TWO RODE TOGETHER. The serial version differed significantly from the original paperback edition published by Bantam Books under the title COMANCHE CAPTIVES and later reprinted under the title TWO RODE TOGETHER. It was the author's agent who proposed breaking this entire saga, of which "Comanche Captives" was only a part, into a number of disparate books. These parts have now been restored to form one book in three volumes based upon the author's own typescript, so that A SAGA OF TEXAS as Will Cook originally wrote it may at last appear in print for the first time.

PART ONE

1874

Chapter One

Since his election as sheriff of Oldham County, Texas, Guthrie McCabe set his hour of rising for eight and rarely varied it. Some people considered this lazy and swore that, when election time came around, they would throw their vote to a more industrious man. McCabe lived in the hotel, second floor, third door on the right, facing Tascosa's wind-brushed street. There was a small upper gallery just off his room, and each morning he would stand there for a time, looking at his town, his adobe-mud town with its eternal dust and eternal wind to shift it about and a near constant sun to keep everything beneath it properly roasted.

Beyond, southward, stretched Texas with its bigness and rivers, and the *Llano Estacado*, the Staked Plains, the flat, lifeless scar of land with moaning winds and scant water. A place where a man could lose himself or find himself, if that were his purpose. This was Guthrie McCabe's country—his because he wore a badge and ruled it with his rules, invented as necessity arose or thrown away or broken if expedience dictated.

After his look came a careful shave, the knotting of his tie, the buckling on of his big pistol and finally his badge, his authority for all to see. McCabe was a big man, even for Texas, who liked her sons tall and hard. Without his boots he stood six foot one. With them he was much taller, for he was just vain enough to wear the two-inch Mexican "spikes," un-

9

dercut so much that he seemed to walk a-teeter on his insteps. His face was like a cocoa bean, a brown that went deeper than a surface tan. The eternal wind had eroded lines around his eyes, which had nothing to do with his thirty-four years. There was no mark of worry or care on his face. He had brown hair and a full mustache, curled at the ends. Sideburns came to the hinges of his jaw and were trimmed daily to blade sharpness. Although his job required only occasional riding, Guthrie McCabe was never without his spurs, full Mexican rowels, four inches in diameter. They dragged with each step, scuffing floors, making a bell-like jangle that announced his approach.

He took his breakfasts in the hotel dining room at eight-thirty, and the Mexican waiter knew exactly what to bring, for Guthrie McCabe's habits were definitely established in Tascosa. He never hurried at the table, and, afterward, he put a match to a short Mexican cigar. While he took this brief pleasure one morning, he saw a small cavalry patrol pace the length of the street, then pass on to dismount at the stable near the street's end.

The hotel clerk came through the dining room, gathered McCabe's dishes, and took them into the kitchen. He dumped them a-clatter into the sink, then paused at McCabe's table on the way back. "Wonder what the cavalry wants this time?" the clerk said.

McCabe lifted his glance briefly, then worked the cigar to the opposite corner of his mouth before speaking. "Go down the street and ask the lieutenant and, when you find out, come back and tell me."

"Too hot," the clerk said. "You ever see such heat? Ain't it ever going to rain?"

"In September?" McCabe scraped back his chair, then walked out through the lobby.

10

A glittering sun bounced a-dazzle from the tawny street and turned the adobe walls of the buildings to gold. McCabe watched the cavalry detail farther down. The officer in charge detached himself and walked back toward the hotel, saber in hand to keep it from flogging his leg. He was a young man, twenty-six or -seven, and already hardened by a tour of frontier duty. His hair was blond, ragged beneath his battered campaign hat, and the solitary first lieutenant's bars sewn into his shoulder boxes were faded and frayed by innumerable launderings.

When he stopped at the porch edge, he took off his hat and grinned. "What is it, McCabe? Ninety in the shade?" The lieutenant needed a shave, and dust lay heavy in the creases of his clothing. "Trade you jobs."

"Army pay is poor," McCabe said. "How's Fort Elliot?"

"Dull, hot, and dusty," the lieutenant said. He swiveled his head around and looked up and down the street. A few horses stood idle by the hitch rack in front of the saloon, and, farther down, a freight wagon was making up for the run to Red River Springs. "You don't have it much better." He twisted his yellow neckerchief around and wiped sweat from his face. The dust in the cloth left muddy streaks from temple to neck.

"You want a bath?" McCabe asked.

The lieutenant's manner brightened. "At any price." Then he let his pleasure fade. "No, it wouldn't look right, Guthrie. I mean, me showing up shaved and bathed while my men stayed itching-dirty." He put his hat back on and pulled the sweatband down to his eyebrows. "What kind of a mood you in this morning, Guthrie?"

McCabe shrugged. "Jim, does it really matter much?" He squinted at Jim Gary. "Did you ride all the way here to see me?"

11

"Partly," Jim Gary said. "Can I buy you a drink, Guthrie? I've been thinking of a beer all the way in from Spindly Creek."

"Nothing in town but hot slop," McCabe said. "Not fit to drink."

"The men will appreciate it anyway," Gary said. He frogged his saber high, then stripped off his gauntlets. Sweat had soaked through the leather and darkened the backs of the fingers. "The colonel wants you to come to Fort Elliot, Guthrie." He did not look at McCabe when he said it, but, after it was said, Gary raised his eyes to study him.

McCabe said: "Can't that man take no for an answer?"

"Doesn't seem like it, does it?" Gary smiled. "We'll leave tonight and travel while it's cooler."

"*If* I go." McCabe looked down the street at the waiting detail. "Well, now," he said, "you brought some help, huh?"

"If you think I'll need it," Gary said. "Sorry, Guthrie, but the invitation is official."

McCabe remained thoughtfully silent for a moment, then laughed. "Gary, it's going to be a long ride for nothing, but I might as well go and get it over with for good."

"Thought you might see it that way. You'll have supper with me? Good." He slapped McCabe across the stomach with his gloves, then walked down the street to his waiting troopers.

McCabe spent the day idling around town, and in the evening he went to the stable and saw that his horse was saddled, his gear properly stowed. Then he walked back to Tascosa's main street and found Gary in a small Mexican restaurant, sitting with Sergeant O'Reilly and Corporal Buskin, at a table near the door.

When Gary saw McCabe, he pushed back a chair so McCabe could sit down.

"You know O'Reilly and Buskin?" Gary asked.

"How are you?" McCabe asked absently, not expecting an answer. He sat down. "Too late for me to order something?"

"No," Gary said, and signaled the cook, who had a plate ready. The two enlisted men were through eating and murmured their excuses before leaving. The cook brought a plate of chili beans and tortillas, and McCabe began to eat.

Gary studied him for a moment, then said: "Are you going to turn the old man down again?"

"In person this time," McCabe said.

"Why?"

"Because this is Army business. Let the Army handle it."

"It's been my observation," Gary said, "that the Comanches, particularly Iron Hand, would rather do business with a civilian than a soldier. Every time he sees dirty-shirt blue he remembers a lot of his dead friends." He reached into his pocket for a key-winder watch, glanced at it, then leaned back in his chair. "We'll leave in thirty minutes. That suit you?"

"I'm easily satisfied."

Gary frowned. "Are you, Guthrie?"

McCabe looked at him. "What's that supposed to mean?"

By rising, Gary ducked the question. He was standing on the sidewalk, enjoying his cigar, a habit he had acquired after serving under General Tracy Cameron, when McCabe came out of the restaurant. O'Reilly was putting the detail together down the street, inspecting it, finding fault, seeing that all flaws were corrected.

"Is the Army going to put the Comanches on reservation?" Guthrie McCabe asked.

Gary turned and looked at him. "No, I haven't heard anything about it. Why?"

"They ought to. Indians ruin a country. They make people nervous just by being around. The counties south of here could be full of ranches and farms if the Comanches were on reservation. Jim, people just won't believe that an Indian is peaceful, treaty or not."

"You figure it that way?"

"I figure what's best for Guthrie McCabe." He looked at O'Reilly and found him standing at the head of the waiting detail. One of the troopers had gone to the stable for McCabe's horse. When the trooper returned, he ducked under the hitch rail and stepped into the saddle. "You coming, Jim?"

"Sure," Gary said, and mounted. The cavalry detail formed a small group. Gary gave the hand signal that turned them, and they left Tascosa, taking the road south, McCabe and Gary in the lead.

Twilight gave the plain a purple immensity, and the grasses nodded to the day's last breeze. Even though the sun died, heat radiated from the ground as though some fire had been banked there, and the wind dwindled to a hot, feeble breath, as though someone had shut a door, closing off the draft. The wind would stay down until the day's heat left the earth, then it would spring up again, bringing with it all those wild flavors of uninterrupted miles.

The column stopped every two hours and dismounted on the hour to walk the horses. Canteens came out, with a popping of corks and gurgling. There was no other sound, and the slightest noise seem magnified for a moment before it was lost in the vastness.

There was little talk until they reached Squaw Creek, when Lieutenant Gary ordered a twenty-minute stopover to refill the canteens and water the animals. Guthrie McCabe lit a cigar and squatted by the creek. The heat was dying off, leaving perspiration salty on his skin, leaving him unpleasantly gamy. Around him swirled the thick aroma of nitrogen and the sweetness of cut-plug chewing tobacco and the strong skunk-odor of bodies unbathed for three weeks.

When the men were at ease and Gary was satisfied as to their comfort, he came over to McCabe and hunkered down.

"You fuss too much," McCabe said.

Jim Gary grinned. "I'd argue that point with you."

"It's my opinion. But every man shoes a horse differently, Jim."

"True. You know, when I was at the Academy, a colonel gave us a lecture on leadership, and he never said a word. He just cut a ten-foot length of rope and laid it on the floor. Then he took the hind end and tried to push it. When that didn't work, he walked around to the other end and pulled it. That's the way I want to handle men, Guthrie."

"I'm a pusher," McCabe said. "And up to now I've had no trouble making a man go."

"But the idea is to get him to go and like it." Gary laughed. "You don't care whether a man likes it or not, so what am I talking about? Let me have one of your good cigars."

"You ever try buying your own?" McCabe handed him one.

"Not on a lieutenant's pay. I've got two younger sisters to support."

"I didn't know that."

"Well, I don't talk much about it," Gary said. "My father was in the Army, too, you know. A sergeant major in B Company." He paused to light his cigar. "He was killed in battle. I was ten years old at the time. Cora and Alice were in pigtails."

McCabe said: "I had no idea you had it that tough."

"Not tough," Gary contradicted. "Just not easy, that's all. Relatives raised us . . . my mother's folks . . . on a farm in

Iowa. They died six years ago in an accident. The horse balked at a railroad crossing, and the Rock Island Limited hit them. We sold the farm. It gave Cora and Alice enough money to buy a place in town and leave a little in the bank. Since then I've been keeping twenty dollars for myself and sending sixty a month home." He chuckled. "Now you know why I don't buy nickel cigars."

"One of these days," Guthrie McCabe said, "they'll up and marry, and you'll never hear from them again. Then you'll wish you'd kept some of that money for your own pocket."

"No, I wouldn't wish that. I never expected to get it back." He twisted his lower body, trying to find a more comfortable position. "You have to do for your kin. They probably will get married one of these days, and then I can quit sending them money, but it's nice to know that they never really wanted for anything or had to take in washing to make a living."

McCabe sat in silence for a time, then he said: "Jim, why is it that all the good men are fools?"

"Meaning me?"

"Sure. You have to look out for yourself."

"That's a philosophy you get from being alone," Gary said.

"Alone?" McCabe laughed. "Jim, I've got eleven brothers and sisters . . . somewhere. You didn't know that, did you? Well, I never talk about it. They don't know I'm alive, and I don't know where they are." He fingered ash off the end of his cigar. "The old man was all prod and talk. When we moved across the country, things got tough. Mouths became hard to feed. He started kicking the boys out a hundred miles from Saint Joseph. The oldest was the first to go. Ma did a lot of crying over him, but a few hundred miles and six sons later she got used to it. He put me out of the wagon not more than

16

twenty miles from here. Ma never even looked around when they pulled away. There was a place on the prairie . . . I could see it, so I went there." He sighed. "A man takes what's easiest, Jim, so I took Anson Miles's cussedness for ten years. You took the Army."

Jim Gary shook his head. "There's a difference, Guthrie. I like the Army. It's what I want. What do you want?"

The tall Texan thought for a moment, then said: "I want to walk down the main street of any town in Texas and have people smile and tip their hats at me."

Gary raised his head suddenly and peered through the gloom at this man, cocked his ears to the voice, for he had never heard this tone before or suspected the drive behind this man's bland manner. "And when I speak," McCabe continued, "I want other men to stop talking and listen to what I have to say, and, when I'm through talking, I want them to jump and do what I want done." He swung his head around and looked at Jim Gary. "Maybe that's too blunt for you, or too big for you to understand."

Jim Gary searched his mind for an answer and found none. "Time to get going," he said, and stood up, brushing dust off the seat of his pants.

Gary signaled for the men to mount up, and they moved in the face of the southwest breeze that was freshening. At midnight the cavalry stopped for an hour's rest, and the troopers immediately stretched out for a quick nap. Jim Gary came in off the temporary picket line and sagged wearily beside McCabe. He folded his gauntlets and put them on top of his hat, making a pillow of the whole thing.

"How long," Gary asked, "since you've been out to Anson Miles's place?"

"A year. Maybe longer."

"His wife asked about you the last time I stopped there."

He looked at McCabe. "If a man was full of meanness and wanted to hurt a man, the easiest way to do it would be to take his wife away from him."

McCabe looked at him steadily. "You sure that's what you wanted to say, Jim?"

"No," Gary said after a pause. "It's none of my business. Sorry."

"Hate to see a man break one of his own rules," McCabe said, "and you've always been set on minding your own business. Now me, I mind everybody's business. I've lived twenty-three years in this part of the country. Know it like a book, every whoop and hollow from here to the Río Pecos. Know most of the Indians, too, over half of them by sight. I don't think there's been a white captive taken, killed off, traded, died, or married that I don't know about. Jim, I'm personally acquainted with every rancher, every badman, cow thief, gunslinger, preacher, widow, and virgin in this part of Texas, although I ought to add that I've reduced the number of the last considerably. To my mind there isn't a shod horse within eighty miles that I can't identify by track, tell you who owns him, or what stud sired him. I call the cattle by name, and the wind sings my song. Twenty-three years I've stood the damned heat and the dust and a lot of trouble to know all of these things, so when anyone wants anything from me, including your colonel, he has to pay for it. If that sounds tough, then just remember that every man has something to sell, and I never give anything away for free."

"You going to tell the colonel that?"

"Sure. How much is he offering for this job?"

Gary shook his head. "He didn't say. How high is your price?"

"A thousand dollars for every one I bring back," McCabe said. "Then, and only then, will I take the job."

Jim Gary thought about this, then said: "The Comanches and Kiowas have had many years of war in which to take women and children. Since they're the only Indians who keep slaves any more, it's natural to think that a lot of them would still be alive. Guthrie, you ought to see the camp outside the post. I'll bet there's thirty families there, all hollering for the Army to bring back the lost, strayed, or stolen. Your price is a little high, seems to me."

"It's the value I place on my services," McCabe said. "You're free to get someone else to go into Comanche country, Jim."

"There isn't anybody who knows what you know."

"Then don't quibble about the price. Look, Jim, I got kicked off a wagon and landed here broke. Anson Miles gave me a hand-out, and that's the way it's been, one hand-out after another until I got smart and began listening and learning and nosing around. Folks began to learn that if you wanted to know a thing, ask the McCabe kid. I've got that kind of a mind, Jim. Pick things up easy and hang onto what I learn."

"You're a hard, practical man," Gary said. "Suppose the colonel goes your price and you bring back twenty or thirty captives. What are you going to do with the money?"

"Buy something," McCabe said vaguely. "Something I've wanted for a long time." He laughed. "You ever hear the saying that money can't buy happiness? It's true, but it'll certainly make misery more comfortable."

Sergeant O'Reilly came around, and Jim Gary got to his feet. Corporal Buskin was having the mounts brought in from the picket line, and the detail formed quickly. The talk between Gary and McCabe seemed ended, yet the silence was unsettled, like the quiet after an argument when both parties expect to resume it more feverishly.

Chapter Two

Through the cool of night and the gauze grayness of early dawn they pushed on. In the east, a streak of light marked the horizon, and then the first orange rays of the sun washed across the flats. In the distance, a little over a mile, Anson Miles's house was plainly visible, a high, three-storied salt-box house with ridiculous gables and scrimshaw work, a thirteen-room monument to bad taste and misspent money sitting alone and weathered on a barren plain. This was a landmark, and it reared, ugly and uncompromising, against the horizon.

"A big house for one man and one woman," Gary said softly. "When I get his age, I want people around me."

"He's got hired hands," McCabe said. He looked sharply at Gary. "Do you think I owe him anything? I worked double for everything he gave me."

"Don't we all?" Gary asked.

When they were several hundred yards away, a dog charged toward them, yapping and showing his teeth. He ran between the horses, causing two to crow-hop. One of the troopers took his carbine by the barrel and cracked the animal solidly across the rump as he dodged about. Surprised and somewhat pained, the dog tucked its tail between its legs and scooted for the shelter of the house.

Anson Miles hobbled out as McCabe and the cavalry dismounted before the broad porch. Miles was a man in his early sixties, unshaven, unwashed, foul of temper and manner now that he was permanently lamed. His wife came to the doorway. A much younger woman, she could easily have passed for his daughter. She shielded the glare of the sun from her eyes with a flattened hand.

"Which of you buggers hit my dog?" Miles wanted to know. He was a small man with a small man's belligerence; he acted as though he were being put upon continually. Miles's face was not unhandsome, yet he wore the pinched expression so common among people who nurse dissatisfaction with living.

"Could we have some water?" Jim Gary asked, keeping his voice pleasant. He looked past Miles, then swept off his hat. "The heat bothering you, Missus Miles?"

"I pay it no mind. It vexes Anson, though."

"I'll live through it," Miles snapped. He flung an arm toward the creek near the barns. "It's nigh dry now. You might as well finish it."

"You'll get rain in another month," Gary said. He dismounted and motioned for Sergeant O'Reilly to take the detail on.

"You said that the last time you was here," Miles said. Then he looked at McCabe. "I don't see much of you any more."

"My own business keeps me busy," McCabe said.

The cavalry was near the big barn, and Miles heard the barn door open. "Damn them soldiers! If they're in my feed bin again . . . !" He stomped off the porch and darted around the house.

Gary slapped his gloves against his thigh and said: "I'd better look into this. Can I take care of your horse, Guthrie?"

"Thank you," McCabe said. As soon as Gary left, he stepped out of the bake-oven heat and into the shade of the porch. When he looked at Carrie Miles, he let his glance soften. She was a shapely woman in her late twenties. Her hair was dark and long, and she liked to wear combs in it to bind it tightly, holding it away from her neck. "I'd like to ask you in," she said. "But you know how Anson feels about you."

"It's all right."

"No, it's not all right." She paused a moment. "I don't get to see anyone out here."

McCabe spoke softly. "Then I should stop by more often."

This pleased her; a flush came into her cheeks. She patted her hair, then smoothed her plain dress. "He doesn't take me to town any more. I guess he thinks I'd run away if he did."

"Do you think of that?" McCabe smiled. "You don't have any money. You wouldn't get any farther than Tascosa. And if he came to town after you and dragged you home, the shame of it would kill you."

"One of these days," she said softly, "the need will be bigger than the shame."

"Find a man. Then you won't have to wait. A man would answer for you, Carrie." He saw Gary approaching and moved to the edge of the porch.

"I'm ready," Gary said.

"All right. In a minute." McCabe waited, and finally Gary walked away again. When he was out of earshot, McCabe said: "I expect Anson goes into town on Saturday and comes back the next Monday?"

"Yes, but only once a month. It'll be three weeks now before he goes again."

McCabe did not look at her but off in the distance. "Be something to look forward to, won't it? Likely my stay at Fort Elliot won't be long. I ought to be passing through here about then."

Gary was already mounted and shooting impatient glances toward the porch. McCabe walked across the interval to the barn and stepped into the saddle. Miles said nothing, and, after thanking him again for the water, Gary turned out, heading the detail.

Fort Elliot lay to the east, a five-hour ride, and Gary took care not to march too rapidly in the heat. They raised the fort before noon, and O'Reilly dismissed the detail and tended the horses while McCabe went to headquarters with Jim Gary. There was not much activity on the post. The heat was oppressive, and only the detail men who had duty moved about. McCabe was surprised at the number of civilians. They clustered about the sutler's place, men, women, some children. They seemed to be waiting for time to pass.

Gary took McCabe's arm and ushered him into the front office. An orderly saluted, then knocked on Colonel Frazer's door. There was a murmur of talk, then the orderly stepped back so they could enter.

McKay Frazer was a man grown old in the service. His hair was shot with gray, and the arid manner of his living seemed to have shrunk him. His arms were thin, and flesh hung in wrinkled folds beneath his chin. He wore a full mustache, the ends upsweeping grandly. Frazer's face was like sun-baked clay, with myriad cracks that ran into each other and recrossed endlessly. His nose was an arch of cartilage, curving, ending in wide nostrils. His eyes were matching agates sheltered in deep sockets and screened by gray, bushy eyebrows.

"Sit down, McCabe." He opened a box of cigars and offered one to each of them. "I'll try to make the long ride worthwhile." Frazer struck a match on the underside of his desk, then leaned forward so both men could take a light. "Did you see the civilian camp near the south gate?"

23

"No," McCabe said. "But there were quite a few on the post."

"They come in for supplies," Colonel Frazer said. "It's good business for the sutler, but hell on the commanding officer." He tipped back his chair. "Most of those people have been out here before, McCabe. Some as far back as twenty years ago. And they all lost a part of their families to the raiding Comanches. Now that there's peace, they want to find the lost ones. They think it's an Army job to return them."

"It is," McCabe said.

McKay Frazer frowned. "We both know that it's a job the Army can't do. Not without trouble, and Washington won't stand for that. Peace came too dear."

"Send the civilians home then."

"No. They write letters, and Congressmen put pressure on the generals, and it all comes back to me." Frazer sighed. "We'll solve it right here, McCabe . . . at Fort Elliot. I need you, and I'll pay you chief scout's wages."

McCabe glanced at Gary who was studying the stitching in his gloves, and then looked at Frazer and smiled. "My price is a little higher, Colonel."

"All right. Perhaps I can stretch the point a little."

"About a thousand dollars a head for every captive I return?"

Blood mounted angrily in Frazer's face. It was a moment before he could speak. "McCabe, this is not a business venture, but a Christian service." He put his cigar into a glass dish. "Shall we consider your remark a bad joke, McCabe?"

"Consider it my lowest offer," McCabe said flatly. He leaned forward. "Colonel, if you take troops south into Comanche country, they'll think it's a violation of the treaty, and you'll have war again. You need a civilian, one who knows them and can come and go without losing his hair. Now, I set the price. You either meet it or not."

"The general would never allow me to spend that kind of money, and you know it!"

"You pay me chief scout's wages, then. I'll make up the balance from the civilians." He studied Frazer's anger, then laughed. "Colonel, don't let your temper get the best of you now. I'll admit my price is steep, but the service is big. I look at it this way . . . you need me badly, Colonel, or you wouldn't have offered this to me twice."

Frazer got up and turned his back to McCabe as though he could no longer bear to look at him. He stared out the window at the shimmering parade ground. "It's a pity," he said, "that we are forced to do business with those who disgust us the most. These civilians know that Lieutenant Gary went to fetch a man. Rumor got out and spread rapidly because it was something they wanted to believe . . . that you were a messiah come to deliver them." He spun around on his heel and stared at McCabe. "That, too, is a pity, that they'd put trust in a man like. . . ." He closed his mouth with a snap. "We'll keep this impersonal. Better that way. And as soon as the job is done, I can throw you off the post with a clear conscience." He waved his hand. "Find him suitable quarters, Gary. I don't mean in the guardhouse, although the thought delights me."

"A pleasure to do business with you," McCabe said, and followed Gary outside.

"I didn't think you'd do it," Gary said. "That's the truth, Guthrie. I thought you'd back down the last minute."

"I don't back down," McCabe said as they crossed the parade toward the officers' picket quarters. "You share the colonel's opinion?"

"Maybe. I've never had a chance to make a lot of money,

so I can't say what I'd do."

The quarters were no worse, no better than any occupied by the junior officers on the post. A small room, one cot, two chairs, a chest of drawers, a desk, and a closet, nothing more. McCabe looked around, then shrugged. "It's not the Palace Hotel in Denver, is it?"

"No. I'll have an orderly bring your blankets later. Do you want to see the civilian camp?"

"Why not?" McCabe said. He smiled. "Jim, tears won't shake my price."

"Tears?" He looked questioningly at him. "Guthrie, you've got it all wrong. They stopped crying a long time ago."

"Then why all the fuss to get their kin back? We both know that, after three or four years, a captive is free to leave when he wants to. Don't these people know that?"

Gary nodded. "They know it, but I guess they still had to come back. Some people have to do the right thing no matter what it costs them." He stepped onto the porch and walked toward the side gate, McCabe following him. "I'd keep out of Colonel Frazer's way, if I were you," Gary said. "He's got five months to go before retirement, and, if it weren't for preserving a good record, he'd throw the book at you."

"He wants a record, and I want money," McCabe said. "Show me the difference, Jim."

"Can't, because I want a few things myself. Not big things, though. I guess you'd say that I think small. It's a failing of mine."

The guard at the water gate brought his carbine to present arms, then passed Gary and McCabe through. The civilian camp was backed up to the creek, occupying the entire cottonwood grove. Tents, lean-to shelters, wagons, all crowded together in disorder as though someone had called a halt to all movement, and, wherever they were at the time, they stayed.

"How long have they been here?" McCabe asked.

"Some since the last rain, nearly four months ago."

"They ought to go home," McCabe said. "The country was too tough for them before, and it hasn't changed much." He stopped as a man walked toward them.

"That's Wringle. He's something of a leader here," Gary said. "Hello there, Mister Wringle." He shook hands while Wringle studied Guthrie McCabe.

"Is this the man we've waited for?" Wringle had a deep voice, and words rumbled in his chest. His clothes were blue overalls and a brown shirt, frayed at the collar and elbows.

"This is Guthrie McCabe," Jim Gary said. "He may take you into the country south of here."

"What's this?" McCabe asked. "Man, I go alone or not at all!"

"Well, I was supposed to explain that to you, Guthrie. I guess it slipped my mind. The colonel wants the grove cleared out, so he thought it would be all right if they all went south with you. There's good land there and. . . ."

McCabe took Gary by the arm and pulled him around to face him. "You knew this in Tascosa?"

"Like I said, it slipped my mind."

"It did like hell! Jim, if I'd have known this, I wouldn't have ridden with you."

"I know it. So I kept quiet about it." He made an appeal with his hands. "Is this asking too much? It'll save you considerable riding time back and forth. Last month I took a patrol south. There's a spring and timber about forty miles from here. They could camp there while you did your looking."

McCabe frowned. "I'll have to think about this." He turned his head and looked at the camp as though studying it, gauging the poverty of it, or its wealth.

"We've come a long way," Wringle said, "and suffered

many years of disappointment to be turned down now on a man's whim."

"Friend, my whim decides whether Iron Hand's Comanches give up their prisoners or not," McCabe said.

"That's right, Mister Wringle," Gary said. "Mister McCabe knows Iron Hand and can do business with him when no one else can."

Wringle thought about this for a moment, then said: "Seems funny to me that one man could be so friendly with. . . ."

"I used to sell whiskey to him," McCabe said, and watched the disapproval rise in Wringle's eyes. "You don't like that, Wringle?"

"Didn't say that." He looked at Gary. "It ain't for me to sit in judgment of a man . . . not when getting my boy back depends on him. You see, I lost my boy about twelve years ago on the way to El Paso. The heart sort of goes out of a man when that happens." He shrugged his beefy shoulders. "All I want is my boy back. Don't care how it's done or who does it."

"I didn't think you did," McCabe said. "Tell your people I'll drop over later tonight. We'll talk about this."

Wringle frowned, then asked: "What's there to talk about? You either go or you don't."

"You don't have the notion that I'll go for nothing, do you?" He took Gary by the arm. "Let's go get a drink." Gary opened his mouth to say something, then thought better of it and followed McCabe back to the water gate. As they stepped inside, Gary looked back at the civilian camp.

"Why did you tell him that lie? About selling whiskey to the Indians?"

"To prove that a man will sleep with the devil if it gets him what he wants. The sutler's whiskey any good?"

28

"No, but I've got a decent bottle in my dresser drawer," Gary said.

"It'd better be full," McCabe said, and cut across the parade.

In his room, Gary set up the glasses and poured. When McCabe had his drink, Gary said: "Guthrie, you don't give a damn whether people like you or not, do you?"

"No. Should I?"

"It's a natural thing for a man to want. Are you going to take them south?"

McCabe shrugged. "After tonight I'll know." He drank his whiskey and set the glass down. "After tonight I'll know if they have any money or not."

"Comes back to that, does it?" Gary sat down on the edge of his bunk. "You want a lot of money. Can a man ask why?"

For a moment it seemed that McCabe was not going to answer. Then he said: "Anson Miles owes nine years of back taxes on his place. I want to buy it."

"That eyesore?"

"All in the point of view," McCabe said. "You ever been inside the place? Well, the hall opens into a big room with the ceiling three stories high, with carved beams and four chandeliers hanging from gold chains. There are tapestries on the walls and polished marble floors. He built it for his first wife nearly thirty years ago. Then the war broke him. She died, and he shut up the house, all except two rooms near the front." McCabe looked steadily at Jim Gary. "When I get that place, I'm going to light all the lamps and open the doors and hire an orchestra and invite everyone just to see what it can be like alive instead of a tomb." He poured from the bottle again. "All the time I lived there, I couldn't touch anything. It was like living in a castle and yet never being allowed off the floor. Does that make sense to you, Jim? To want something just because you want it?" He laughed uneasily. "Maybe, after I get 'it, I'll find that I never wanted it at all."

"That was my thought," Gary said. "I don't think it'll pay you back for all the years you lived under Anson's foot."

"Might be that way. It just might be."

"Then it would be for nothing."

"No," McCabe said. "I'll put a match to the place and have the biggest bonfire in Texas." He raised his glass. "This is good whiskey, Jim. It sort of evens it out for the cigars."

"That's a funny thing to say."

"Is it? I guess I'm naturally suspicious of any man who doesn't indulge himself in something." McCabe smiled. "But now I won't have to be, will I?" He chuckled. "What's the frown for, Jim?"

"Just trying to figure out how much in you is good and how much is bad. Right now it seems important that I know," Gary said.

"When you find that out about any man," Guthrie McCabe said, "then tell me, because it wouldn't be fair just to have one smart man in the world."

Chapter Three

The invitation to have supper with Colonel Frazer took Jim Gary completely by surprise. He barely had time to shave and change into a clean uniform before it was time to dine. In the back of Gary's mind always lay the hope that someday he would advance to this rank and occupy a big house with three enlisted servants and live graciously, or as graciously as one could under frontier conditions. This occurred to him again as he was ushered into the colonel's parlor and handed a glass of sherry.

"Short notice, I know," Frazer said, "but I'm glad you could come, Gary."

"It was kind of you to invite me, sir."

"Have a chair. Try that leather one. I think you'll find it comfortable." Frazer sat down across from Gary. "Somehow a good sherry is made better by company." He put his glass aside. "I suppose McCabe is at the camp pinching purses."

"He told them he'd speak to them this evening, sir."

Frazer drummed his fingers for a moment. "I hate a man like McCabe, always after something more than he has." He sighed heavily. "Well, in a few more months I'll be out of this, Gary. With luck, I'll retire a brigadier." He studied Jim Gary from beneath the thicket of his brows. "How long have you been in grade?"

"Nearly four years, sir."

"Where do you stand on the list?"

"Twelfth, I think."

Frazer nodded solemnly. "That'll mean another year at least, Gary. Seems a shame. You're a good officer with a lot of promise."

"That's very flattering, sir."

"It's the truth. That's why I said it. I rarely flatter a man just to be doing it. Care for some more wine? No? I think I'll have some. A good wine always adds something just before a meal. We have damned few graces on the frontier. You didn't know my wife, did you?"

"No, sir. It was never my pleasure."

"A good woman," Frazer said. "She took the heat and the discomfort for twenty-seven years, God bless her, and I never once heard her complain, although she had reason to." He smiled. "Is there a woman some place for you, Gary?"

"No, sir. There was a time when I thought there was, but. . . . well, she ultimately decided that she couldn't accept the sort of life she would have to live on the frontier. We came very, very close to marriage, but it just didn't happen for us, after all."

"I'm sorry to hear that. It's a lonely life without a woman, Gary. You best find one." He waved his hand. "There ought to be someone in the civilian camp, some pretty girl no one has noticed."

"I'll have to look, sir."

"You do that. Consider it an order." Frazer drank some of the wine. "Ticklish business, this trying to locate lost relatives. As a final assignment to cap off a clean career, I can think of things more preferential. And this man, McCabe, will make trouble. A thousand dollars a head!" Frazer snorted briefly. "If I had more time, I'd send him packing and find another man.

You've known him for some time, haven't you, Gary?"

"Yes, a few years."

"Strange," Frazer said. "I mean, you and McCabe being friends. One man by training and instinct a gentleman, a man of honor, and the other a profiteer of the lowest sort, a man obviously with neither honor nor conscience." He shook his head. "There's an old saying about strange bedfellows, Gary. Most apt in this case."

"McCabe has always been honest with me, sir."

"Has he? Wait until he wants something from you. No, I must tolerate him, but I'll never trust him. That's why I'm placing you on detached duty, Gary. You'll go into the Comanche stronghold with him . . . out of uniform, of course." Frazer finished the wine and pushed bottle and glass aside. "Gary, I'll be frank with you. The general has given me a difficult assignment, and, if I want to go out a brigadier, I'll have to complete it without trouble. Do you think I'll enjoy a decent night's sleep until McCabe leaves my province? I'm sure I won't. But it will ease my mind if I know you're there, to take over in the event he gets out of hand. Gary, I can pull some weight in Washington, and I can have you set up on the promotional list. This isn't a promise, mind you, but a strong possibility exists that you'd make captain within three months . . . six, on the outside." He leaned back and folded his hands. "I'm sorry to rush you like this, but there isn't much time. I'll need an answer tonight."

"Just what is it you want me to do, sir?"

"Keep McCabe from exploiting those people."

"How can I do that, sir? He's a strong man who does what he wants. When he was elected sheriff, the county wasn't fit to live in, with rustlers getting fat and toughs running the town. McCabe cleaned them out in three months. He's that kind."

"You're a resourceful young man, Gary. Think of a way. I'll give McCabe chief scout's pay, but not a cent more. The job will be done at my price, Gary, and that's final."

"Colonel, I thought you agreed. . . ."

"With a rogue like McCabe?" Frazer laughed and got up from his chair. "I believe dinner is served, Gary. Come along, and don't let your conscience trouble you where a man like McCabe is concerned." He took Jim Gary by the arm. "You've got a career to think of. A captaincy now will mean a majority before you're forty. What does McCabe matter when you think of that?"

"I guess it doesn't matter," Gary said, and sat down at the table, his manner grave and troubled. The soup was excellent, yet he ate mechanically, thinking about the things McCabe had said to him, about all men wanting something, wanting it badly enough to push aside all else to get it. And in that moment, Gary understood why he had tolerated the man. They were not dissimilar at all, except in method, and there McCabe was perhaps the more honest, for he never hid his desires, even from himself.

Later, Gary left the colonel's quarters and walked across the dark parade to the water gate. He stood there for a time, watching the fires from the civilian camp. On impulse he walked over.

A woman sat before the fire, shelling peas. She looked up as Gary stopped, then said: "The men are gone. There's a meeting at Wringle's fire."

"I know about that," Gary said. He started to turn to move on, then decided not to and stood there, watching the peas drop into the pan on her lap.

"There's some coffee left if you want some. The cups are in that chest over there." She pointed, and Gary helped himself, conscious of her inspection. He placed her age as early twenties, but he wasn't sure about this, for hard work and sun had darkened her skin and brought small wrinkles to the corners of her eyes.

"Your husband at the meeting?" he asked.

"My father and brother," she said. "Sit down if you want. I'm Jane Donovan." She squinted at his shoulder boxes; the fire did not give off much light. "You're an officer?"

"Lieutenant Gary. I'll be going with you, if McCabe goes."

"A lot depends on this man, doesn't it?"

"He knows the country and Iron Hand. Not many white men does Iron Hand call friend." He sat down on the wooden box and cradled the tin cup between his hands. He could see her face better now, oval, framed in dark hair. She had a long, straight nose and nice eyes, appraising, frank. He did not resent her open study of him nor was he made nervous by it.

"You brought this man to us, didn't you? McCabe, I mean."

"Yes," Gary said.

"We're in your debt," Jane Donovan said. She put down the pan of peas and poured some coffee for herself. "It's my brother we seek. He was two when we lost him, nearly ten years ago. If he'd been killed instead of taken, I guess we could have accepted it. But it was my job to care for him, and, when the Indians came, I ran and hid."

"How old were you . . . ten?"

"Eleven," she said. "I shouldn't have run. It's not a easy thing to live with . . . to know that it's your fault . . . a thing like this happening."

"And if you hadn't run," Gary said, "you'd be some buck's wife now, with a couple of half-breed kids."

35

"That would still have been better than this," Jane Donovan said.

"You don't know," Gary told her. "I've been in the villages, and I've seen captives, dozens of them. The women would rather be dead than go back. Do you know what it would be like, being pointed to, talked about, singled out, blamed for something you couldn't help?" He shook his head. "Be glad you ran and hid."

He turned his head as two men came out of the gloom and stepped up to the fire. Both were tall, bearded, and the older of the two stared at Jim Gary.

"You from the Army? I don't want soldiers around here."

"This is Lieutenant Gary, Pa," Jane Donovan said. "My pa, Sean Donovan . . . and my brother, Liam."

Gary acknowledged the introductions, and, before he could say anything else, Sean Donovan spoke. "This fella McCabe is taking us south. Leave day after tomorrow."

"Lieutenant Gary is going, also," Jane said.

Her father and brother looked intently at him. "Was my understanding," Sean Donovan said, "that the Army couldn't go into Comanche territory without stirring up a ruckus."

"I won't be in uniform," Gary said. He stood up. "Perhaps I'd better say good night."

"No need to," Donovan said. "I didn't mean to sound unfriendly, but with a single woman. . . ." He let the rest drop. "Sit down, unless you're in a hurry." He put his hand on Gary's shoulder and pressed him back. "Fine fella, McCabe, giving his time like that for folks he don't even know. There ought to be some way to pay a man back for his trouble."

"Didn't you talk about that?" Gary asked.

"It never came out in the talk," Donovan said. "Did it, Liam?"

"Nope."

"It's a good feeling the way folks will help a man when he's got troubles." Donovan shook his head sadly. "A man's dreams and hopes are pretty fragile, Gary. They get smashed all-fired easy. We sold out in Iowa ten years ago and bought land here. After the lad was taken, we never went on . . . never saw that land again. Had to sell it. Had to buy again in Iowa, too. That's enough right there to break a man, Gary. And on top of it, she's got to grieve." He reached out and put his hand on Jane's head. "I've been telling her every day that it wasn't really her fault, but I guess that don't do any good when you feel different inside."

Gary watched her carefully, observing the sudden tightness of her lips. Suddenly she pulled from beneath her father's hand and walked rapidly to the nearby trees.

Sean Donovan's expression was one of hurt. "Wish she wouldn't do that. Running away from a thing don't solve it."

"You went back to Iowa," Gary said softly.

"That's different," Donovan said.

"I suppose it is," Gary said, getting up again. He thought about going over to the trees and speaking to Jane Donovan, then decided not to. Cutting away from the fire, he walked toward the wagon park, stopping at another camp.

For nearly two hours he moved about, listening to the talk, hearing the same thing over and over again, about how much they had lost and why they had turned back instead of going on. He was touched by their talk and irritated at the same time, for they had all been defeated a long time ago, and had lived with it for years. There wasn't a teaspoon of hope in the lot of them, just excuses and reasons that sounded good to no one but themselves.

Finally he left the camp and went back to the post, going to Guthrie McCabe's room. The tall Texan was stretched out on his bed, patiently cleaning the grit from the bore of his pistol. He turned his head when Gary knocked, then motioned toward the chair.

"Been out to the grove, huh?

"Yes," Gary said. "I'm going with you, Guthrie."

"Good. I can use the company."

"Donovan thinks you're the patron saint. A lot of them think that way." Gary dropped his hat to the floor and crossed his legs. "I wonder if they'd feel the same way if they knew you'd put a price tag on the deal. Why didn't you say anything about that, Guthrie?"

"You ever trade horses?"

"Sure."

"Then you ought to know that price is the last thing you talk about." He swung his feet to the floor and reassembled his revolver, then loaded it, and slipped it into his holster, which hung on a wall peg. "Jim, after I look around a bit and turn up someone, then I'll talk about price." He looked squarely at Jim Gary. "The old man send you along to keep tabs on me?"

"He didn't say that exactly."

Guthrie McCabe laughed. "Don't play poker, Jim. You're a poor liar." He took out some sack tobacco, rolled a cigarette, and passed the makings over to Jim Gary. "I wish you wouldn't be such a do-gooder. It makes me nervous." He accepted a light, then leaned back against the wall. "What did you think of the pack living at the grove, Jim?"

"They're good people."

"They're rubbish," McCabe said flatly. "Cowards, quitters, failures. Something tough happens to them and they fold in the middle and run back home where it's safe."

"A pretty harsh judgment for such short notice," Gary said.

"I'm right, and you know it."

"Sure," Gary said. "You're right, but I'll be damned if I want to talk about it." He sounded angry. "I can look at the town drunk without sermonizing. Be a good idea if you did the same. What these people are is no concern of yours. How can you live among people when you don't respect them, or even like them?"

"Because they don't matter to me, that's how. The trouble with you, Jim, is that you try to do everyone a favor. One of these days, when the cards are down and the bets are made, you'll find out that the only one worth looking after is yourself. To hell with the other guy."

"McCabe, you're honest about it, I'll say that much." Gary took a final pull on his cigarette, then got up to throw it out the door. "If you're so busy taking care of yourself, how come you ran for sheriff? Isn't that buying someone else's trouble?"

"No. If someone had tried to clean up the county, I'd never have run for office. But someone had to do it, and I did it for myself. Let me tell you something. If you and I were in a tough spot together and it was run or die, I wouldn't hang back to save you. Not if it meant my own neck I wouldn't."

"I'd try to save you."

"And I'd call you a fool for it."

"And I wouldn't believe you," Jim Gary said. "Guthrie, there must be two hundred people in the grove. For every four, there's a relative lost. How many do you think you can bring back?"

McCabe shrugged.

"Ten?"

"Maybe ten." He looked intently at Gary. "What do you want me to do . . . go out there and tell them that their sisters and daughters are squaws now with Comanche kids? Or that their sons and brothers are Comanche warriors who've raided and killed? Go on, you're the do-gooder. You go and tell them."

"You're the tough one," Gary pointed out. "Why didn't you tell them?"

"Because they wouldn't believe it," McCabe said. "Not after farming a broken-down section and saving their money to come back and look. Jim, it's a shame that people care so much. It would be a lot better for everyone if they cared less, and stayed home."

"You're working yourself up to a boil," Gary said, smiling. "I thought you didn't give a damn."

"I don't. If I did, I'd go back to Tascosa and sit with my feet on the desk. That dumb deputy of mine probably has everything messed up by now." He rose and walked to the door to stand. Someone came across the parade ground and onto the porch. Gary caught a glimpse of skirts and recognized Jane Donovan's voice when she spoke.

"Mister McCabe?"

"Yes."

She looked into the room and saw Gary. He stood quickly, then came to the door. "Won't you come in?" he asked.

"No," she said. From a pocket in her apron she produced a tintype. "This isn't a very good picture, Mister McCabe, and he was very young when it was taken, but it's all I have." She handed it to him. "I've been saving it, thinking that it might help, but it's been ten years, and I don't suppose he would even speak English. He could only say a few words and. . . ."

Jim Gary took her arm. "Perhaps I'd better walk you back to the grove."

"No, it's kind of you to offer, but I'll be all right." She turned then and hurried across the parade, and Guthrie McCabe watched her for a moment. When he turned back into the room, he kicked the chest of drawers solidly.

Jim Gary said: "Kind of gets you, doesn't it? I mean hanging onto so thin a hope all these years."

"Damn' fools! They're all blind fools who can't understand that there isn't any hope." He tossed the picture on the bed, not looking at it. "I don't know what they're thinking, Jim. Probably that all I have to do is ride into Iron Hand's village and tell him to cough up the prisoners. There must be twenty villages between here and the Río Bravo and, if I do find someone, getting them back won't be easy. They just won't want to come back." He blew out a ragged breath. "I should have stayed in Tascosa."

"Maybe they'll see it after we camp south of here," Gary said. "Like you say, they're not hard to discourage. They went back home once. They might do it again."

"That's a thin hope. For twenty years Texans have been fighting Comanches, hoping that someday there would be peace. Look at it now, just a big mess to paw over and try to clean up. During the war there was an officer in charge of graves and burial, and I used to watch him go around after the battle, poking around the dead, going through their pockets, trying to identify them. His sleeves would get bloody, and he'd get mud on his pants from kneeling, and I used to think then that it would be a hell of a lot better if they just buried them where they lay and forgot about it." He waved his arms. "Prisoners are traded and killed, and they die. It'll be like combing a dog for fleas, then trying to match up the parents with the children. And what about the years in between, Jim? All those years of living like an Indian? Thinking like an Indian? What do they do when they've been reunited? Take him back to Iowa or Indiana and let people stare at him because he eats with his fingers and farts at the table?" He slapped his hands together and sat down. "She brings me a picture! A god-damned picture taken when he was two years old and hopes I can see the resemblance ten years later."

"Give it up, then."

McCabe shook his head. "No, there's been too much giving up in that camp. Would you give it up, Jim?"

"I might because I'm not as tough as you. I'm the kind who cries at funerals."

"You'll never learn," McCabe said, "but then, with some people, it's just as well." He took out his watch and wound it. "I figured we could move out day after tomorrow. They can pack up and be ready to leave by tomorrow night." He put the watch back in his pocket

Jim Gary picked up his hat and turned to the door. He paused there and said: "I'd have tried to tell them the truth about how hopeless this all is. I'd try because I'm soft, and I can feel sorry for them. Maybe you're doing them a favor, Guthrie. I mean taking them back to where it all began and rubbing their noses in it for one final time. But I don't know. There ought to be an easier, a kinder way."

"There is. I could go back to Tascosa and leave them standing there." He sat down and took off his boots. "But there's no profit in that. For them or for me."

"Yes, I guess it all boils down to that when all's said and done," Gary said. "I'll see you in the morning." He stepped out and walked rapidly down the walk toward his own quarters.

Chapter Four

Gary had a letter to write to his sisters next morning. Then he changed out of his uniform, rolled what gear he would need, and carried this to the stable, along with his rifle. The sergeant would see that his horse was saddled and that everything was stowed. He spent the remainder of the day in the grove, helping the families get ready to move in the morning.

The farrier sergeant checked their stock, and Colonel Frazer detailed C Company to help them with their wagons and buggies and buckboards. One man drove a brewery wagon, the barrel racks removed so he could carry his possessions. At four in the afternoon an orderly summoned Gary to the office of the commanding officer. Guthrie McCabe was there, his chair tipped back against the wall. Frazer maintained an unfriendly silence until Gary closed the door.

"Take the other chair, Lieutenant." He rustled some papers, stuffed others in a dispatch case, and handed it to Gary. "Here is the list of missing, classified as to name, age, when taken, and any physical description . . . hair, eyes, scars, or marks. I want a thorough check run on anyone returned by Mister McCabe."

"Yes, sir."

McCabe cleared his throat. "Which brings us to the trading goods. I thought I'd better mention it."

"What trade goods?" Frazer asked.

"Well, you don't expect them to give up a slave just because I ask them to, do you? I'll have to dicker a little, offer a trade. That's what I mean, trade goods. Something to exchange."

"I could have sent anyone down there to trade," Frazer said. "McCabe, I wanted you because we could dispense with that nonsense."

"Not nonsense to the Comanches," McCabe said. "No trade goods, no prisoners. I suggest you load two wagons from the sutler's and take them along. This is just another little expense you're going to have to absorb, Colonel."

"I'm afraid he's right, sir," Gary said. "Shall I attend to it?"

"Yes," Frazer said. "But in a few minutes. That will be all, Mister McCabe." He waited until the Texan went out, waited until the door closed and his footfalls had receded. "Take an inventory of the trade goods, Lieutenant, and keep accurate records. I don't want anything to find its way into a Tascosa hardware store."

"Yes, sir."

"And there's one more thing. When someone has been recovered, to the best of your ability make certain that he is returned to the proper family. God knows I don't want someone to say later that we pawned off someone else's kin."

"That might be difficult to establish, sir."

"Difficult? Likely it will approach the impossible, but this whole thing is impossible, a political move to make the voters happy."

"Will that be all, sir?"

"Yes, and the best of luck. You'll be in a country rarely frequented by white men, and you'll be dealing with basically hostile forces, regardless of the treaty. On top of that you'll have to ride herd on a group of people who were never meant to live here, and you'll have to keep your eye on that thief with a sheriff's badge." Frazer spread his hands. "A captaincy comes hard, Gary, but I'm sure you'll earn it."

They shook hands briefly, and Gary left the building. McCabe had gone back to the civilian camp, so Gary had two wagons brought to the sutler's place and began to select trade goods. He and three enlisted men loaded tools, blankets, bright cloth, beads, trinkets, and two cases of worn-out military rifles. Gary was smart enough to select mainly the things a woman would want, for he knew that any buck who lost a slave would soon have to replace her with a wife, and that would take trinkets.

That evening the sound of music and laughter from the grove drew his attention. They always had been a solemn lot, and these sounds seemed out of place, alien to them. He left the post and walked to the creek, stopping at the Donovan wagon. Sean and Liam were sampling a jug while Jane sat on the food box and tapped her foot to the saw of violin and the wheeze of a small accordion.

"Not dancing?" Gary asked. He spoke to Sean Donovan, but his eyes sought the girl.

"The night's young," Donovan said, and offered the jug. "Good to be leaving tomorrow. A man thinks of something for a long time, and then it comes to pass. You've been south. What's the country like?"

"Brush, hills. Water's scarce, though. It'll populate now that the treaty's been signed. Land can lay for a long time, then someone who won't take no for an answer puts up a mud hut. The next thing you know, you got a town."

"I like that," Sean Donovan said. He tapped his son on the arm. "Let's go see where the fun is." He looked sternly at Jim Gary. "You keep good company with my girl . . . you hear?"

He stomped off, followed by his son, and, when they were

45

gone, Jane said: "He embarrasses me sometimes."

"No need to be," Gary said. "You don't mind my being here?"

"I'm glad you came," she said. "How long have you been in the Army?"

"Over five years."

"Always out here?"

"Most of it."

"It must be lonely for you," she said.

"Yes, it is, but a man can't have everything. You see, I always wanted to be one of those men who forged ahead, found new horizons, but I've never had the courage to do it alone. In the Army, with men around, acting under orders, I can do those things without fear of failure. You might say it's a combined strength. The Army holds me up a little, and I like to think I help to hold it up."

She looked at him quite frankly. "Doesn't it bother you to admit that?"

"No. Should it?"

Her shoulders rose and fell slightly. "It's something I'd want to keep for myself, something I'd be ashamed of." She was silent, then: "Lieutenant . . . ?"

"Jim. I wish you'd call me that."

"All right, if you like. Jim, I hope Mister McCabe doesn't find my brother. I hope he's dead." She put her hands over her face and rubbed her eyes. "That was a terrible thing to say, but I've been thinking it a long time, so I decided to say it. It's not easy to say and harder to keep thinking, but I'm not strong enough to live around him and have him know that I once deserted him when he was helpless."

"How many in the grove stuck by when the Indians attacked them? How many of them carry some secret loathing within them, Jane? How many do you think blame themselves for something that couldn't have been avoided?"

"I don't know, but, even if they all felt that way, it wouldn't help me." She got up and pushed the blackened coffee pot nearer the fire. Then she turned and looked squarely at him. "Jim, haven't you ever done anything you've been ashamed of? Haven't you ever wanted something you knew you had no right in having?"

"Sure, but I always got over it." From his pocket he took a cigar and bit off the end before taking a twig from the fire for his light. "Jane, suppose McCabe is lucky. Suppose he finds your brother. What then? I mean what will you do? Go back to Iowa?"

"I suppose. The farm is all we have, and Pa spent the last ten years working his fingers to the bone, paying for it." She got two cups out of the wooden locker and filled them with coffee. When she handed him his cup, she asked: "Is it important what we do?"

"It would be to your brother. No one is really going to understand or make allowances, not even here in Texas. It'll be much worse in Iowa."

"We never thought of that. You ought to talk to Pa about it." She sat down across from him and folded her hands in her lap. "You think we're wrong, coming here now that there's peace, don't you?"

"Yes, it was a mistake. With good intentions, but a mistake. You did your crying once. Why do it again?"

"Because a thing isn't really done until it's finished," she said. "And until we know whether or not he's dead, it never will be finished."

"I understand," Gary said softly. "When I was a kid, I remember this preacher who came into the saloon every night to deliver his sermon against drink. Every night the boys threw him out, but he came back. Nothing could stop him,

Jane. It was like he had a disease that only dying could cure."
He finished his coffee and threw the grounds into the fire.
"It's late, and we have an early start in the morning. Good
night."

"Good night," she said, and watched him turn away.
"Jim!"

He stopped, looked back.

"Jim, you don't like us very much, do you?"

His frown was only momentary. "I never thought of it that
way," he said. "Perhaps you could say that I don't understand why, since you found failure and heartbreak once, you
would subject yourself to it again."

"Then you don't hold much hope that we'll find our kin?"

"I'm afraid I don't." He tipped his hat and walked rapidly
back to the post. As he passed through the water gate, he saw
the courier arrive from Tascosa, mail pouches swollen. Perhaps there was something there from his sisters. He started
toward headquarters to check the mail, then changed his
mind, and went to his room. If there was anything, Sergeant
O'Reilly would pick it up.

His window was bright with lamplight, and Gary opened
the door. McCabe was on the bunk, reading. He put the book
aside when Gary hung up his hat and pistol.

"I thought you'd be at the whoop-up," Gary said.

"Later," McCabe said. "There's some pretty fair-looking
women in that camp." He patted his pockets for a cigar,
found one, and tipped the lamp toward him for a light. "I
think we ought to have a little talk, Jim. About how it's going
to be when we get into Comanche country." He thumped
himself on the chest. "It's going to have to be my way, the way
I say, and no arguments."

"I'm not going along to argue with you, Guthrie."

"Sure, sure, but you wear that soldier suit and the colonel

48

gives you orders that I don't know anything about, and you're the kind who obeys orders." He looked steadily at Jim Gary. "Don't buck me, Jim. I won't stand for it."

"Then you play it straight," Gary said.

McCabe gave him a look of complete innocence. "Why, sure. What did you think?"

"I'm saving that for the time when you tell them that Guthrie McCabe never works for free."

A smile built on McCabe's face, then he laughed. "I never charge more than the traffic will bear. That's why I get so few complaints. I charge high, but a man gets his money's worth with McCabe." He got up from the bunk, the book still in hand. He glanced at the title, then tossed it on the chest. "You understand that stuff? Hell, I can't even pronounce his name . . . G-o-e-t-h-e."

He walked out, and Jim Gary closed the door, sliding the bolt. The brooding, forbidding presence of Guthrie McCabe remained in the room, along with the aroma of his cigar. This disturbed Gary. He was a little in awe of McCabe, and a little afraid, for the man seemed to reach out and squeeze, and afterward nothing was the same. There was a tremendous capacity for good in the man, and a latent talent for evil, and in Gary's mind he could never quite separate the two.

He thought it strange that he could go through life with all good intentions, yet actually accomplish very little that was materially good. Gary did his job with exactitude, and a certain amount of imagination, and, when the job was finished, the edges were smooth, the details taken care of, but the mark remaining was never very lasting nor very deep. McCabe, on the other hand, cared little for good intentions, and never entertained them, yet he left a wide path for a man to see, leaving in his wake something of a mess. Yet much of value came out of the things McCabe did. He was a builder, a rough, fast-working, self-centered builder, building for himself, working for himself, but the litter remaining was of great value to others.

Like McCabe and Iron Hand. It had been worth a man's life to travel south into the Comanche stronghold. Some who tried never came back. Then McCabe hit on the idea of trading with the Comanches. They'd run down wild horses, and McCabe would trade for them. Most men said it couldn't be done, but McCabe did it. He made a lot of money and broke a few local horse ranchers in the process, but Gary knew that McCabe had broken the trail for other traders, and that trail widened soon into a full peace negotiation with Iron Hand and the United States Army.

Running for sheriff had been an entirely selfish move on McCabe's part. He'd been rustled and didn't like it, and, when no one else would do anything about it, he did it for himself. Some said that he could be bought, and Gary halfway believed it. But for all that, he did clean out the country so that it could grow.

Settling down for the night, Jim Gary thought it strange that he could respect and resent a man at the same time. He was in awe of McCabe, and afraid of him. He admired and disliked him simultaneously.

I've got to get over this, Gary told himself. *I've got to live with him for a while, so I've just got to get over this. Damn it, I'm my own man!*

Chapter Five

A day south of Fort Elliot the land began to change, opening into gullies and rising to low ridges that made traveling more difficult with wagons. The first night they camped on the flats near Joe Sutro's place. This was the last white habitation for nearly eighty miles. Some of the travelers talked with Sutro and stared at his graveyard. A wife and nine children were buried there, all killed by Comanches during the raids to drive him away.

Gary had supper with Sutro. He liked the withered, rawhide-tough little man. The meal was simple—some sowbelly and beans and coffee strong enough to float a railroad spike. Sutro believed that coffee ought to be a meal unto itself.

"Surprised to see you with this bunch," Sutro said. "The Army ain't often given to foolishness." He filled his mouth with beans and chewed rapidly; he had only four front teeth left. "How far you taking them?"

"Sand Creek," Gary said. "McCabe will go on alone from there."

"McCabe?" Sutro put his knife and fork down. "I didn't see him." He grunted once and began eating again. "Don't want McCabe around here. The sooner he moves on, the happier I'll be." He looked at Gary and grinned. "Nothin' personal, you understand, but I traded horses with him once. He talks too good, and I persuade too easy. Trouble is, I need McCabe, but I don't know how to tell him without lettin' myself wide open to a slick deal." He pushed the tin plate away from him and hunched around in his chair. "A month ago I lost some saddle stock. Couldn't afford to lose 'em, either. A dozen horses represent a lot of money. Some of Iron Hand's bunch stole 'em, but I'll be damned if I'll risk my hair to go after 'em."

"You want McCabe to do it?"

"He could, if he would," Joe Sutro said. "Likely his price'll be high."

"I'll see what I can do," Gary promised. He finished what was left of his meal and walked over to where the wagons were parked. He asked at three different fires for McCabe, but no one knew where he was. Gary turned to the Donovan wagon, parked on the other side of the camp.

Jane was alone, washing the pots left over from supper. "Have you seen McCabe?" Gary asked.

"No. Is there something wrong?"

"I just can't find him, that's all." He put his hands in his pockets and rocked back and forth on his heels. "Don't you ever stop working? I mean, every time I come around here, you're busy." He observed her a moment longer, then reached down and took the wet cloth from her and kicked the dishwater into the fire. "Let's go for a walk, Jane."

Her eyes were round and surprised. "I can't."

"Sure you can." He took her arm and started her away from the steaming fire. "Out there the grass is talking and the night is black and the earth smells good. I want you to listen to the sounds and feel the darkness like a touch against your skin." He started to walk, and she held back slightly, then gave in to his whim and walked beside him.

"Pa'll be roaring mad," she said.

"Let him be mad. I'll stand up to him if I have to." She seemed willing to let him have his way, and he wondered whether or not he should relax his grip on her arm. He was reluctant to do so, for her flesh felt warm to his touch, and he had almost forgotten how soft a woman was.

When the camp was a little distance behind them, they both paused and turned to each other. Jane caught her breath and seemed about to speak, then hesitated.

Gary said: "What is it, Jane? I have the feeling you want to ask me something."

She laughed softly. "I do . . . but I'm afraid you'll think it impertinent."

"Try me."

"Well, I've been wondering why someone as nice as you has never married?"

He grinned at her. "That is a bit impertinent, but I guess I'll tell you anyway. The answer is . . . I almost did a few years ago. Her name was Elizabeth Rishel, and I fancied myself totally devoted at the time." He paused a moment.

"What happened?"

"In retrospect, I can see now that it was lucky for us both she was honest enough to admit that she simply couldn't face a life on the frontier. It really does take a special kind of woman to put up with the hardships of living with a career Army man in the West."

Jane was silent for a time, then she said: "Well, I suppose it would depend on how much the woman really loved the man, wouldn't it?"

As though by mutual agreement, they turned and continued walking together into the soft, fragrant night.

Fifty yards from the camp, Gary stopped.

"What's the matter?" she asked, then gasped when a man reared up from the knee-high grass.

Guthrie McCabe reholstered his pistol as they came toward him. He said: "I thought fifty yards was far enough.

Maybe I should have made it a hundred and fifty." He peered at Jim Gary. "You had a lot of other directions to take to do your courting. Why pick this one?"

"An accident," Gary said. "I've been looking for you, Guthrie."

"So? If I'd wanted to be found, I wouldn't be out here."

"Just why are you out here, Mister McCabe?" Jane asked. "I'd think you'd want to be around people. Do you like it alone?"

"McCabe's afraid to have friends," Gary said, half joking, then realized that he had inadvertently hit upon the truth, for McCabe stared at him rudely, then sat down.

"You're here. You might as well stay a while. What did you want, Jim?"

Gary took off his coat, so that Jane wouldn't have to sit on the ground. "I was talking with Joe Sutro. He's lost some horses."

"And he wants me to find them?" McCabe asked. "All right. Tell him I'll do it."

Gary did not try to hide his surprise. "No hitch, Guthrie?"

"Sure, but one Sutro wouldn't care about." He waved his hand to the south. "In three days I'll be leaving you, going into Iron Hand's country. But I've got to have a reason, one he'll buy. Joe Sutro's horses will do nicely. After I move around from village to village, looking for the horses, I'll have some idea of how tough this job is going to be, and who's left to bring back, or who'd be fool enough to come back." He laughed. "I was figuring to run some stock south as soon as we camped permanently on Sand Creek. Sutro's saved me the trouble."

"Mister McCabe, why is it that no one likes you?" Jane's question was so pointed, so blunt, that he could only look at her, his mouth slightly open.

54

"That's a good question," Gary said. "I'd be interested in your answer, Guthrie." He waited for McCabe to speak. "Or maybe you don't care to give it." He got up and took Jane by the arm. "Let's go on back. He wants to be alone."

"Hold on a minute," McCabe said. "Sit down. Here, Jim, have a cigar." He scratched a match on his belt buckle, and, in the brief glare, Gary studied him. Then McCabe whipped out the match and broke it before throwing it into the grass. "Miss Donovan, you just stuck your nose into my business, and I've never liked that from anyone. But since you asked, I'll tell you why no one likes me. It's because I don't want them to like me. Does that make sense to you?"

"No," she said, "because it goes against human nature. You care, Mister McCabe. I know you care and, because you do, I wanted you to tell me why. You haven't, you know."

"Figure it out for yourself," McCabe said flatly. "I never give free hand-outs, and that applies to advice. The world's full of mean people and sad stories, and, if a man caught all the kicks that were aimed his way, or listened to the stories, he'd be aching or crying all his life. A friend always wants something, and I've never felt obligated to give. No one gives to me."

"Perhaps they would, if you'd let them," Jane said. She got up and handed Gary his coat. "I'd really better be getting back, Jim. If Pa and Liam found out I'd gone off . . . well, I'd just better get back."

"Of course," Gary said.

McCabe rose. "I'll walk back with you." He slung his coat over his shoulder and trailed them into the wagon park. As they approached the Donovan wagon, Gary saw Sean and Liam turn. There was a scowl on the old man's face.

"I'll have a word with you, Mister Gary!" He waved his hand. "Get in the wagon, girl."

"Pa, don't say anything! Not anything at all!"

"You want me to be silent?" He looked at Gary. "I spoke to you before, but it seems you ignored my advice."

"We went for a walk," Gary said. "I don't know what you can make of it, but it seems that you're going to try."

Sean Donovan took off his coat and laid it to one side. Then he rolled up his sleeves carefully and hitched up his pants. Gary stood there while the promise of trouble collected a crowd, and he wondered what he should do—talk or fight. Talk would make him look weak, and fighting would be something he'd have to answer for to the colonel.

"My daughter is a good girl, Gary, and a good girl has nothing but her good name, which is an easy thing to lose. Then she has nothing." He pushed his son aside. "Are you ready, Mister Gary? Or do you wish to strike the first blow?"

Jane put her hands over her mouth, then whirled to McCabe. "Can't you stop him?"

"What for?" McCabe asked. "This is Gary's ball."

Sean Donovan was not a man who liked to wait for anyone. When Gary just stood there, he lost patience and charged, arms working like a two-bladed windmill. One fist caught Gary alongside the head, then he side-stepped the rest and danced back, fists cocked, but making no attempt to strike. Drawn up short, Donovan whirled and came in again, and this time Gary tried to smother the flurry of fists, getting a cut lip for his trouble, and a smarting patch on the cheekbone. He heard McCabe say: "You going to dance with him or fight him, Jim?"

He was right, Gary knew, and he hit Sean Donovan, the blow a solid, axing drive that propelled him backward into the side of the wagon. In Gary's past was his share of barracks fighting. He knew the dirty tricks and had a gentleman's reluctance to use them. But when Donovan came at him,

56

spitting blood, Gary hooked into him, making him goggle-eyed.

Donovan was the heavier of the two, and he chose to wrestle, hugging Gary around the neck with a vise pressure, then flinging him over his hip to the ground. Donovan intended to fall with his weight on Gary's abdomen, but the young officer had seen that once before and swayed to one side, leaving Donovan nothing but hard ground to break his fall. Raising his arm up and over, then locking the fingers, Gary forced Donovan's head back until he could raise a leg and hook the back of the knee behind his chin.

With a surge of power he brought Donovan head down to the ground, then twisted and carried him over to land flat on his back. For several minutes the two men strained against each other, one to hold and the other to get free. Finally Donovan broke away, and they both came to their feet, more cautious now and more determined.

They drove together like two bulls in the first battle rush of spring, pawing, striking, grunting, cutting the earth with their boots, then Gary caught Donovan behind the knee with a leg chop and hooked him to the ground. He hit him, a dry-twig-breaking sound, and strength ran out of the Irishman.

Quickly Gary got to his feet and stood over Sean Donovan as the man tried to rise, but could not make it. Liam, his son, was at his side then.

"Pa! Get up, Pa!"

Donovan shook his head. "Can't. You finish this."

"I'll sure do that," Liam said, and started to peel off his coat.

When it was halfway down his arms, Jim Gary struck him, knocking him clear off his feet. Liam Donovan rolled twice and ended on his face and knees. He struggled to his feet, ripping free of the coat. He threw it aside while Jane jumped between them.

"No! Liam, no!" She grabbed his arms while she made an appeal to Guthrie McCabe. "He can't fight two in a row! Help him!"

McCabe rolled his cigar from one corner of his mouth to the other before speaking. "I make it a point to keep out of another man's fights."

Liam shoved his sister aside and went after Gary, who was more tired than he realized. Sean Donovan had mauled him, worn him down, sapped his young first strength, and his speed. The two men rammed together, and it was Gary who gave ground this time, backing quickly to keep out of Liam's way.

He went down once, but was hardly conscious of it. The young Irishman was like the wind, coming in, bowling him over, then retreating to strike from a new direction. Gary put up his fight, but it was not enough. Each second that passed seemed to take more out of him, and then he passed that point when he knew he could not possibly win this. Just stay as long as he could stand.

Blood ran from Gary's nose and his mouth and a cut over the eye, but he seemed numb, and, when Liam hit him, he did not feel pain, only the jar of the fist landing. Twice more he fell, and somehow he got up and was promptly knocked down again.

Then someone fired a gun, and he looked around to see who did it and saw Jane standing there with a cap-and-ball pistol in her hand, smoke issuing from the barrel and cylinder. Liam was by the fire, shirt in shreds, blood and a surprised expression on his face.

"That's enough!" Jane said, tears flashing in her eyes. She looked at the curious gathered around the fire. "Get out of here. Get!"

They moved when she flourished the pistol at them. Her

father was standing by the wagon, and Liam joined him. McCabe remained back a few paces. Then Jane put the pistol down and picked up the water bucket. Using her apron for a wash cloth, she bathed Jim Gary's face gently.

Finally he sat up and drew up his knees, resting his head on them. He felt sick and angry and sorry that he hadn't whipped Liam Donovan.

McCabe said: "You did all right while you lasted, Jim."

Gary remembered that he was there and swiveled his head around so that he could look at him. A new anger came to him, the anger of being let down, deserted, like that time when he was a boy, and a "friend" had agreed to help him beat up two other boys, then ran out and left Jim Gary to do it alone. Gary said: "Guthrie, you'd better hope the day never comes when you have to ask me for anything."

"You'll turn me down?" He shrugged casually. "What does it matter, anyway? I've never asked you for anything yet, have I? One way to look at this is that I did you a favor. You'd have had to fight both of them anyway . . . they're Irish. So a man might as well do it at one time and get it over with."

He turned then and walked back through the grass to his lonely camp. Gary stared after him for a moment, then murmured: "A man doesn't know what to believe, whether he was lying to cover himself or telling the brutal truth." He looked at Jane Donovan then as though he expected to read the answer in her face.

She only helped him to his feet.

Chapter Six

In the week it took to establish a permanent camp at Sand Creek, Lieutenant Jim Gary began to know and understand the people he was forced to live with. Timber was handy, and water, and they began to build cabins, to establish themselves with permanence. He was positive of this when Clyde Twokerry faced Hank Swilling with a rifle and ordered him off his "property."

Guthrie McCabe was gone, with a pack horse and trinkets. He intended to scout the Comanche villages to the south and east in search of Sutro's horses. Jim Gary was in charge of the camp. Unlike the many movers he had known, these people stayed to themselves, bound by their clans, their families, their selfishness. There was very little "hand lending." They shifted for themselves.

The Twokerrys were from Minnesota—the old man, Clyde, his three boys, a talkative wife, and two young girls, the older in the first full bloom of womanhood. They had lost two, a boy and a girl, and, after talking to Twokerry, Jim Gary came to the conclusion that he wanted them back not because he loved them, but because they were his and they had been taken from him. Twokerry was a man who disliked losing things to other people, whether it be a pocket knife or a child.

Burchauer was from Illinois. He spoke broken English, and his wife spoke none at all. They had three children, nearly grown, but they spoke only of the one who was gone, and ignored the three they still had. Next to them, the McCandless family erected a crude shelter, and, of all the people there at the creek, Jim Gary felt most sorry for Mrs. McCandless. The tragedy years before had robbed her of her reason, and she would sit in the sun for hours and sing to herself, and her children would have to feed her and take care of her every need.

McCabe failed to return on the tenth day, and Jim Gary began to worry, not about McCabe, but about the people in the camp. They were an impatient, restless lot. Gary tried to reason with them, to explain that this would take time, perhaps many months, but they did not believe him, for it was something they did not want to hear. Several offered ultimatums. If McCabe did not return in five more days, they would go into the Comanche country themselves.

He had to take a stand, and he did not want to, for this gave them something solid to buck, something to vent their disappointment and anxieties against. The Twokerry boy, Ralph, was the one Jim Gary watched, for Twokerry was the pusher, and Ralph had just enough of the old man's antagonism in him to be the first to try to override authority.

McCabe still did not return, and time was running thin for Jim Gary. He knew this when Ralph Twokerry selected the best of the horses from their small stock, packed his bedroll, and prepared to leave the camp. Everyone else seemed content to stand by and see how this would go, and Gary dared not fail, for, if Twokerry got out of camp, they would all go, trampling him in the process.

Twokerry turned this into a game, bringing his horse to the edge of the camp and picketing him there. He intended to wait for the hour, the exact moment of his father's deadline, then to leave whether Gary liked it or not. Gary studied Ralph Twokerry, trying to decide how to handle him. Twokerry was young, in his early twenties, and the immensity of the land seemed to open the tap to his native wildness. He wore a pistol in a holster that had been pared of excess leather, and Jim Gary speculated on how good he might be. Certainly the will to use the pistol was there. The only thing that troubled Gary was the man's possible skill. If it were poor, he might succeed in disarming him, knocking him down with his fists; that would end this germ of rebellion. But if Ralph Twokerry could shoot, and chose to shoot, Gary was not at all certain of what he would do.

Five o'clock. That was about the time. Jim Gary left his own camp and walked over to where Twokerry stood by his horse. People began to gather, standing silently to watch.

Twenty yards separated the men when Jim Gary spoke. "Take your horse back, Twokerry. You're not leaving."

"Yes, I am." He reached down and yanked the picket pin. "All you Army men know is to hurry up and wait. My pa told you, Gary. We're through waiting."

"You know I have to stop you," Gary said flatly. "Twokerry, if I let you go, how could I hold the rest?"

Twokerry shrugged and put his hand on the butt of his pistol. "Kind of looks like that's your worry, soldier boy." He grinned. "And a lot depends on how far you're prepared to go to stop me."

"I thought I'd wait to see how bad you wanted to leave."

"Pa said to go," Twokerry said, "and I'm going." He drew his revolver and cocked it. "Now, step aside, soldier boy."

This was, Gary decided, no different from the time that drunken corporal had thrown down on him at Fort Laramie. He flipped to one side and hit the ground, rolling. Twokerry's bullet nipped into the dirt inches from his face, then Gary had the flap of his holster unbuttoned and was jerking his own gun free.

He shot to wing Twokerry, but the man had crouched down and fired again, and Gary's bullet took him flush in the breastbone, knocking him flat. Twokerry lay there kicking, gagging, staring with his eyes all white as though they were inverted in their sockets. With a cry, his father rushed toward him and flung himself down and lifted his son. Then, suddenly, he dropped the boy and snatched up the .44. He aimed it at Jim Gary and fired, but Gary rolled twice, came up with his elbows braced, both hands steadying the gun, and broke Clyde Twokerry's shoulder with one shot.

The echo of the shots dwindled to a flat, breathless silence. Gary was surrounded by a sea of shocked faces. They had not believed this could happen, could still not believe it. This was a hard, uncompromising discipline, the Army kind, unapproachable, beyond argument.

Slowly Gary got to his feet and reholstered his pistol. He stood there and faced them. "Go back to your wagons. Germaine, you give Twokerry a hand. Get that bullet out of him if you can." He singled out two more men. "Put Ralph in a blanket. We'll bury him after supper."

The man gave him a hard-eyed stare. "I expect you'll read over him. You killed him."

"I will," Gary said. "Now you listen, you people. McCabe said to stay at the creek until he came back. So you'll stay. The Army is doing all it can to see that your kin are recovered. And as a representative of the Army, I'll go by Army orders."

"You didn't need to kill him," one woman said. "Ain't there been enough death and heartache among us?"

"The decision was mine," Gary said. "I was the one he shot at."

He turned then to leave them, to be alone with the sickness he felt rising, but this was not to be. His path was blocked by Jane Donovan, her father, and brother. There was censure in Sean Donovan's eyes, but he could not read any in Jane's, which gave him some small comfort.

"I wish he hadn't pulled his gun," Gary said. "The last thing I wanted to do was to shoot anyone."

"A bitter thing," Sean Donovan said, "that a man should have to die because he was a little foolish."

Gary pushed past him and walked on. Then he realized that Jane was trotting to keep up. When they were out of ear-shot, she said: "I'm sorry for you, Jim. Sorry you didn't handle it differently."

He stopped and faced her. "How would you have done it?"

"I don't know, but there must have been another way. I'm sure you know that and are wondering why you didn't try it." She took off her bonnet and shook out her hair. It fell past her shoulders in waves that caught the light. "Do you mind if I talk, Jim?" He shook his head. "I don't think Twokerry or his boy ever dreamed that there'd be shooting over this. Back home, where all of us come from, we're not really punished for our mistakes, and I don't think we develop a proper re-spect for the severity of consequences. The first time, when we came through this country, we made mistakes, and we lost something, a life here and there, and for the ones who turned back it broke us. Broke us inside. I know it did me, and Pa. We could never accept it as a consequence of something we had done, or failed to do. So we've spent years asking our-selves how it could possibly have happened to us, or what we had done to deserve it. Poor Twokerry. The tragedy of it all was that he never knew what he was doing when he told Ralph to go. Couldn't you have told him, Jim? Told him of the con-sequences?" Then she shook her head. "No, of course, you couldn't. I don't suppose anyone could have made him be-lieve what he never wanted to believe. Jim, what's going to happen to us? How many of us are going to die out here?"

"I don't know, Jane. Some. Some always do." He found a cigar and lit it with hands that trembled slightly. He took a long pull on his cigar. "Since I've been on the frontier, I've seen a lot of movers. Jane, I've worked hard to keep them alive! I've talked and begged and advised and threatened, and it hasn't done much good. They've gone on and made their mistakes and died because of them." His voice contained bitterness and a genuine regret. "I've tried all my life to do what was right. You know what would have happened to Ralph Twokerry if he'd left camp and gone into Iron Hand's country? They'd have caught him and killed him. So I had to stop him. I killed him to stop him! Sure, I'm a do-gooder, and I end up doing no good at all. The harder I try, the less I accomplish." He took another pull on his cigar. "I'd like to be like Guthrie McCabe . . . hard, not caring about anything. He's the last man in the world you'd expect anything from, yet he's done more good for Texas than any man I know."

"Don't be like McCabe," she said. "Don't be hurt and lonely and afraid. Be warm, Jim. Warm enough to care and cry a little, and to keep on trying."

"Thanks," he said. "I guess I can't do anything else, can I?"

She drew his attention onto the flats by pointing. "Who's that out there? No, a little south and east. There! Is that McCabe?"

"I wish I had my binoculars," he said. They stood there in silence for ten minutes, then Gary said: "It is McCabe. Come on, we'll go and meet him."

They walked for nearly a mile, then stopped, and let Guthrie McCabe come the rest of the way. He was a man bearing the mark of many miles traveled. His beard was heavy and dust lay in the creases of his clothes. Dismounting, he stamped his feet to restore the circulation.

Then he said: "Did you kill that fellow, Jim?" He laughed when Gary's mouth dropped open. "Oh, I saw it all through my field glasses. Came as a surprise, because I didn't think you had the sand to stand up to a gun. I'd have let him go."

"And let the Comanches get him?"

McCabe shrugged. "It's what he wanted, wasn't it? Then there was the off chance that he'd have smartened up a little and learned how to live cold, to do his traveling at night, and not leave a trace of where he had been." He shook his head sadly, like a father trying to push the lessons of life through his offspring's thick skull. "Jim, when you ever going to learn to let a man do what he wants to do? That fellow would have run up against his stone wall. Every man does, sooner or later."

"You ever hit yours?" Jane asked.

He looked at her, then smiled. "Girl, you've got your heart set on picking on me, haven't you? Do I fascinate you or something that you've got to keep prying and poking?" He looked at Gary then. "I suppose shooting was the best. Least-ways, you won't have anyone bucking you now. They'll be too scared to try."

"You took your own good time out there," Gary said. "The Army paying you by the hour or something?"

"A lot of country to cover," McCabe said. "And then, Sutro's horses have been swapped, strayed, and stolen three or four times." He arched his back to remove a kink; several small bones popped. "Iron Hand and I had a long talk. He's going to try to get the horses back, and I'm to take in a lot of trinkets. I gave him my word that this was as far as the movers would come, and he seemed satisfied."

"The devil with Sutro's horses," Gary snapped. "Did you see anyone in the camps who was white?"

"Oh, a few. Maybe four." He scratched his whiskers.

66

"There was a boy in Lame Bear's camp. Somewhere near fourteen, I'd judge, but it's hard to tell. Then east of there, a day's ride, I saw this girl, eleven or twelve. Pretty yellow hair and gray eyes and wild as a deer. Be hell to bring her back."

"We'll start in the morning," Jim Gary said.

"Whoa, now! I'll go, but you stay here."

"We both go," Gary said flatly. "McCabe, I won't argue about it. I can leave Wringle in charge here. But this is a two-man job and you know it."

"I like to work alone," McCabe said. "Another man always complicates something that's basically simple."

"Not this time. It's settled."

"All right," McCabe said. "But get it straight, Jim. If you get into a tight one, don't expect me to pull you out."

"Don't waste your worry. I know where we stand and so do you."

McCabe pursed his lips. "Then be ready to leave before dawn." He started to step into the saddle, then paused. "Let me have that list of missing kin you've got."

"It's in my dispatch case. What do you want it for?"

"Why, I've got to do some matching up, don't I? And when I do, then it'll be time to talk about money."

"Just what do you mean?" Jane asked him.

"How much money has your old man got with him?"

"About nine hundred dollars," she said. "If it's any of your business."

"Well, if I find a young man that fits your brother's description, you're going to find out that nine hundred is my fee for bringing him out alive and unharmed." He eased into the saddle and rode on toward the camp.

Jane Donovan turned to follow him with her eyes. Without taking her attention from Guthrie McCabe, she said: "Jim, you made a mistake today. You shot the wrong man!"

Chapter Seven

Jim Gary was not present when Guthrie McCabe held council. He knew that he could not stand idle while McCabe stated his price, yet by staying away he endorsed the man's methods, which was worse. In his own way, Jim Gary was ducking responsibility by thinking that what he didn't see and hear didn't concern him, yet he understood now that sooner or later he would have to stop McCabe, and the longer he waited, the more difficult it would be.

Jane Donovan attended the meeting, or a part of it. Then she came over to Jim Gary's fire and sat down. She thumped the coffee pot to see how much was in it and helped herself.

"What's the matter?" Gary asked. "The meeting isn't over yet, is it?"

She shook her head glumly. "I couldn't stand to look at Missus McCandless when he told about the girl he found. They had to carry her back to her wagon."

"You're going to see a lot of that. High hopes, then dropped and broken." He looked at her. "What was McCabe's price for bringing her back?"

Jane Donovan frowned. "The McCandless family is poor, Jim. They don't have a hundred dollars all told." She set the coffee cup aside. "Jim, you're a good man. Can't you help?"

"How?"

"You're going with McCabe. You bring her back." She

reached out and took his wrist. "Jim, do you want her to live out the rest of her life with vacant eyes and a mind that understands nothing? If she could see the girl, maybe it would help her. Isn't it worth a try?"

"Yes," Gary said. "But as I recall, the McCandless girl had brown hair, and this girl is blonde and. . . ."

"Jim, does it really matter?"

He frowned deeply. "Jane, it's my job . . . the Army's job . . . to see that all captives are returned to their rightful kin. Suppose I went along with this. Just what have I accomplished? It's like digging a hole to get the dirt to full another hole."

"Will you talk to McCandless?"

"No, I don't want to talk to him. What could McCandless say to me? What could he say that I don't already know?"

"You could listen and find out." She got up and stood there, looking down at him, and, when he could stand it no longer, he sighed and got up, also.

"I'm a fool," he said, and circled the camp with her to where Jake McCandless had his wagon parked. He had three walls and part of a fireplace constructed, but he seemed uninterested in building. His manner was almost listless.

He sat on the dropped wagon tongue, and they approached his fire and stopped before he looked up, and then he moved his head slowly. "I'd offer you something," McCandless said, "but we've got nothing." He was a small man, thin in the shoulders and chest, and his skin was as coarse as grained leather.

"This is Lieutenant Gary," Jane said.

"Know him by sight," McCandless said. Then, in half apology, he added: "Got little more than a howdy for anybody these days. I've run out of talk. Run out of everything, I guess. Feel like sittin' and not gettin' up. What's the use?"

"How's Missus McCandless?" Jane asked.

"Same's always. She don't change much. She's either starin' or yellin'. Faints when she gets excited." He shook his head. "I'm used to it. Had ten years of it. Every time she sees a girl about Esther's age, she starts bawlin' and kickin' up a fuss. Three years ago she jumped out of a moving wagon and broke a leg." He patted his shirt pockets. "You got any tobacco, Lieutenant?"

"A cigar." He handed it to McCandless, who bit off an inch of it and chewed it. "Mister McCandless, wouldn't it have been better if you'd stayed home? I mean, your wife can't stand much shock."

"Oh, she's tough enough, I guess. But I saw no harm in comin' back. What could I lose, with her light in the head as it is? I guess she ain't ever goin' to get better. Be a blessin' if she died. Somehow, though, I kept thinkin' that maybe there'd be one left over, a little girl, I mean. Not one that really belonged to anyone, but one that was left over, one no one else wanted. She ain't ever goin' to know what's real and what ain't, and, if I can give her comfort in a lie, then I guess God won't kick me out of heaven for it."

"Did you talk to McCabe?"

"No use," McCandless said. "That boy he saw could be Wringle's young one. I guess Wringle will come first. Most of the others, too, but it don't matter. I've spent my life waitin' on another man's pleasure. And time don't mean anythin' to my woman, Lieutenant. However, it'd please me to get her to look at me and know me just once before she died."

"I'll talk to McCabe," Gary said. "That's all I can promise."

"Promise?" McCandless seemed puzzled. "Son, I don't ask a man to promise anything. And talkin' to McCabe won't do any good. The McCabes in this world don't listen to men like me because I've got nothing to say worth listenin' to." He shook his head and spat tobacco juice. "I got to wait, and, if some sunshine comes my way, then I'll stand in it until a McCabe pushes me out. Fightin' don't do any good. Resentin' it don't help, either." He shook his finger at Gary. "Just one that someone's thrown away, that's all. Keep that in mind and, if she's half-Injun, my wife'll never know the difference."

"Let's go," Gary said, and turned away.

Jane Donovan said nothing for a time. She walked with her arm in his. "There's nothing left in him, Jim. It kind of twists you inside when you see it, doesn't it? I mean, he'll be happy with the slops and swill of life. The part that gets you is when he thanks you for that."

"Jane, what am I supposed to do? I'm in the Army. I've got to go by the book. There's no room for me to interpret the rules."

"No. I suppose there isn't. But you will talk to McCabe, won't you?"

"Yes. I'll beg him if I have to." He laughed without humor. "That'll amuse McCabe. He likes to rub a man's nose in his weaknesses, but right now that doesn't seem important. The trouble is, I think I'm afraid of McCabe, in a way. I guess all men are a little afraid of each other."

Someone ran past them, stopped, and came back. "Lieutenant? I've been looking for you. Mister McCabe is saddling his horse. I think he's going to leave the camp, sir."

"Thanks," Gary said. He touched Jane Donovan gently on the arm. "Go back to your fire. I'll see you later." He turned then and cut across the camp, casting quick glances at every fire, searching for Guthrie McCabe. He found him on the picket line, selecting a fresh horse.

Gary stopped. "Where do you think you're going?"

"Back to Tascosa." McCabe did not bother to look around when he spoke.

"What about this?"

"It'll keep," McCabe said, "but my business won't." He pulled the cinch tight, dropped the stirrup, then turned to Gary. "Don't get grumpy with me, Jim. I'll be back in a week or ten days." He waved his hand toward the camp. "You think time's going to mean much to them? Now step aside so I can mount."

Jim Gary did not move. "This business here is more important than any you could have."

"What the hell do you know about my business?" He laughed. "I made a date with a lady, and I just about have time enough to get back and keep it."

"Anson Miles's wife?"

Guthrie McCabe stared for a moment, then shrugged. "I guess you see more than I gave you credit for. But, fortunately, Anson is not so bright." He put a foot in the stirrup and reached for the saddle horn. "Ten days, Jim. You can wait that long."

Because he was confident, McCabe made a mistake. He ignored Jim Gary, who quickly unflapped his holster, whipped out his long-barreled pistol, and whacked McCabe over the head with it. The big man sagged to the ground, and the horse shied, stepping away from him.

"Reese! Cassidy!"

The two men appeared on the heels of Gary's shout. They saw McCabe and stared at him.

"What happened here?" Cassidy asked.

"Never mind. Get him across that horse and tie him there. Reese, have my horse saddled and a pack horse loaded with trade goods. McCabe and I are leaving right away."

"Ain't you going to wait until he comes to?" Cassidy asked.

"I said now." He started off, then stopped. "Tie him good."

Gary ran to his own fire, and from his bedroll he took a pair of elkhide shotgun breeches, an extra blanket, and his rifle. Jane Donovan saw him and came over. "Where are you going? Did McCabe leave?"

"We're both leaving. I hit him on the head. When he wakes up, we'll be miles from here."

She was more worried than displeased. "Jim, was that the right thing to do?"

"How do I know?" he snapped. "When I try to do right, it turns out wrong. Anyway, I felt like belting him, so I did." He gathered his gear to leave, then turned to look at her. "Jane, you're a darned pretty woman, and I never seem to get around to telling you that. Trouble is, I'm always in a hurry. Wish I had more time."

"Take time."

"Invite me when I come back."

Her smile was impish, but it made her eyes bright. "I might do that."

"Just so you don't forget," he said, and, freeing one hand, he pulled her against him and kissed her. When he released her, she stood close to him, not touching him, but very close, and the clean scent of soap rose from her hair, and he could almost feel her body warmth.

"Jane!"

They both turned and found Liam Donovan standing ten feet way. He seemed outraged by what he had seen.

"I'll be back," Gary said as he gathered up his gear and walked away, passing Liam Donovan by a few feet.

Donovan reached out, hooked Gary's arm, meaning to spin him around. "Mister, you don't learn."

Gary came around, rifle barrel lifted, and Donovan's pull

brought it solidly against the side of Donovan's own head. The blow knocked him off his feet, and he sat on the ground, rubbing the side of his head.

"What the devil did you do that for?"

"Because I haven't got the time to fool with you," Gary said, and ran toward the picket line. Cassidy was there with the horses. The pack horse was tied by a lead rope, as was McCabe's horse. Gary stepped into the saddle and slid the rifle into the boot.

"You're sure in a hurry," Cassidy said as Gary lashed his roll behind the saddle. "What'll I tell Wringle?"

"Tell him good bye," Gary said, and left the camp.

An hour south the land began to change, opening up into gullies and rising into distant ridges. The brush was becoming more dense, and now and then a jack rabbit startled him by dashing across his trail. A breeze pushed dead brush along and lifted dirt into a swirl. Gary tipped his head back and studied the sky—dark, starless, a black cap for the world.

McCabe's groan stopped him, and he waited while McCabe was sick.

"Untie me," McCabe said.

"Can you behave yourself?"

"I'll beat your damned head off for this."

"Then you'd better stay tied." Gary nudged his horse into motion, knowing how painful this was for McCabe—a man is not designed to ride belly down on a saddle.

A hundred yards later, McCabe said: "All right, all right! Have it your way."

Gary dismounted and untied McCabe, who would have fallen to the ground had not Gary caught him. There was a welt on the side of McCabe's head, and, before he could think to do anything about it, Gary lifted the pistol off him and kited it into the brush. This enraged McCabe.

"I paid fifty dollars for that!" The burst of temper pained him, and he pressed both hands to his head. "Damn you, Gary, I'll square this with you."

"After we get back," Gary said flatly.

McCabe suddenly became aware of his surroundings. He whipped his head in four directions, then stared at Gary. "What is this anyway?"

"Army business first, Guthrie. You knew I came along to ride herd on you. You said so in Fort Elliot. All right, we're riding, and, if I have to use the spurs, I will."

"You're not tough enough," McCabe said. He sat down, head pillowed in his hands. "My head's full of hammers." He sat that way for a moment, then looked up at Gary, who was a vague blackness surrounded by the inky night. "All right, you want to go into Comanche country, then we'll go. But I won't guarantee you'll get back."

"I didn't ask for any."

McCabe grunted, then pulled himself erect, using the stirrup for support. "Jim, it's a big country where a man can cash in almost any place. Don't expect anything from me. A favor, help, or advice." He grinned. "Why should I sweat to give you some lumps? I'll let you make your own mistakes."

"All right," Gary said. "Let's ride."

He started to move away, but McCabe took his arm. "What about my gun?"

"What about it?"

"Be tough to find it in the dark, that's what about it."

"You just lost your gun," Gary said, and mounted. He sat there, waiting for McCabe to pull himself into the saddle. Finally he said: "Maybe I ought not to admit this, but it would suit me fine if you rode back to Miles's place and stayed there. I don't enjoy your company. But this is something I've got to do, Guthrie. I've got to be a sucker. I can't help myself."

He turned then and rode on, staying now to the higher ground, following the ridges. There was no talk between them, no trust, no friendliness, and this filled Gary with misgiving.

They camped in a pocket, picketing the horses in some nearby brush, but Gary couldn't sleep. He lay in his blankets, shivering in the dawn chill, watching Guthrie McCabe, listening to him snore. He was afraid, and that was bad enough, but McCabe made it worse just by knowing he was afraid —knowing, and enjoying it like a spectator enjoys a fight with one certain outcome.

Chapter Eight

Through the next day's travel, Guthrie McCabe did not speak once to Jim Gary, but, every time Gary turned his head and looked at McCabe, the Texan smiled faintly, as though he enjoyed a private joke.

For his evening camp, Jim Gary chose Chino Creek, and without consulting McCabe he built a small fire and put on the skillet to heat.

This brought McCabe out of his silence. "You want to call Comanches? It'd be easier just to holler."

"I'm not trying to hide," Gary said. He mixed some flour and water, added a little starter, then cooked the wheat cakes. Pushing some sowbelly toward McCabe, he said: "You can slice that."

"No knife."

Gary gave him his. When the hotcakes were done, they folded them around the strips of sowbelly and ate while the coffee boiled in the frying pan. Finally Gary said: "Just when I think I'm beginning to understand you, you do something stupid, like wanting to ride back to Miles's place. Has she got her hook into you that bad, Guthrie?"

"Her?" He laughed. "Don't be a fool."

"Then why?"

McCabe shrugged. "She'll own the place one of these days. Just say that I'm covering all bets."

"I see," Gary said. "If Miles dies, the place is hers; providing she pays the back taxes. Being a friend, you'd loan her the money and move in. But if Miles doesn't die, you'll pay the taxes and claim the property, then move in."

"After I kicked her off," McCabe said. "Too bad you didn't know Miles in the old days, before the horse crippled him. He built the place as a monument to his money and importance, and his ignorance. He can't read or write, and he can hardly draw his name, but he wanted everyone to see the house and be so dazzled that they'd forget that just a stupid old man owned it. When I first came there, you couldn't cross Miles's land in a three-day ride. His first wife was alive then, but he was on the downside, losing stock to rustlers, drought, and dumb foolishness. I've seen him order a thousand dollars' worth of whiskey for one party. Even when he spent his last borrowed dollar, Miles kept up the pretense. That's what I grew up around, Jim, a squandering old man who never appreciated the things he had. I read the books Miles showed off to his friends, the ones he pretended to read, and little by little the place became more mine than his. I belonged there, not him, and he knew it and he hated me for it."

"What happened to all the land? I understand that less than a thousand acres goes with the mansion."

"He claimed it by right of possession. Small ranchers, farmers . . . they all nibbled away at it until all he had left was the house, and that's buried in back taxes." He used the brim of his hat to wrap around the handle of the coffee pot, then he filled both tin cups. "The place belongs to me. I've felt that for years, almost from the first time I saw it. And I'll have it, Jim. It's everything I want."

"So you can light it up and fill the yard with carriages?" Gary shook his head. "McCabe, you've lost your mind." He held the cup between his palms and leaned forward. "You know what I think? I think you're the loneliest man in Texas. Your favorite song is that you never do anyone a favor, but I think that's a lie. You're always doing something for someone, but you're covering it up with a lot of selfish talk, like you were ashamed to be human. You know something, Guthrie? You like to have people owe you. It makes you feel real good to have people in your debt, even when they don't want to be. But don't count on that from me. With me, you've got to pay your way, and I don't mean to buy it, either."

"Jim, you're real mixed up about me."

"No, I've got it straight. Guthrie, the thing you want is a friend who likes you because you're Guthrie McCabe and nothing else. But you've been kicked too hard, by your pa, and by Miles, and now you think that no one would ever like you for yourself. That makes you afraid. You want to stick out your hand, but you're afraid one more man will snap at it." He got up and threw the coffee into the fire, then scraped dirt over the fire until it was out. "Let's ride."

McCabe stared at him. "What's the hurry?" He continued to watch Gary. Then, after a moment, he got up and brushed off the seat of his pants. "All right, Jim, let's go. I hate a man who likes to be the boss all the time."

Gary laughed. "You just can't stand to be told what to do, can you, Guthrie?" He felt pleased with himself, less fearful, for with this knowledge of McCabe's character came weapons, to turn his will, to make him angry. Gary found that he had strings to pull and that McCabe would react.

"I've had enough," McCabe said, and took a swing at Gary. There was only time to duck, and even this upset his balance so that he fell backward, with Guthrie McCabe launching himself to keep him from getting up. Gary was partially rolled out of the way when McCabe landed, and then

Gary felt McCabe's hand fumbling at his holster, trying to unbutton the flap, to take possession of the pistol.

Gary hit him alongside the head with his elbow, then McCabe jerked away, the pistol in his hand. Quickly Gary grabbed for the frame and cylinder, locking it tightly, which prevented McCabe from cocking the piece and firing it. They came to their knees, both struggling for the gun, both tugging, resisting, trying to wrench the other free of it.

Somehow Gary managed to trip McCabe. When he fell, his grip on the pistol relaxed, and then Gary stepped back, covering him. His breathing was ragged, and he looked steadily at McCabe, who sat on the ground, braced against stiffened arms.

"You want this badly enough," Gary said, "I'll make you eat it, barrel first."

"Don't get sore," McCabe said. "A man's got a right to try."

He partially turned, then came erect with a rush, his hand stabbing for the gun as Gary pulled the trigger. To his surprise, the pistol failed to discharge. Then McCabe cried out in sudden pain. He danced about, clutching his left hand, and strangely, the pistol dangled from it, flopping about as though it were invisibly fastened.

Gary grabbed him and held him, and McCabe quieted, but he was hurt.

"Get it off!"

He held up his hand, and Gary saw what had happened. In grabbing the gun, McCabe's hand had gone too far, and the hammer had fallen on that web of flesh between the thumb and forefinger. The pointed firing pin had gone deeply into the flesh, preventing the cartridge from being ignited. Cocking the gun again, Gary freed it from McCabe's hand and let the hammer down before dropping it into his holster.

The wound bled badly, and McCabe clutched his wrist, his face chalk-white. "My God, that hurts!"

"Let me look at it."

McCabe jerked away as Gary reached for his hand. "You get away from me! You've been nothing but trouble to me." He stripped off his neckerchief and bandaged the wound tightly. Pain was still biting him. It put a saw edge in his voice and a pinched look around his mouth. "Let's get out of here before you kill me."

He walked over to his horse and climbed into the saddle. Then he sat there, bent forward, head down, nursing his pain. Gary almost tried again to help him, then decided to let him alone. He packed his gear, tied it behind the saddle, and mounted.

"You can lead on from here," Gary said. "This is as far south as I've ever been. We'll try Iron Hand's village first."

McCabe nodded and led out. He kept his shoulders rounded, and Gary studied him as they moved along. The wound was painful, he knew, but he could not help but wonder which pained worse, the wound, or the knowledge that he had been bested by a lesser man.

I was lucky, Gary told himself. *But maybe the next time I won't be.*

Iron Hand's camp lay a half day beyond the dawn, and they sighted it when the sun was high. They made their approach in the clearing and rode through the racing children and the dogs snapping at the horses' hoofs. Two hundred penny-colored faces stared at them as they moved between the stinking lodges toward the center of the village. Both men dismounted there, and Gary took picket pins from his saddlebag and tethered the three horses. Guthrie McCabe stood with his left hand tucked into the front of his shirt, turning his head now and then to watch the outer fringe of women and children. The bucks formed a ring around them, their expressions gravely neutral, neither savage nor friendly. War was too fresh a memory to allow them open trust of any white man, even Guthrie McCabe.

Jim Gary took off his pistol belt and hung it on the saddle horn as a gesture of peace. Then Iron Hand came from his lodge, robed, beaded, poker-faced. One hand was hidden, and he approached them, his copper face inscrutable.

Iron Hand spoke remarkably good English, and Gary recalled that he had once gone to an Indian school. "McCabe returns as he has said, but he brings a stranger here to my fire."

"He is a trader from the north," McCabe said.

Iron Hand thought about this for a moment. Then he saw that Gary was unarmed and decided that it was all right. "What does McCabe and the trader seek?"

"A place by your fire," Gary said. "The hand of friendship."

"Will the trader accept my left hand of flesh, or the right which gives me my name and has no warmth?" He exposed his hand, which was a leather cuff laced high on the forearm. A bent piece of polished steel formed a hook.

"I will take the cold hand in peace," Gary said, "for it gives you the name, Iron Hand. That name is known where all men walk."

This flattery pleased the Comanche, and he smiled through his eyes. "Come to my lodge," he said, and turned away.

In a soft voice McCabe said: "You can talk like a horse thief when you want to, can't you?" They followed Iron Hand, who waved his hand, and a woman rushed forward with a bowl of food. The Comanches held wolves and their kind sacred, including dogs, but to Gary the odor distinctly suggested dog meat, and a lot of other ingredients best not thought about, but he ate it anyway and nodded an appreciation he did not feel at all.

In Indian fashion Iron Hand let time pass and a lot of small talk, before he came to the main issue, the reason for their visit. "The winter will be severe, McCabe, and my people have not hunted well this year. The horses of Sutro have not been returned. Perhaps more gifts. . . ."

"We'll speak of that later," Gary said. "The third horse bears gifts."

He wondered if it would be impolite if he looked around the camp, then decided not to. Under the guise of looking for the horses they might be permitted to remain a few days. There would be plenty of time. Still he wondered how the subject could be switched from horse trading to slaves. Perhaps McCabe had an answer; he seemed full of them.

Iron Hand was speaking. "I do not live alone on a mountain top. The horses will be returned. Then we can speak of trade." He paused. "If I could see the goods, I perhaps might find the horses sooner."

"Three men may unpack the horse," Gary said.

A signal from Iron Hand sent them scrambling, fighting to be the first to unlash the pack. McCabe gave Gary a disapproving glance but dared not say anything. Watching the Indians—he had an excuse now—Gary noticed a tall young man who kicked and bit and cursed his way through the milling group. The young man was as brown as a nut, yet his hair was light, and, when he turned his head, Gary saw that his eyes were gray. He judged his age to be fourteen, although it was difficult to tell when they grew up wild. Other than the hair and eyes the white blood had been bred out of him, leaving him pure Comanche in thought and action.

Iron Hand seemed satisfied with the quality of the goods, and the talk resumed, mostly lies told by Iron Hand in an effort to convince them how honest he was, how he lived with honor and had never stolen a thing in his life. They sat through the speech, then listened to different braves swear to the lies. Gary let this run in one ear and out the other. This took all afternoon and much of the night, and Gary began to understand that nothing would be settled that night. He got his blankets off the horse and lay down by the fire and went to sleep.

The next day he wandered about the camp unmolested. Iron Hand had made an attempt to find the horses because the Comanche was smart enough to know that, if he failed to produce them, the gifts would stop. Yet Iron Hand was an Indian, proud, vain, and he would never admit that any member of his village had taken the animals. He went through a long rigmarole to find the horses. Iron Hand claimed that the horses had been stolen by someone else, and that members of his tribe were trading for them, and that he would have to give many buffalo robes, but, as a gift to the two white friends, he would hand them over. Still there was some hedge in Iron Hand's talk. He kept referring to the bad winter coming, and how valuable a horse would be, and the more he talked, the more convinced Jim Gary became that he was about to hit on something, like an easy way to switch the talk and the trading for white captives instead of Sutro's horses.

He wanted to talk this over with McCabe, but the man kept wandering off, clearly indicating his preference for being left alone. Gary wandered about, looking for the white boy, and found him, with his coup stick and war-making implements. The Comanches always practiced war, even when they talked peace.

A direct question was impossible, so Gary passed out some cigars among the women and loosened a few tongues. He knew enough of the language to understand them. Yes, the boy was white. He had been taken quite young; the women could not remember when exactly, but the boy was the faithful son of Lame Bear and had counted coup against the white soldiers before he was ten.

This was, Gary assumed, Wringle's son. Now it was his job to get him out of the Comanche camp as peacefully as possible. A trade might be in order, yet Gary did not feel in the least cheered by this. He had watched the boy and now wondered if he could lead such a wild animal back to his rightful parents. Then there was the matter of keeping him, teaching him those thousand subtle things a young man had to know to be even halfway acceptable to society.

Right then, at that moment, he saw that Guthrie McCabe was right. This whole business was a mistake. It should be left alone, a thing over and done with and best forgotten. But he knew it wouldn't be that way.

Chapter Nine

There was nothing in Jim Gary's nature that made waiting easy, yet it was something he had to do now, and with all the outward signs of enjoying it. He could not help but worry some about Wringle and how he was making out at the Sand Creek grove. The responsibility for the civilians' conduct and safety was Gary's, passed on to him by Colonel Frazer, who hoped to hold this balance for another few months, then get out of it completely. Now Gary had passed it on to Wringle, temporarily, who really could not be held accountable at all if anything went wrong.

By dark, no one had returned to Iron Hand's camp with Sutro's horses, and during the evening meal Gary spoke of this to McCabe. "I'm getting tired of waiting. Let's press Iron Hand now and make the best of it."

McCabe shook his head. "Been looking around some and we'll have to play this cozy. Iron Hand will fetch the horses when he's ready, and then we can talk. He'll want to keep the horses. After he argues, we'll offer an alternative. That boy could be Wringle's."

"You've been thinking the same thing I have," Gary said wryly. "I thought I was one jump ahead of you."

McCabe smiled. "That'll be the day." He motioned with his head. "Tonight wander around and see what you can see."

"What do you think I've been doing?"

"Wake up," McCabe said. "You've seen what they want you to see. Get away from the camp. Go to the water hole, or where there's wood to be gathered. If a Comanche's got a slave he doesn't want you to see, he'll keep him in the lodge during the daytime."

"All right. Where will you be?"

"With Iron Hand, shooting the breeze."

"That's a soft job," Gary said, and drank what was left of his coffee. He left McCabe with the meal clean-up and knew that he would resent it, but it gave Gary pleasure to sting this man. McCabe's left hand was heavily bandaged, Gary noticed, and he did not use it at all. Later, Gary decided, he would make another attempt to dress it properly, if McCabe would let him. The trouble with men who liked to do for themselves was that they usually lived in fear of appearing weak, less sufficient than they were. Gary couldn't see the disgrace in accepting help when it was needed.

He had been in the Comanche camp long enough not to attract any attention no matter where he went, so he eased past the last group of lodges and made his leisurely way to the creek. A fringe of cottonwood trees lined both banks, and Gary walked to the end of the trail and stopped there, a few feet from the water, his back against a tree. His wait was long and tedious and without reward. He gave it up and walked along the creek bank, venturing nearly a mile before angling back through the trees to the camp. The night was ink, and he could see nothing farther than a few feet in front of him.

He heard a twig snap ahead of him, and he collided heavily with a woman. He identified her sex by her sharp gasp. She had an armful of kindling and dropped this. In unmistakable English she said: "You clumsy savage! Why don't you watch where you're going?"

"I'm dreadfully sorry," Gary said, and raked a match alight to see to whom he was apologizing. He had only a glimpse. She was strikingly attractive, with large eyes and a full, curved mouth. Gary whipped out the match when it singed his fingers.

The woman stared at him. "You're white!"

"I'm Lieutenant Gary. What's your name?"

"Janice Tremain." She held her hand against her side where he had bruised her. "I thought a stranger was in camp. I haven't been allowed out of the lodge in the daytime." She started to cry, then checked it quickly. "To hear someone speaking something besides Comanche is more than I can. . . ."

"How long have you been here?"

"Five years, I think. Yes, it's been five years."

He took her arm. "Are you sure you're not hurt? I fetched you quite a whack."

"I'm really all right, but we can't talk here."

"Then where can we talk?"

She thought a moment. "We'll go bathing in the creek."

"What?" He was quite shocked.

"It's the custom for couples to bathe. No one will bother us. Besides, it's dark, and if we go upstream a few yards. . . ."

"Hang the custom," Gary said.

"If we stay here, some squaw is bound to come along. She'll see us and tell Stone Calf. Then he'll try to kill you."

"Stone Calf?"

"My husband," she said simply.

"Good heavens!" Gary said. He wiped a hand across his face. "I think the creek is the lesser of the evils." She pushed past him then, and he followed her to the water's edge. Farther downstream, someone splashed water and giggled. Janice Tremain looked at Jim Gary, then untied the drawstrings to her simple dress and shed it. His intention was to turn his head, yet he did not. He had a moment's glimpse of a firm, well-rounded body. She waded into the creek until the water reached her shoulders. He heard her laugh, then she said: "At least take off your boots, Lieutenant."

This embarrassed him, and he shed boots, shirt, and trousers. Hang the underwear, he thought, and went into the water with her. Within moments a half dozen couples were bathing, each keeping a respectful distance from each other. Moving close to him, Janice Tremain said: "If a woman wants a lover, they bathe together. If the angry husband bursts upon them, both can say that they were only washing. It saves his face."

"Forget the customs of aboriginal tribes," Gary said. "How the devil did you get here in the first place?"

"A stage was attacked," she said. "I was going to join my father at Fort Elliot."

"That's my post!"

"I'm an Army brat. My father is Captain Tremain. Is he well?"

For a moment Gary couldn't place the man, but then he remembered the talk. It had all happened before his assignment at Fort Elliot. "I don't have time to put sugar on it," he said softly. "He's dead."

She did not cry or betray emotion. "I'm glad. I wouldn't want him to know me now. How did he die?"

"He took his own life."

She nodded. "I thought it was like that. He was a man of honor, and was touched deeply by many things. He withstood pain well, but he was easily broken by grief. When my mother died, he. . . ."

"Janice, do you want out of here?" He asked the question abruptly, almost as though he feared she might say no.

"It's all I've thought of, but I'm not sure." She shivered and crossed her arms over her breasts. "I have no children. That way I'm lucky. But they know I'm barren, and Stone Calf has another wife who bears his children. So life hasn't been easy for me here. They've worked me hard."

"Let me take you back," Gary said. "You must have relatives."

"An uncle," she said. "Senator Tremain." She touched his arm. "I've been gone too long now. Stone Calf will come looking for me. I'll meet you here tomorrow night."

"I may be gone by then," he said. "Janice, let me take you back."

"Let me think about it. This is so quick, meeting you, finding hope again. Tomorrow night? Here?"

"All right," he agreed.

She waded ashore, and he waited until she was dressed and gone before leaving the stream. Quickly slipping into his clothes, he meant to follow her, then let the idea go. He might invite danger by such an action, danger to them both.

He returned to the main camp and McCabe's fire. The Texan was rolled in his blankets, but he turned around as Gary sat down. McCabe saw the dampness on Gary's clothing.

"Been having some fun in the creek?" McCabe sat up, eyeing him curiously.

"I met a white woman. Been here five years. Guthrie, I'm going to get her away from here."

"Wait a minute," McCabe said. He looked around to see if anyone was within earshot. "This wouldn't be Stone Calf's wife, would it?"

"She's Janice Tremain," Gary said. "A white woman."

"Yeah, yeah, and Stone Calf is Iron Hand's brother, too." He settled back and pulled the blanket around him. "You leave her alone, Jim. I don't want half the Comanche nation down on my neck."

"You knew she was here?" He was incredulous.

"Sure. There's a hands-off sign on her. Make sure you read it right."

"That won't stop me."

"No? Then I will," McCabe said. "Hang it, Jim, I want to go on living." He made a few tugs on the blanket. "Now shut up so I can sleep."

There was a lot he wanted to say, even an anger to express, an anger at the sudden knowledge that politics invaded so basic an act as freeing a white woman prisoner, an Army brat at that. Gary felt almost honor-bound to rescue her. McCabe, he knew, regarded him as a wide-eyed innocent that no amount of experience would temper, and Gary supposed the Texan was right in this judgment. Yet he felt no shame because he was this way. He did not consider it an unforgivable character flaw.

The horses were produced the next evening, along with Iron Hand's long-winded account of how they were borrowed by mistake and how much he had to give to get them back. Both McCabe and Jim Gary listened to this. It was all part of the game a man played when he dealt with Indians.

Talk of trade began. Iron Hand set his price high, often reminding both McCabe and Gary that horses were most valuable with a cruel winter coming on. McCabe played his game, trying to lower Iron Hand's price, while Iron Hand held it as high as he could.

Gary wondered how long this would continue. Already they had talked for two hours. Then McCabe pulled the switch—suddenly, without warning. He offered to trade all the goods Iron Hand asked for the horses for the yellow-haired boy.

This called for a conference. The Indians drew to one side, and McCabe put a match to a cigar.

"We'll get the boy," he said softly.

"You sure?"

"Yes. Iron Hand will kick up a fuss, but he'll see it our way." McCabe rubbed his jaw. "Now to figure out how to get him back. These are the only folks he remembers. Probably have to tie him to the pack horse."

"I'll put our gear together," Gary said, and left the fire. He rolled their blankets and stacked them near the fire, and then went to the picket line on the pretense of looking at the horses. After wandering about for a moment, enough so that the guard no longer paid any attention to him, Gary ducked away and hurried to the grove of trees near the creek.

He stood around for a few minutes, listened to several couples already in the water, then slowly walked upstream to the spot where he had met Janice Tremain the night before. He heard someone splash water in the creek and took a chance. Undressing quickly, he went into the water and found her at midstream.

"I thought you hadn't showed up," he said.

"Running Wolf brought the horses back," she said. "When will you leave?"

"Very soon. Will you come?"

"I'm afraid now . . . but not for myself."

"You must come, Janice. I'll see that we cross the creek farther up. Be waiting." He took her arm and shook her. "Janice, it's now or never. There is no other way out."

"All right."

He started to leave. Time was pressing him like a hand at his back.

She touched him, and he turned. "What will I do? It's been five years."

"Let me take care of it," he said. He knew what she meant—how could she explain five years and yet remain socially acceptable? Rashly he said: "Janice, let me take care of everything. Do you understand? Everything."

"Can you?"

"Yes, I know I can."

He left her then, dressed, and returned to McCabe's fire. The Texan was ready to leave. The boy was bound and mounted, firmly tied to the pack horse. McCabe saw the dampness of Gary's clothes and only frowned.

"Let's go," he said, stepping into the saddle. He was a bit awkward with the reins, being able to use only one hand, and Gary knew that it pained him badly.

"I'll lead," Gary said, tying the lead rope to his own saddle horn so that the boy rode between himself and McCabe. Iron Hand raised his hand in a token of peace, all the while silently congratulating himself on the slick horse deal he had made.

Gary made certain their exit was casual, but he glanced back often to observe the boy, who sat stone-faced, only his eyes alight with hatred.

McCabe said nothing until Gary turned and started to cut across the creek close to the cottonwoods. "Hey, that's the wrong way!"

"Shut up," Gary said.

He edged his horse closer. Suddenly Janice Tremain ran from the woods and came up to him. He took her hand, and she put her foot in the stirrup, mounting behind him.

McCabe swore softly, then said: "You did it now, you damned do-gooder! We'll be dead by sunrise."

Chapter Ten

Once away from the camp, Jim Gary increased his pace in order to put as much distance between himself and Stone Calf as he could. He knew that an hour might be all he could gain. He dared not hope for more. He rode double and was slowed by the boy, who already fought his bonds, and McCabe was riding humped in the saddle, his hand paining him. Stone Calf would have very little trouble making up that hour.

They had to stop or kill the horses, and Jim Gary hated the thought of either. He dismounted and helped Janice Tremain down. A glance at the sky assured him that dawn was yet some time away. Then he looked at McCabe and found him standing near the boy, who remained tied to the horse.

"I'll watch him," McCabe said softly. He spoke to the boy in Comanche, and the boy spit at him, earning for his effort a slap in the face.

"Cut that out!" Gary said. He started toward McCabe, then let it go and sat down beside Janice Tremain. "How much time have we got? The truth now."

"Before Stone Calf misses me?" She shrugged. "I would say that he's left the village." She folded her hands together. "Actually, I think he will be glad to get rid of me, but pride will force him to follow."

"Will pride make him come alone?"

Janice frowned. "He might, but he has three young sons.

They might come with him in the name of family honor."

"We'll have to figure it that way then." He got up to get his canteen and offered it to her first. "You're not sorry?"

"No. Just frightened." She looked at Guthrie McCabe. "Who is he?"

"McCabe. Haven't you seen him before?"

She shook her head, and he opened his mouth to tell her about the man, but decided to let her judge for herself.

He walked over to McCabe. "Stone Calf is probably behind us. Got any ideas?"

"Leave her here," McCabe said bluntly. He fumbled in his pocket for a cigar, found one, and put a match to it. "She's got no business with us, Jim. When you going to stop doing favors for people?"

"She's white. And she's Army."

"That may be enough for you, but not me." He shifted his injured hand, trying to find a more comfortable way to carry it.

"That beginning to bother you?"

"I can live with it." He looked at the boy, who sat silently, his attention seemingly elsewhere. "I think he understands what we're saying."

"So?"

"So that makes him doubly dangerous." He rolled the cigar to one corner of his mouth. "Jim, when we started, I told you I wouldn't stick around and pull you out of any holes you got into. You going to give the woman up?"

"No," Gary said.

"Damn, but you're stubborn." He shrugged. "All right. I'll say good bye now. It's likely I won't see you back in camp."

"Are you running out on me?"

"Depends on the point of view. Like the little kid holding

the cat's tail. The cat does all the pulling. Me, I'm leaving because it's a good way to stay alive. Still, I wouldn't set you up for Stone Calf. You take my horse. I'll go on, riding double with the boy." He reached out and tapped Jim Gary on the chest. "Look, this will be better for you. And don't get the idea you can stop me. Stone Calf will have his sons with him, so hitting me on the head would only increase your troubles, not solve them."

"Thanks for nothing," Jim Gary said.

McCabe stared at Gary. Then he clamped his cigar firmly between his teeth and swung up behind the boy, reaching around him for the reins. "I'll travel fast and straight, Jim. You'd better take the round-about way. There's some badlands about twenty miles from here. Good for holing up during the daytime."

In spite of himself, Gary said: "I'll give you my rifle. You'll need a gun."

McCabe shook his head. "Stone Calf will be after you, not me." He started to lift the reins, then thought of something else. "You're mad at me, Jim, and I guess you think you have a right to be, but I told you some time ago how it would be. It occurs to me that I could get shot in the back as I leave, but then I guess you're too much of a gentleman to do a low thing like that."

He drove his heels into the horse's flanks and rode out, the hoofs clattering as he drove down the draw. Then the sounds faded until Jim Gary could hear nothing. He was filled with an immense sense of loneliness.

Janice Tremain came over. "Where is he going?"

"His own way. McCabe always goes his own way."

"He's leaving us?"

"Yes," Gary said. He took her arm and led her to McCabe's horse, boosting her into the saddle. "We've stayed

96

here too long. McCabe was right about that."

He led the way, and she followed him closely, but they did not speak. He was inclined to silence, and she was observant enough to see that and respect it. Perhaps she was also observant enough to sense his misgivings. His decision to rescue her had been spontaneous, possibly regrettable. Yet he was also the kind who finished what he started. He seemed terribly determined not to make mistakes.

There was in Jim Gary's mind the sure knowledge that he was only an adequate man who continually overreached his native ability. He was not brilliant or brave or even outstandingly resourceful. His record at the Academy and his service sheets proved that. Given a job, he would do it, but he could never rise to greatness for he felt that it was not in him. He was regretful now that he had taken Janice Tremain from the village. His own inner qualms caused this feeling, for her presence placed him in personal jeopardy. Yet his instincts, his training, forbade leaving her—his conscience and sense of duty grappled for the upper hand. He could even envy McCabe for his lack of conscience, the selfishness that permitted him to do what was best for himself and never think of others.

From behind him, Janice Tremain said: "It's not too late for me to turn back." After she said it, she regretted it, for it put him in an impossible position, even if he wanted her to turn back.

"Be daylight in five hours," he said. "We'll be in the badlands by then."

Somewhere off his left flank, McCabe would be pushing through the night with the boy. Gary wondered how much Wringle had promised to pay McCabe for the safe delivery. Enough anyway to make McCabe strike out on his own rather than stay and risk losing the boy. This was something else that troubled Gary, his failure to prevent McCabe from fleecing the civilians. Colonel Frazer liked to have his orders obeyed, and Gary would have to report complete failure. Wringle might be willing to pay, as would some of the others, but there were some in the grove who felt the world owed them a hand-out, and they would file a complaint against the Army, which Frazer did not want at any price. He wouldn't get his brigadier retirement, and Gary wouldn't get his captain's bars. And the civilians wouldn't get what they wanted, either. Just McCabe, who was tough enough and smart enough, would get it all.

The first rise of dawn found them in a barren waste of jumbled rock and gorges. This was a breathless, lifeless, forgotten land, and somewhere in the back of Gary's mind he remembered hearing that the Indians had deep superstitions about the place. They avoided it unless desperately pressed by their enemies.

They hid the horses and stretched out to rest, but there was no lasting shade. As the sun climbed, the cool shadows disappeared and a molten heat lay trapped, making breathing a chore. Gary tried to sleep. He was bone-weary and his eyes burned and the unshaved stubble on his face itched, but he could not rest.

Finally he sat up and tipped his hat low over his face. Janice Tremain tried to use the horses for shade, but they kept moving about, so she gave this up. She unlaced the front of her dress to the waist and let it hang loosely, trying to keep reasonably cool. Gary glanced at her once, then studiously avoided looking at her again. He did not want to think of her as immodest. He supposed five years as the common wife of a Comanche had caused her to forget for the moment that she was a proper lady, an officer's daughter.

"Who commands Fort Elliot?" she asked.

"Colonel Frazer. He's up for retirement soon."

"I don't know him. What will I say when I go back?"

"Tell them you're glad to be back and let it go at that," Gary said.

"Yes, a man could say that. But not a woman." She tried to do something with her hair, to brush it with her fingers, but it was long and ungroomed and unmanageable. Her complexion was dark from exposure to the sun, and her fingernails were cracked from difficult work. Her dress was thin buckskin, all she had to her name. She lifted the hem of it, looked at it with disdain, then let it drop as though she did not want to think about it any longer. "I was engaged," she said softly. "He was a junior officer at Fort Elliot. Lieutenant Culver. Perhaps you know him?"

"Hardy Culver? He was transferred to Fort Yuma three years ago." He turned and looked at her. "His wife went with him. She was going to have a baby."

His desire had been only to tell her the truth, so that she would not show disappointment before anyone, yet his words hurt her deeply.

"If you're going to say you're sorry, then don't," she said. "What did I expect, anyway?"

"A world that hasn't fallen apart."

She turned her head slowly, and he saw tears in her eyes. "Yes, that's exactly what I expected. And why isn't it that way?" Her voice rose in volume, in anger. "Why is it that it's all happened to me while everyone else gets off scot-free? Am I being punished for something I didn't know I'd done?"

Along the pathway of Jim Gary's life there were strings of hurt birds, homeless small animals, all lovingly nursed, and it was natural for him to put his arms around her and hold her against him while she cried over the unspeakable injustices of living. He understood her fears, for they were real. Somehow the world was always too busy to offer sympathy. She would find very little of it at Fort Elliot. Sure, they would have a dinner in her honor, and everyone would be polite to her, but that would wear off and they would soon be wondering how many lodges she had shared. In time the commanding officer would politely question her presence on the post. After all, she no longer had any direct connection with the Army. They could not keep her because of a dead father and a fiancé who had quit grieving and married another.

"I have two sisters," he said softly. "You could go back East for a while and live with them. They'd love to have you." When she did not answer immediately, he thought she hadn't heard him. She disengaged herself from his arms and wiped her eyes.

"Strange, but I thought there were no more tears." She did not look directly at him when she spoke. "I couldn't impose on them, Jim. Sooner or later I'll have to stand by myself, so we'll make it sooner." Perspiration ran down her cheeks and stood out in small globules on her upper lip. "I think that's what frightens me most . . . the fear that I won't be able to stand by myself and look anyone in the eye who asks me what it was like to be a female prisoner. Jim, if I falter just once, I'm through. Do you understand what I mean?"

"Yes," he said. "I know exactly. We're alike in that re-spect, Janice. Destroy our equilibrium even in the slightest, and we're totally lost. I guess that's why I'll be Army and nothing else. I feel secure in the protocol of the service." He smiled then.

"You know how it'll be with me," she said. "If . . . if you could be by me, Jim, just at first, I know I'd be all right." This was only a hope on her part, a hope she knew was faint, for he had his duty and that came first. "I'm sorry. I've asked too much of you already."

"We'll work it out," he said, and got up, climbing high in the rocks to view the back trail. The sun smashed down, raising rippled heat. He turned his head and spoke to her. "McCabe has a pair of field glasses in his saddlebag. Would you bring them up here?"

She found them and climbed to where he lay, stretching out prone beside him. He took the glasses, adjusted them, and spent many minutes carefully scanning the distant flats.

"Nothing," he said, genuinely puzzled. "I don't understand this. From here I can see ten or twelve miles. Stone Calf ought to be out there somewhere."

"Could it be that he didn't leave camp?"

"No, no," Gary said. "We've got to figure the worst and prepare for it. And I keep thinking of McCabe, who knows Comanches very well, and he was worried about Stone Calf. No, he's out there all right, and I'd give six months' pay to know just where."

Chapter Eleven

By mid-afternoon the heat in the rocky pocket became so oppressive that Gary put aside his caution and decided to leave, hoping that sunset would catch them on the edge of the flats. They walked slowly down to the lower levels, leading the horses, and Janice Tremain did not speak. Gary was not sure whether it was the heat and weariness that made her withdrawn, or her thoughts of going back to civilization. The first night they had met, he had promised to help her, and it had been a promise hastily given, one he might not be able to keep. Another failure. Only this one bothered him more than the others.

Gary was careful, working his way down to the flats, and he took his time, trying to think ahead in the event he was walking into an ambush. Having left the highest ground, he had no vantage point from which to survey the terrain and spot his enemy. He could only blunder on now, pitting his intelligence against the hunting craft of the Comanche.

By his judgment he had another hour among the rocks, another hour of soft footing along with the nettle sting of fear-sweat on his face. He could not make up his mind where safety lay—in a quick dash across the flats, or waiting for darkness, then taking a round-about route. Either way, he would leave sign that Stone Calf could follow. Either way, the Indian stood a good chance of catching him and killing him.

At the last fringe of rocks, Jim Gary hunkered down and

took out the field glasses, carefully searching the flats before him. He saw nothing and put the glasses away.

"We'll go straight north," Gary said, his decision made. "By my reckoning, the Fort Elliot patrol will be out there somewhere. I'd rather look forward to them for help than the civilians in the Sand Creek camp." He uncorked the canteen and offered it to Janice first, pulling it away when she tried to drink too much. "That water has to last another fifty miles. A swig three times a day . . . that's all we can afford."

"Are we going to wait for darkness here?"

"We'll wait a while longer. You need the rest."

"He didn't come for me," she said softly. "I don't know whether I'm happy or insulted." She wiped her hand across her face, leaving streaks in the dirt and sweat. "Don't look like that, Jim. I've shared his blanket for five years. Do you want me to feel nothing?"

"I don't know what I want," he said. "We'd better go."

When he stepped near her, she took his arm, turning him to face her. "Let's be honest, Jim. The thought of me with an Indian fills you with fury, doesn't it?"

"Yes," he said. "God, Janice, you were born for a white man!" He realized how stupid that sounded, yet he had spoken his true feelings, revealed to himself another facet of his personality that he had only before suspected. He stood there, shaking his head back and forth. "I guess it all boils down to the fact that I'm white and I'm better."

"Are you, Jim?" She asked the question because she wanted him to find the answer for himself, not to give it to her. "You're right. We'd better go on."

"I want to do the right thing," he said.

She smiled at him, then said: "Jim, don't we all?"

He put her on the horse, then turned to his own as a rock

skip-clattered down the side of a nearby rise. Gary whipped his head around and caught a glimpse of doom. Stone Calf had his rifle leveled, and Gary reacted, flinging himself down, letting the bullet smash into the neck of his horse. The animal screamed and went down, then Stone Calf discarded his single-shot rifle and bounded off the ledge, knife flashing, his throat filled with a war cry.

Gary had enough time to regain his feet and meet him, hand grabbing for the wrist, fending off the knife. Even then it bit slightly into the flesh of his shoulder, driving him to renewed strength. The two men stamped about, feet drumming the dust, trying to lock legs, trip each other. They fought breast to breast, cheek to jowl, sweat and spit and hate blending. Then they fell and rolled, arms and legs beating the barren ground, grunting at each other as though this were an animal language that both understood.

Gary did not know when he turned the knife or how he did it; he only felt it bite deeply, and he threw his weight on the bent wrist and drove it deeper. Stone Calf cried out, then fell back, and Gary got unsteadily to his feet.

Janice Tremain vaulted off the horse. She rushed to Stone Calf and lifted his head. He was dying, and the knowledge was in his eyes, and his last strength was spent when he lifted his hand and brushed her cheek.

"Stone Calf . . . comes alone," he said. Then his head rolled and his eyes assumed a vacancy, and she gently let him down until his hair mingled with the dust.

"He kept me alive because he favored me," Janice said softly. "What can I do for him now?"

"Forget him," Gary said. "Now the past is truly dead."

"Yes," Janice said.

Then she knelt by his head and began to chant the Co-manche death song, and she rocked back and forth and threw dust in her hair while Jim Gary watched with mounting horror.

"Stop that!" he shouted.

If she heard him, she gave no sign, and he moved toward her.

"In the name of God, I tell you to stop!" He pushed her, then struck her heavily in the face with the back of his hand. She fell back and looked at him, and he saw that she was crying, and this enraged him completely. "I wish I'd never brought you away if you loved him so much!" He whirled away from her and mounted her horse. He cooled his anger and forced himself to speak civilly. "Get mounted, Janice."

"Why?" she said, rising. "Why should you take me back, feeling as you do? Because I'm white, and you think each kind should be with his own?"

"Something like that," Gary said. "I don't think trying to explain it will help anything. Not now."

"No. We'll never understand each other."

She pulled herself up behind him into the saddle and rode with him into the growing darkness, never once looking back at Stone Calf.

Three hours after Guthrie McCabe parted company with Jim Gary and Janice Tremain, he stopped and told the boy to dismount. Leaving him tied hand and foot, McCabe built a very small fire and cooked a meal. The firelight flickered in the boy's eyes, and he watched McCabe carefully, noticing the injured hand, measuring the Texan as though figuring out the odds of escape.

McCabe was aware of the scrutiny and spoke in Comanche. "You might as well forget it. I'm two jumps ahead of you."

"You are without weapons," the boy said. "And your hand is in pain."

"A kid like you I can handle with one hand," McCabe said. He picked up a stick of wood. "Try anything and I'll break this over your head."

"Your heart can be cold. But it can be warm, and that is weak." He smiled. "You were kind to the other white man, but it will do no good. Stone Calf might follow the horse carrying double for but a short way, then know that you have tricked him. He will know that I would not be taken into the badlands."

McCabe's manner was one of respect. "Smart kid, you are. All right, but I bought Gary and the woman some time. It was the best I could do."

"I have seen you many times in the camp. You are friend to no man."

"Why should I be?" He offered the boy something to eat, feeding him with his fingers rather than untie him. McCabe's injured hand was nearly useless, and the slightest movement caused him intense pain. He had not looked at it for a day, but it was badly swollen and ached continually so that he found sleep difficult. The boy was a man by Comanche reckoning, and, because of this, McCabe respected the danger he represented. And the boy saw more than he let on, too. Probably he had it all figured out, the why of it and everything, about splitting up with Gary and the Tremain woman. Gary was such a sporting ass, full of gallant nonsense, and McCabe knew that he would never have agreed to split and let McCabe draw Stone Calf away, even for an hour or two. Gary would start a spiel about McCabe's being hurt and all that nonsense, and McCabe didn't want to listen to it.

The boy spoke, breaking into McCabe's thoughts. "Why must I leave my home, my family, to be bound this way, a prisoner?"

"I'm taking you back to your mother and father,"

McCabe said. "Your real parents."

"My real parents are in Iron Hand's village."

"These are real decent people who've come a long way to get you back. They cried over you."

"Others will grieve for me. But why do I speak of this? They cannot hold me. I will run away."

"Maybe," McCabe said. He stood up. "Get on the horse. We're getting out of here."

"And let Stone Calf see the fire?"

"Something like that."

The boy laughed. "Stone Calf is a man of many summers, very wise. He will find the woman and take her from the white man and leave his bones to bleach in the sun."

"That could be," McCabe said. "We'll see."

He tied the boy to the horse—hard work with only one hand—and then the boy flipped out his knee and bumped McCabe's bad hand. A sunburst bloomed in McCabe's skull, and he fell to the ground, crying out, writhing, and the boy dashed off, wheeling around, guiding the horse with his knees.

Before McCabe could gather himself and give chase, the boy had a hundred-yard start in the wrong direction, but he began pursuit while a hammer tormented his skull and his hand flamed. The boy made a game of it, yapping like a noisy dog leading another in play. He raced around McCabe, who was afoot and helpless.

McCabe yelled: "Do the Comanches teach their young to run like women or count coup?"

This was a desperate chance, and the boy took the bait, wheeling the horse to ride McCabe down, to touch him before riding back to his village to boast of the deed. At the last possible moment, McCabe whipped aside and flung out his arm, catching the boy in the stomach. He knocked him back, spooked the horse, and set him bucking, thrashing the boy

107

around like a stick on the end of a string. McCabe lunged again for the bridle, caught a trailing rein, and got the horse and prisoner again under tow.

He longed to rest a moment, to nurse the pain in his hand, but he dared not show further weakness to the boy. He was as wild as any animal and infinitely more dangerous. Mounting behind him, McCabe asked: "You have your fun?"

"Dancing Bear is too old for games. I will kill you."

"Sure you will," McCabe said. "Or maybe get yourself killed." He gigged the horse into motion and tried to ease his hand so that it pained him less. He wished now that he had let Gary take a look at it. Most of these frontier officers were half doctor from patching up their own wounded. The trouble was, Gary would have made a fuss over it and left McCabe feeling that he owed him something. A man had to pay as he went along. It was the only way to live. Or perhaps it was because he had never known genuine kindness. Everything that had been given him had been given selfishly. You worked for your bed and board and usually ended up giving more than you got in return, and, if you did a man a favor, he'd come back for another, a bigger one. Or if you let him do the favor, he'd remind you of it soon enough and expect something better in return.

The way he figured it, the hurt hand was just something that had to be. He took his chance on getting shot, so he couldn't really complain about the hand. He decided that, when he got back to the movers' camp on Sand Creek, he'd bathe the hand in hot water and take out the soreness—but after he'd delivered the boy and collected from Wringle.

McCabe wore out the night traveling, and, when dawn came, the boy spoke. "Stone Calf has killed the white man by now. He will take the woman back to his lodge and beat her properly."

"You know something? You're not worth all the bother I'm taking with you!" The boy turned and looked at him, his pride injured. Indian fashion, he wanted torture, brutal treatment. It was a value of his worth as a man. Only women and children were killed quickly or disregarded.

"Yes, sir," McCabe said. "You're just a kid who ought to be licked. Now, when you get among your own people, you act right, you hear?"

"I am Comanche!"

"You'll never be Indian," McCabe said. "No more than Stone Calf's wife is Indian." He sighed. "What am I going to do with you, anyway? Don't you remember anything about your real folks?"

"I am a Comanche," the boy said.

"All right, all right," McCabe said in English. "Lord, why can't people leave a thing alone? Poke around, stir it up, shake it, cry about it. They'd be better off if I turned you loose. But I can't even do that, boy. Too late for that."

Chapter Twelve

Guthrie McCabe remained near the Wringle wagon, not because he wished to be sociable, but because he smelled trouble and wanted to avoid it if he could. It seemed that everyone in the Sand Creek camp was congregated around Wringle's wagon. They stared at the boy and pestered him with talk he did not understand.

He was frightened and trying not to show it. He believed that he had been brought here to be tortured, then killed. This was what he would have done had one of them fallen into his hands. Wringle and his wife were pathetic. She cooked a meal for the boy, a homecoming meal that had been long planned and was the best she had, and he picked up the laden tin plate and threw it in her face. Wringle did not know whether to hit the boy or forgive him. He touched him, and the boy seized his arm and bit it deeply. Wringle retreated, blood dripping from his fingers.

From McCabe's elbow, Jane Donovan spoke. He had not heard her approach. He was not sure how long she had been standing there. It was easy to come and go in this crowd. "Can't you do something?"

"What can I do?" He looked at her. "Wringle's got to handle this his own way."

"Speak Indian to the boy. Make him understand."

"He understands," McCabe said. "I talked to him on the

way in." He hunched his shoulder, trying to position his hand more comfortably. "Wringle's got to understand that he's made a mistake . . . having the boy returned. He'll never tame him."

"How much did he pay you?"

"Enough," McCabe said shortly. "You want the exact amount?"

"No. I know what heartbreak costs." She paused. "Where's Jim Gary?"

"With a woman he found." McCabe waved his hand. "Out there some place, trying to stay alive."

Wringle was talking to the camp members, asking them to leave because they were making the boy nervous. He might as well have spoken to the night, for they remained around his fire, their eyes curious, each wondering if this would be happening to them. Even Mrs. McCandless was there with her vacant, wandering eyes. She studied the boy, and, when he saw her, his attention remained on her like a magnet.

"Someone ought to get her out of there," McCabe said. "The boy has been raised by Indians, and they don't like anyone who is sick in the head."

"What happened to your hand?" Jane asked curiously.

"Hurt it."

"I can see that."

Wringle's wife was moving slowly toward the boy, speaking softly, smiling, trying to touch his heart with words. He waited until she was within reach and pounced on her, bore her to the ground, his hands locked in her hair, trying to drub her head against the earth. Wringle and two men pulled him free, then Wringle picked up a strap, raised it, and finally dropped it and stood there with tears running down his cheeks.

"I've seen enough of this," McCabe said, turning away.

Jane moved with him. "Come to the wagon. I want to look at that hand."

"Feeling sorry for me?"

"Yes, but for a different reason probably than you think."

At her fire she heated a kettle of water as McCabe removed the bandage from his hand. He had to jerk the last bit free, ripping off a scab. Pus drained from it, and his face was chalky from the pain.

Jane lighted a lantern so that she could see better. Her expression tightened when she saw the wound so badly festered. She used a salt and boric acid solution, and, when she pushed McCabe's hand into the pan, he gasped, then clenched his teeth.

"Can you feel that draw?"

"Lord, yes," he said tightly.

"What will Wringle do with the boy, McCabe?"

He looked at her for a moment. "You change the subject mighty fast when you get a notion." Then he shrugged. "Let him go. He can't keep him. The boy was taken too young. Maybe they'll learn from this. I hope so."

"Is that why you brought the boy back . . . so this would happen? So they'd all see and give it up?"

"It was in my mind," he conceded. "But you always hope that this one will be different. It never is. How long do I have to soak this?"

"Until I say it's enough. The hand is infected. You want to lose it?" She made him rest the hand on a towel while she reheated the water.

"You see the way Wringle was? He'd take anything for the boy's sake . . . kicks, insults, abuse. That's not right, Jane. It makes you sick to see what wanting something will do to a man."

"Are you sure this is Wringle's boy?" She studied him

when she said it. "You're not really sure, are you, McCabe? Here . . . put your hand back in the water."

He ground his teeth together for a moment, then said: "There's a good chance the boy is Wringle's, but who can be sure? What difference does it make, anyway? None to Wringle. If I'd brought in a monkey with the hair shaved off, it would have been the same. A long time ago he made up his mind that he'd do anything, take anything, just to get the boy back. That became an excuse, a password, with Wringle. God knows how many failures it's covered."

"You don't feel pity for him," she said, "just disgust." She dried his hand, took out a sharp knife, and heated the blade.

"What are you going to do with that?"

"I'm going to cut that open so it can heal."

"Oh, no! The way you feel you'd push that extra deep."

"What would it matter? I couldn't touch your heart." She leaned forward and looked steadily at him, her eyes large and bright in the firelight. "Do you want to lose your hand? You know I'm not lying to you, don't you? Let that hand go and you'll lose it, maybe the arm, too. And Guthrie McCabe couldn't live with one arm. He'd be half a man. That's very important to you . . . to be right and strong and better than anyone else." She smiled. "Perhaps I might go a little deeper than someone who didn't know you, but it shouldn't matter. You have very few feelings. You pride yourself on that. Then, too, you can't have it all your own way. Someone is bound to hurt back, just a little."

"You're as hard as a man . . . as hard as I've ever seen." He took a cigar butt from his pocket and lighted it. "Go ahead and cut, but don't expect me to yell."

"Naturally," she said, and made the incision quickly, deeply.

McCabe's eyes were like white eggs, and the cigar

dropped from his mouth; then he fell over, the cigar singeing his vest until she flicked it away. Her father came up as she was putting a bandage on McCabe's hand. He looked down at the Texan and asked: "He sleeping?"

"He fainted."

"The hell you say!"

Donovan filled a cup with coffee, then squatted until she was finished. She made a sling for the hand and said: "Help him over to the wagon. Liam can get his bedroll."

"I don't want him sleeping here," Sean Donovan said. Then he put the cup aside and got up. "Oh, all right. I guess it'll be all right."

"The crowd still around Wringle's?"

"Some have had enough. The boy's a real savage."

"What did you expect?"

"A savage," her father said. "But, then, what a man expects is a lot different from what he gets. We all expected him to be wild, but we also thought something could be done about it." He shook his head sadly. "It makes a man wonder if he's done the right thing about coming back."

He walked off into the night, and Jane Donovan straightened McCabe's legs, trying to make him more comfortable.

By cutting north and keeping up a steady march, Jim Gary hoped to intercept the Fort Elliot patrol, and his luck ran well, for he sighted it late in the afternoon of the third day, a thin column reaching across the flats, a dark line moving sluggishly with only the guidon to mark the head of it. Gary emptied his pistol into the air and listened to the reports soak into the immense miles. Then he saw the column increase its pace, change direction slightly, bearing down on him.

Captain Winslow Scott was commanding, a razor-jawed man in his middle forties. He dismounted, leaving the detail in charge of the sergeant, then took off his hat and bowed when he saw Janice Tremain.

"In heaven's name, Gary, where did you find her?"

"Iron Hand's village . . . Janice, may I introduce Captain Scott . . . ? Janice Tremain, Captain."

A look of awe and wonderment came into Scott's gaunt face.

"Not old Pistol Britches' daughter? Sergeant, on the double here." He put his arm around Janice's shoulder, a completely unnecessary gesture, for she could have out-marched him any day of the week. Yet she permitted this. It was a gallant part men liked to play, and she did not wish to deprive him of it. "Sergeant, have the detail dismount and light squad fires."

"Here, sir?"

"Damn it, you heard the order. Take Miss Tremain with you and see that a shelter is put up to protect her from the sun."

"Really . . . ," Janice began, but Gary's touch closed off the rest. "You're back in the Army now," he said. "Go with the sergeant. Everything will be all right."

"Of course, it will," Scott said. "Get on with it, Sergeant." He took Gary's arm and led him a dozen yards away so their talk would not be overheard. "The old man is on needles and pins. He hasn't received a report from you."

"I've been busy."

Scott smiled. "Indeed, you have." Then his gaiety faded. "Has McCabe made any progress?"

"One boy was recovered."

"Just one?" Scott frowned. Like most men in command, he wanted everything done yesterday. "Tell McCabe to work a bit faster. These civilians are an impatient lot. We don't want them complaining of Army inefficiency to their Congressmen. A thing like that could go down the line and land on some first lieutenant's neck."

"Well, mine's way out, sir."

"Yes, I know." He turned his head and looked at Janice Tremain, who was sitting beneath the newly erected shelter, a canvas stretched on four poles, the back side of it staked to the ground to block out the smashing sunlight. "She may save your bacon, Gary. Her father was well known in the Army. Does she have any relatives?"

"Some politician."

"Ah, yes, I recall now. I'll dispatch a man to go on ahead and send a wire. Naturally I'll mention your name."

"You don't have to," Gary said.

Scott frowned again. "Gary, you sound morose. Is there anything you want me to include in my report?"

"Tell them to ship me a box of cigars."

Scott laughed and gave Gary what he had left in his case. He shook hands briefly. "I don't envy you this duty, but, when there's no fighting to do, the Army has the last mess to clean up. Besides, you always have the next batch to look forward to."

"What's this?"

"The camp in the grove outside the fort is beginning to fill up again. Four wagons when I left and a report that more were on the way."

"Oh, no," Gary said, and walked over to the shelter. "You're in good hands now, Janice. Good bye."

She stood up, and he noticed absently that she was nearly as tall as he was.

"I'd embarrass you if I kissed you, wouldn't I?" she said.

"Yes."

"I won't, then." She offered him her hand. "You've been most gallant, Jim, and I'm sure you've done the right thing as far as the Army is concerned. Will I see you again?"

"Perhaps, if you remain at Fort Elliot."

"You know I can't do that." She let her shoulders rise and fall. "You'll have to forgive me for not thanking you for bringing me from something to nothing. With Stone Calf I had a halfway home, but all that's gone now, so I can go back to no home at all. My father, my fiancé, even Stone Calf are all gone. So I can't really thank you, can I?"

"No," he said.

"All those years, I dreamed of getting away, but now I no longer want it. Good bye, Jim." She turned away from him with the abruptness of a closed door. He stood rooted for a moment, and then stomped angrily to his horse.

In passing, Scott said: "All the details are not clear in my mind, Gary. The circumstances under which you found her ought to be included in the report."

"She was gathering firewood. I asked her if she wanted to go back, and she said yes."

"Is that all?"

"Yes, sir," Gary said. He mounted then and turned out, moving in a southerly direction. Behind him, Scott yelled something, but Gary ignored it completely and kicked the horse into a run. He did not pause for nearly a mile. When he stopped and looked back, Scott had the detail moving toward Fort Elliot.

The sight saddened him, not because he was alone in this immense land, but because he had done what was right and somehow it had come out wrong. Wrong for Janice Tremain. Had he left her with Stone Calf, he supposed she would have always longed to go back, just as the civilians at Sand Creek wanted something they didn't have. But time would have softened this for her, and eventually made her content with her lot. That was, Gary decided, the key to being happy, anyway—to be satisfied with what you had and to keep the wishing just that—wishing.

117

Chapter Thirteen

The last thing Jim Gary thought he would see on the prairie was three wagons moving north. He spotted them at dawn and rode toward them, unable to understand why they were there.

Silas Barnstalk had the lead wagon. He drew up as Gary wheeled his horse around. Barnstalk's wife, riding inside the wagon, looked out, saw who it was, then pulled her head in, no longer interested.

"What's the matter?" Gary asked.

"We've had enough," Barnstalk said. "That's what's the matter."

Two men from the other wagons dismounted and came forward on foot. They looked at Gary but said nothing, just stood there with their hands tucked into the bibs of their overalls.

"Did McCabe get back with the boy?"

"Boy?" Barnstalk laughed without humor. "By God, a mountain cat would be more like it. Wringle's having one hell of a time. His woman's thrown up her hands and won't go near the kid. No, we seen that and that's enough! My Jess was three when we lost him. Be seventeen now. If that's what he's like, the Comanches are welcome to him." He motioned to the other men. "Lige and Sam feel the same way. I guess a man has to learn the hard way."

"Yes, so it would seem."

Sam Ludlow said: "Wringle's wishin' now that the boy was back with the Comanches."

"All he'd have to do is turn him loose," Gary said. "The boy'd skip out during the night."

"Funny you'd say that," Barnstalk said. "Wringle's turned the boy loose, but he still hangs around. Seems like he's watchin' something, waitin' for something." He took out some cut-plug and worried off a chew.

"When you get to Fort Elliot, try to tell all this to the new folks living by the creek."

"Another batch, eh?" Barnstalk laughed dryly. "Well, I won't be going to Elliot, Lieutenant. Besides, a man has to find out things for himself. What's right for me is wrong for another."

"There's some truth there," Gary agreed, thinking of Janice Tremain. "Good luck to you."

"Same to you," Barnstalk said.

Gary mounted and waited while the wagons filed past him, and then he rode on toward Sand Creek. He wondered how many of the others would be following Barnstalk. A good many, he hoped. The more who gave up, the better it would be. Since they'd all given up before, and that sort of thing got to be a habit with some men, it would get easier each time.

Another night on the prairie, then he saw the grove before noon, and entered the Sand Creek camp while the sun was high. He thought the place oddly silent; people stood around in clannish groups, not working much, and talking less. He saw the boy near Wringle's wagon, sitting in the shade, staring at a spot of ground between his outstretched legs.

Gary went on to the Donovan camp and found Jane there. She was washing the midday pots and dropped them with a clatter when she saw him. Gary put his arm around her and walked with her to the fire.

119

"Haven't had a decent cup of coffee since I left," he said. "Where's McCabe?" His voice assumed a flatness when he said the man's name, and Jane's eyes took on a questioning expression.

"In our wagon." Gary forgot about the coffee and unflapped his pistol holster. Jane put out her arm and stopped him. "McCabe's flat on his back, Jim. His hand became infected." She took his arm. "Come on, sit down. You look like you rode to hell, measured it, and rode back." Her hands pushed at him, then handed him the coffee cup. "Let's talk, Jim. Then you can do what you think you have to do."

"Sure," he said. "Why get excited?" He tried the coffee and smiled. "Man, that's good. Real good."

"McCabe said you had a woman."

"I took her north and met the Fort Elliot patrol. She's Army."

"Oh. It's good to be somebody, isn't it?" She squatted down across from him and watched him. "You look good to me, even with the whiskers." She lifted the pot. "Better have a refill on that coffee before Pa and Liam get back."

"The camp seems unusually quiet," he said.

"It's Wringle's boy," Jane said. "Nothing has been right since McCabe brought him back."

"I met Barnstalk on the way in. Lige and Sam were with him."

"There'll be others going. It doesn't take much to discourage them any more, Jim."

"And you?"

"Maybe. Pa and Liam are trying to buy some horses. They've been talking about returning to Fort Elliot and wintering there before going East."

"Winter's five months away," Gary said. The trend of the

talk began to alarm him. "What about your brother?"

She shrugged. "I hope he's dead. I've seen enough, Jim. I think all of us have, but they don't want to admit it yet."

"Captain Scott told me another camp was building at Fort Elliot."

"People like us?" She shook her head sadly. "The fools! The utter fools."

"Sure they are, but you can only teach fools one at a time." He got up and walked over to the back of the wagon and looked in. Guthrie McCabe was stretched out on a pallet of folded blankets, his hand a pillow of bandages.

"Heard you talking," McCabe said. "You caught me when I'm down, Jim."

"What I've got is good enough to keep until you can stand."

"Now you're sore. I see you made it, though. The woman in camp?"

"The Army's taking care of her."

"I'll bet she likes that," McCabe said. "Do me a favor and roll up the sides of the canvas top. It's like an oven in here."

"Kind of gives you a taste of what hell is like," Gary said, but he rolled up the sides.

Jane was cooking some back fat and beans for him. He again settled by the fire. "He's been a better patient than I thought he'd be," she said.

"Why not? He can't help himself . . . yet." He looked around the camp. "Wish a fight would start. The quiet gets you, doesn't it?"

"Jim, why doesn't the boy run away?"

"I don't know." He took the plate from her and began to eat, but he had hardly cleaned up half of it when someone yelled in a long, drawn-out wail, and a sudden and mixed shouting came from the other end of the camp.

Gary dumped his plate and started to run even as a crowd gathered around the McCandless wagon. He used his elbows and fists to batter his way through, then stopped quickly, having come to the inside of the perimeter.

The boy was there, glaring at them, an animal ready to pounce at the first sign of antagonism. Mrs. McCandless was there, too, on the ground, her normally vacant eyes now made permanently so by death. Gary saw the stout stake, carefully sharpened, the butt protruding from her chest, and he knew with a terrible certainty that the boy had killed her, although it seemed completely senseless at the time.

Around him was utter silence, shocked silence. McCandless stood there, looking at his wife, then at the boy. This seemed to be a signal. For the crowd suddenly vaulted into action, roaring, yelling, driving forward, grabbing the boy, beating on him with their fists as though he were a demon representing all the accumulated hurt they had known in their lives.

Gary tried desperately to stop them, but they mowed him down like a new reaper in a field of wheat. He rolled and thrashed to keep from being trampled beneath their feet. Suddenly they were free of him, moving away, the boy suspended above their heads, gripped by a dozen angry hands. They were a roaring, savage animal mob, and the boy's screams rose above the sounds they made.

Gaining his feet, Gary staggered after them, drawing his pistol, then remembering that he had failed to reload it after firing the signal shots at the Fort Elliot patrol. He tried to use it as a club, to knock men asprawl, but a few turned on him and took it away from him. He was completely helpless against them.

Someone produced a rope and threw it over the limb of a tree while others fastened the loop around the boy's neck.

Eager hands hoisted him aloft, and he jumped like a toy on a string, his eyes popping, tongue bitten through. His hands clawed at the rope around his neck, and the man on the other end began to jerk on it, making him jump and swing while they yelled their venomous hatred at him.

Gary could only stand there and watch and listen until the sawing parted the strands of the rope, and the boy fell like a shot bird. Instantly the yelling ceased. It was like water pouring from a ruptured dam, at last finding a sane level, leaving only a trickle now in place of a torrent.

The boy was dead, and they lost interest in him, turning away, going back to their wagons without a word. Only one man remained, Wringle, who looked at the boy and cried silently. In time he turned away to get a shovel to dig the grave.

Wringle saw Gary standing there, and said: "I wanted my boy back. That's all I wanted. A man must have a curse on him to have all this happen to him."

"I'll get some help for you."

"No, he's mine. I'll bury him. Let each bury his own."

Gary went back to Jane Donovan, sick, sorry, ready to give the order to pull out. Couldn't they see by now how it was? He was surprised to find McCabe leaning against the wagon. He was very weak, and Jane was trying to help him back inside, but he stubbornly resisted her.

"They killed him?" McCabe asked.

Gary nodded. "Not the easy way, either. Like animals."

"What else are we?" McCabe asked. "He killed her, huh?"

"Yes," Gary said. "How did you know?"

"A guess," McCabe said. "Just a guess." He became angry then. "If I'd suspected, don't you think I'd have warned McCandless?" He wiped a hand across his sweating face. "Indians fear anyone who's not right in the head. Evil spirits live there. Usually they kill off their own when they're that way.

123

The boy did what he thought he had to do." He let Jane help him sit down. "When I heard the first yell, I had that feeling. Then I remembered how the boy looked at Missus McCandless the night I brought him into camp, but it was too late then." He saw Gary's torn clothes, the blood on his face from the cuts he had received during the struggle. "I can see you tried to stop them. You could have got yourself killed."

"But at least I tried."

"Yeah," McCabe said. "Well, we never learn anything, just keep on trying." He accepted the coffee Jane handed him, then sat with the cup in his hand. "Jim, be smart and call it off. Pack 'em up, kit and caboodle, and take them back to the fort."

"You know I can't do that."

"What's to be gained by staying? Neither one of us is going to be popular with Iron Hand. Didn't Stone Calf chase you and the woman?"

"Yes."

McCabe frowned. "I'm afraid to ask the next question."

"Then I'll save you the trouble. He's dead."

McCabe groaned, but not from pain. "Lord help us! That's Iron Hand's brother." He drank his coffee and handed the cup to Jane. "Help me in the wagon. I want to lie down. I feel sick all over again."

"What the devil did you expect me to do?" snapped Gary.

"Just what you did, only I hoped you wouldn't." He leaned on Jane's arm and crawled over the tailgate. She came back to the fire and stood there for a moment.

"Were my father and brother . . . ?"

"Pulling on the rope," Gary said, not feeling disposed to be kind about it. "They went wild. Everyone went wild. All except Wringle. He's left with the burying."

"How could anyone ever live in such country?" she asked.

He raised his head and looked at her. "You just live and forget about the rest."

She waved her hand in the direction of McCandless's wagon. "How can you ever forget that? I think it ought to stay with you as long as you live."

"Did you think for a minute that it won't?" Gary asked. He left her then, went to his horse, and took off the saddlebags. At the creek he bathed, soaked to soften his whiskers, then lathered his face and shaved. He seemed to find a measure of comfort in this simple, familiar task.

McCabe was probably right: the best move would be to get out of the country before Iron Hand let his medicine man work him into the mood for war. Sooner or later someone would trail Stone Calf—his sons, probably—and, when they found what the buzzards had left, they'd be mixing paint and loading cartridges.

By going back to the fort, Gary supposed that he could gain a temporary reprieve from Comanche wrath, but what would going back really solve? The civilians would still be howling to the politicians for their loved ones, and the Army would still have the job of recovering them.

He'd have to come back, anyway, and do the hated job all over again, so he decided to stay and try to figure a way out of this. If he failed, it wouldn't matter because the Army would have a hard time court-martialing a dead man. And if he won, there wouldn't be a need for it.

There were no certain odds on a thing like this, Gary decided, but he guessed that he ought to go to Iron Hand and have a talk. The possibility occurred to him that, if he said the wrong thing, he might end up head down over a slow fire, but he surprised himself by not being frightened by this prospect.

"You made your bed," he said to the creek. "So now you sleep in it."

Chapter Fourteen

Jim Gary read the brief funeral service over Mrs. McCandless, and everyone in the grove was there except Wringle, who had reading of his own to do. After the headboard had been set in place, McCandless took Gary's hand and thanked him.

"She's at rest now. Poor woman, she's had a heavy load to carry these years." He looked past Gary, past the last fringe of wagons to the lone man and his own mound of earth. McCandless's eyes pulled into fleshy slits, and his expression grew thoughtful. "Don't seem right that a man should have to stand alone over his only son. There's something indecent about it." He stepped around Gary and walked slowly toward Wringle.

McCabe, who stood by Jane Donovan, said: "Help me over there."

She looked at him oddly, almost joyously, then gave her arm for support. He was not a well man, not strong, but he was determined and closed the distance without faltering.

Jim Gary looked at the others. "Anyone else? Or aren't you big enough?"

They knew what he meant, but not one budged, although the desire to do so was evident in their eyes. Finally, he turned away and walked over to Wringle and the mound of earth.

McCandless was staring at the crudely carved headboard.

Then he said: "In a way, neither knew what they was doin', Wringle."

The other man nodded. He kept his head tipped forward as though studying the brass eyelets in his shoes. "Everything was against him from the very start, wasn't it?" He took out a handkerchief and blew his nose. "When I was a kid, I used to spend time cryin' when the cat would have a litter. Out of five or six, only one would live. The others would get stepped on by a horse, or run over by the reaper, or killed by dogs. I guess the Lord figures we're animals, too, 'cause there's so many of us who get killed off, and there don't seem to be much we can do about it."

"I'm sorry," McCandless said. "Sorry for my woman and your boy, and plumb sorry I went crazy like I did." He put his hand briefly on Wringle's shoulder.

"I suppose you'll go back now, Mister Wringle," Gary said.

After a moment, Wringle replied: "I guess not. I'm going to build right here. Right here on Sand Creek." This was, Gary guessed, more than an idle boast or a spur-of-the-moment statement. Wringle meant it. He put the shovel on his shoulder and went back to his camp.

McCandless commented: "Nothing for me here now, but if Wringle can stay, so can I."

"Go back to where you came from," McCabe said flatly. "For once in your life, be smart."

"Who wants to be?" McCandless asked.

At evening time, several more families broke camp, made up their wagons, and announced their intention of leaving this forsaken country. Jim Gary did nothing to stop them. They left early in the morning, just before sunup, a quiet departure with no good byes. They just pulled into a string and started north across the prairie. In an hour they were only vague dots against the heat shimmer, and soon after that they vanished. Gary likened this land to the sea, with its changing moods and unforgiving character. A man could easily vanish on its face and leave not a trace.

He wanted to talk to McCabe about Iron Hand and the advisability of remaining at Sand Creek, so he went to Jane Donovan's wagon and found her alone. McCabe, she told him, was at the creek, bathing. He walked downstream to a thicket of rushes, guided the last twenty-five yards by splashing and off-key singing. McCabe jumped when Gary parted the rushes and sat down on the bank, then relaxed and went on with his bath.

"Thought it was a woman," he said, smiling. "Somehow they find me irresistible."

"I find you irresistible, too," Gary said. "You feeling better?"

"Jane's cooking did it." He canted his head and looked at Gary. "Still carrying a grudge?"

"It can wait. Right now I need some advice."

"Pinches like hell to ask for it, doesn't it?"

"Some, but I can live with it. What's Iron Hand going to do?"

"Froth at the mouth. Dance and sing songs and tell everyone how the white man lied and double-crossed him." McCabe got out of the water and dried himself with an old blanket. "And you did, Gary. I told you to leave the woman alone."

"This is all my fault?"

"You took the woman and killed Stone Calf." He slipped into his underwear and pants. "Of course, he'll blame me because I brought you into the camp as a friend. McCabe's name is mud now."

"The honor is richly deserved," Gary said.

McCabe laughed. "What's going on in your do-gooder mind?"

"I've decided to go back to Iron Hand. I don't know how, but I've got to make him listen, to understand that I was forced to do what I did."

"He'll take the hide off you a layer and an inch at a time. Then, in a week or so, if you're still alive, he'll cook your brains out over a slow fire." He slipped into his shirt and buttoned it with one hand. Putting on his cartridge belt was more of a chore, but he managed it, even to tying down the bottom of the holster. "Jim, what makes you so stupid?"

"I work hard at it," Gary said, determined not to rise to McCabe's bait.

"Maybe I put that the wrong way. What makes you so damn' set on saving these people? Let them get discouraged and go home." He wiped a hand across his mouth. "I've tried to help you, but you keep fighting me all the time. One of these days I'm just going to throw up my hands and. . . ."

"Help me?" Gary shouted this. "McCabe, you've bucked me every step of the way!"

"Show me where?"

The man's gall, his coolness, angered Gary unreasonably. He had to take three deep breaths before he could speak. "How about that trouble I had with the Twokerrys? You sat out there on the prairie and watched it instead of coming in and giving me a hand."

"You haven't heard a peep out of them since, have you?"

"What's that supposed to mean?"

"Simply that you settled it yourself. Suppose I'd come in and backed you. Every time you'd give an order after that they'd look at me to see if I approved. I did you a favor, Jim."

"You've got a slick way of twisting things around," Gary

said. "All right, we'll skip that and go to the main issue . . . your running out on me and Janice Tremain."

McCabe laughed. "You were riding double, Jim. Stone Calf knew that the boy and I rode single, so he was following the horse that made the deepest track." He watched a blank amazement come into Gary's expression, then went on to add: "So I took the boy on one horse. Bought you a little time that way, too. I'll bet Stone Calf rode ten hours before he found out he was following the wrong man."

"I might have known you'd have some crazy, twisted-up reason, Guthrie, but it won't work with me. Just get that hand healed up so you can fight. We're going to have it out, and the winner of this will only be able to crawl away."

"You're stubborn as well as stupid," McCabe said, and stepped past him. His right side was hidden from Gary, and McCabe sneaked the draw on him, cracking the young man heavily on the head with the barrel of the gun. Gary wilted instantly, and blood oozed from the long slit in his scalp.

McCabe wiped the barrel on his pants leg, then reholstered the pistol. He looked down at Gary and shook his head. "Hang it all, you're the hardest man to do anything for. You go into Iron Hand's village and you're dead, and you're too pure to die. There aren't enough like you as it is."

He left him lying in the rushes and walked back to the grove, thinking that it would be better if he just saddled up and rode out without saying anything to anyone. Still, he couldn't do that. He'd have to speak to Jane Donovan. He felt compelled to say something, give her some reason.

She was washing clothes, boiling shirts in a kettle, when he came up to the fire.

"Too hot to do that," he said.

"Hot or not, they get dirty. Where's Jim?"

"At the creek," McCabe said. "I came to say good bye."

She frowned and deserted the washing. "Why?"

He let his shoulders rise and fall. "Because I've had enough, too. I'm getting out."

"No, that isn't what I meant. Why say good bye to me?"

"Because you're the first woman I haven't . . . well, worked for something. Or maybe because you hated me yet treated me like you'd treat Jim Gary."

"I could have changed my mind about you, Guthrie."

"No reason to," he said. "Given a chance, I'd still lift the pennies off a dead man's eyes." He looked at her and found her regarding him carefully. He pulled his glance away. "No, I guess I wouldn't do that any more, either. I'm just sorry about the whole thing. Because of you, and I guess Jim, it leaves a bad taste in my mouth." He reached out and took her hand. "Jane, I've never had a friend in my life who didn't want something from me. But you've been that to me, and I like it."

"Don't be afraid of people any more. They won't hurt you."

"Yes, they will. But it's worth it." He dropped her hand. "Look, when you see Jim again, tell him good bye. Tell him that I like him in spite of the things I've done and said to him."

"He's at the creek, you said. You can tell him yourself."

"No, no. Jim's sore at me, but he'll get over it in time." He laughed. "He's the closest thing to a friend I ever had, the foolish do-gooder." He looked at her, studied her as though fixing the image of her in his mind. "Jane, would you let me kiss you?"

"You could have taken a kiss," she said. "I'm sure you know how. You must have taken plenty."

"No, not this time. If it isn't given. . . ."

"Of course, it's given," she said, and put her arms around

him. He held her for a moment, as if she were a flower, full of delicacy and sweetness, and then released her.

"I'll remember that," he said. "Remember it for a long time." He turned away from her, then stopped, and looked back. "Jane, why don't you marry Jim Gary? I mean, he's your kind of man, Jane. When you're both old, you can look back at the mistakes he's made, but you won't feel a bit ashamed of any of them."

She opened her mouth to speak, but he wheeled and went to the picket line, there saddling his horse. He figured the tap he'd given Gary should keep him sick long enough for him to clear out. He had wasted enough time with Jane, but somehow he couldn't go without saying his piece. Probably she thought he was a liar. Why not? A man is judged by what he has been, and there wasn't much in McCabe's life that reflected pride or instilled confidence in others.

There wasn't much of a plan in McCabe's mind, except that he couldn't let Gary go to Iron Hand's village. They'd kill him before he could state his case. Still, McCabe knew that he himself would hardly be welcome. Indians did not single out men to blame for their troubles. They blamed them all, took out their hate on those handiest, usually some innocent traveler who died wondering what it was all about.

Nobody can accuse me of being innocent, McCabe thought. He'd lost that the day his father kicked him off the wagon and shoved him into a cold world without a blanket. He felt sorry for Jim Gary because, no matter how this turned out, Gary's head would roll. That old colonel was due for retirement and had himself covered like a dirty shirt. Gary was positioned and primed to fall when the axe let go higher up the line. And this disturbed McCabe, for he found a great worth in Gary.

With this thought came McCabe's reason for being again on the prairie, for riding back to Iron Hand's village, which was the most foolish thing he had ever done in his life.

"I'm a no-good fool," McCabe said to his horse. "And now I want to do one thing that will make people remember me without getting mad."

Still he was a man who calculated his chances carefully. He fully believed that he could get away with this and return to Sand Creek alive, with his ears still fastened to his head. The chances were against it, but he had never backed away from a risk or two. The thought occurred to him that this might look better than it really was, and there was enough recalcitrant rogue in him, enough schemer, to make him thoroughly enjoy this—a moment of genuine heroism.

He spent the night on the prairie, huddled in a split in the earth, sleeping with one ear cocked, his horse saddled and picketed close by. He was a lone man in a lonely land, and his mind kept going back through the years to other times when he had felt like this. Like when he had lived under Anson Miles's thumb in the mansion, jumping when Miles had told him to jump, and hating every minute of it.

He was riding hours before the sun came up. In the afternoon he came on Iron Hand's camp and rode boldly into it, through a quickly gathered avenue of hostility. He stopped before Iron Hand's lodge.

The Comanche came out, looked long at Guthrie McCabe, then raised his hand a brief inch. Instantly the braves howled and converged on him, sweeping McCabe off the horse. They hoisted him aloft and carried him into Iron Hand's lodge.

Chapter Fifteen

Bertha Stokes, who was nine and unable to stay out of the creek, found Jim Gary moaning in the rushes. This frightened her, so she ran and brought her father, along with four other men in the camp. They carried Gary back to the camp. He was too sick to help himself, and, as soon as Jane Donovan heard about it, she had him brought to her wagon. Her father and brother disapproved of this, but she put womanly pressure on them, and they fell silent. They had learned from her mother how it would be if they pushed her too far: half-done beans, bitter coffee, and dirty shirts to wear. They permitted Gary to be placed in the wagon.

The cut was bathed and bandaged, and he slept through the night while Jane sat outside, quickly coming awake every time he stirred. By morning he was left with only a throbbing headache and a renewed anger at Guthrie McCabe. He left the wagon and had breakfast with the Donovans.

"I suppose he ducked out?" Gary said. "He's great at that."

"He's gone," Jane said. "I think he went to see Iron Hand." She looked at her father and brother. They said nothing, just scooped food from their tin plates.

Gary looked at each of them, a frown building on his forehead. "No, he wouldn't do that. That would be a dumb thing to do. McCabe only does the smart things, the things that are best for McCabe."

"I saw the direction he took," Liam Donovan said. "This time he wasn't heading toward Fort Elliot."

Gary's interest in breakfast vanished, and he got up, pacing back and forth, his lip caught between his teeth. "I was going to go. We talked about it before he slugged me with his gun."

"He didn't want you to die," Jane said simply. "Can't you see that?"

"I can see that it might look like that, but it's not McCabe. He doesn't do things that way."

From the other side of the camp, someone yelled. "*Ri-i-i-ders!* Riders coming!"

Gary walked across the grounds and stood on the north side, where a group gathered. His field glasses were with his blankets, but, by shielding his eyes with his hand, he could make out a four-man detail, unmistakably Army.

"Stay here," he said, and walked out to meet them. This would be Army business, and he didn't want everyone listening to it.

Sergeant Goldman was in charge, a whiskered man with a large cud of tobacco in his cheek. He saluted before dismounting and handed the reins to the man on his right.

"Dispatch for you, sir," Goldman said, producing it. "I met Captain Scott five hours out of Elliot. He told me where to find you. Hurt your head, sir?"

"No," Gary said. "This keeps the sun off." He ripped open the envelope and read the message, then swore. "What the hell does this mean? Report back to Fort Elliot immediately? By heaven, I've got trouble enough here without . . . !" He cut the rest off and blew out his breath.

"I wouldn't know that, sir. I talked with Scott, and he'd sent a rider ahead to telegraph that Tremain woman's uncle, or something. You know how those politicians are, sir. Likely he sent a wire to Colonel Frazer, and now you get your orders."

"But I'm needed here."

Sergeant Goldman shrugged. "I guess a politician is more important."

"Sergeant, I just can't go."

"Lieutenant, you'll get court-martialed if you don't." He wagged his head. "In twenty-four years I haven't yet figured out the way the Army runs, but I just do as I'm told and let the fellow higher up worry about it." He turned to the detail. "Dismount . . . ! We'll start back in a half hour, if that suits you, Lieutenant."

"Yes. Hell, yes. Let's go if we have to." He turned and walked back to the creek where the civilians waited, the question in their faces. He suddenly saw that they did not trust the Army. They depended on it because they had to, but they did not trust military policy. And he hardly blamed them.

"Find Wringle and send him to the Donovan wagon," Gary said, and passed on through.

"What's up?" a man asked.

"You'll find out in time. Just get Wringle for me and don't be all day about it." He hurried back to the Donovan camp. They stood there, waiting for him. "Liam, would you roll my gear and saddle a horse for me?"

"Sure," he said, and left the fire.

"What did the Army want?" Sean Donovan asked. "Some change in plans? We ain't being ordered out, are we?"

"No, but I've been ordered back to Elliot," Gary said. "Not for long, though. I ought to be back in ten days." He was not sure of this, but it sounded good, made them feel better. Wringle came over, a new worry in his eyes. Gary said: "I'm leaving you in charge here until I return. Keep them in camp until McCabe gets back."

"Maybe he won't be coming back," Wringle said. "I hear he rode out toward Iron Hand's country. Wasn't that woman you rescued married to his brother or something?"

"News gets around," Gary said curtly, hoping that would end the prying talk.

"How come you're ordered back?" Wringle asked. "Oh, the soldiers talked. Didn't expect them to keep quiet, did you?"

"I guess not," Gary said. "Wringle, if I gave you an order, would you obey it?"

"I guess I would."

"Then get this straight . . . if I'm not back in two weeks, pack up the camp and return to Fort Elliot." He went on before anyone could stop him. "I know that's not the way it was supposed to be, but I'm trying to do what's right for you people. McCabe's gone, and I don't know if he'll come back or not. Our friendship with Iron Hand was thin to begin with, and now it's shot down the creek because of the woman I took. The responsibility for this is mine, so you have nothing to worry about. The way I figure it, Iron Hand is just as likely to make a raid on you as not. He sure knows what we're here for. I just don't want anyone killed."

"There's many in this grove that haven't given up hope of recovering their kin," Wringle said. "Going back to the fort won't set well, Gary."

"Good heavens, man, we'll do everything we can to recover the prisoners!" He wiped a hand across his mouth. "Maybe we'll just have to make a new start, that's all."

"All this starting is discouraging," Wringle stated. "All right. Two weeks. If you're not back then, we'll pack up and pull out." He turned and walked away to tell the others.

Liam Donovan had the horse saddled and Gary's gear lashed on.

"I'll walk with you," Jane said. He wanted a moment alone with her, but he was to have only that, for Sergeant Goldman was impatient to leave, and the civilians kept gathering around, looking on.

"Some of the orders you get in the Army are really stupid," Gary said. "I hate saying good bye, Jane, especially when I don't know what's over the next hill for any of us. But I'll try to get back."

"Don't, if it means doing anything against regulations." She smiled at him. "You're a very sincere man, Jim, and because of that somewhat foolish. Remember that we're not worth it. If we were, we could do for ourselves." She bent forward and kissed him lightly. "Was she pretty . . . the woman you rescued?"

"Yes," he said. "Why do you ask?"

"Lieutenant, we ought to be going!" Goldman called out.

"Yes, yes! In a moment!"

"Jim, I hope you don't come back," Jane said. "Then we'll leave, too, and we'll never get started again. Believe me, most of us want to give it up, but none of us is honest enough to admit it. We made a mistake, and it's snowballed into one huge mess. I want to go back to Fort Elliot, to give it up. My brother's dead. Let's bury him and get it over with."

"Lieutenant!"

"All right, Sergeant! Good bye, Jane. I'll see you."

He ran to his horse and stepped into the saddle. Goldman was already turning the detail. They rode north immediately, and, when Gary looked back, Jane Donovan was standing alone, her arm upraised like some small statue. He waved to her and then did not look back again.

Guthrie McCabe spent a most unpleasant evening, tied to four solidly-driven stakes while the children amused themselves until bedtime by lighting small twigs and placing them on his bare stomach.

Iron Hand and his favorite braves watched this, but McCabe robbed them of genuine enjoyment by failing to cry out even once, although he had to bite his lips until they bled. Finally, at Iron Hand's signal, the children were shooed away and McCabe was cut free of the stakes.

"There will be more tomorrow night," Iron Hand said grimly.

"I can hardly wait," McCabe said.

He had momentarily forgotten Iron Hand's knowledge of English and complete lack of a sense of humor. McCabe was seized by the hair and beaten soundly with a coup stick.

"Iron Hand does not think McCabe is a friend. There is no honor in McCabe. Soon, when we are through, he will stop laughing. His eyes will not see the things to laugh at, and he will have no tongue to make sounds. McCabe lies and cheats and brings false friends into Iron Hand's village."

"And Iron Hand is an old woman who will not let me speak," McCabe said. "Iron Hand is thick in the head. He should sing his death song and die, for he is not a leader."

The insult was meant to cut deep, and it did. Iron Hand half rose and raised his hand to strike. Then he settled back, his eyes a bright glitter in the firelight. "Why does McCabe return? Does he think Iron Hand will know rest until Stone Calf's killer is dead?"

"Stone Calf was a little boy fit for hunting rabbits, else he would not have allowed himself to be killed by a white man." McCabe laughed. "Stone Calf should have hunted sparrows with a net."

This was worth a kick in the face, and McCabe's head whacked the dirt. Then he sat up again. "Tell me where Stone Calf's sons were?" McCabe asked. "Did they hide in the rushes when their father rode out to bring back what was never his to take?" McCabe shook his head. "I come alone, Iron Hand, but soon many white men will come, and there are not enough men in your tribe to stop them. Soon all Comanches will join Stone Calf, for Comanches are thieves who steal women and children."

"Enough!" Iron Hand shouted. He was on his feet, stiff with anger. "There will be no quick death for McCabe, the enemy of all Comanches. You will be guarded well, day and night, and you will do a squaw's work until your arms ache and your fingers fall to the ground. Naked, you will walk among us, and the children will hurl stones at you and pelt you with sticks, and the women will turn their faces from you. You will rise before all others and sleep only after others have gone to rest. Each time you falter, you will be beaten, and your food will be the slops left over from the dogs. I have spoken, McCabe. Your days will be long and many-numbered, and each day a new death worse than the one before."

"You're a generous son-of-a-bitch," McCabe said, getting to his feet. He bent low at the waist, bowing, and Iron Hand was fascinated by this, thinking it was some part of the white man's ritual. At the proper moment, McCabe uncorked himself, balled his fist, and caught Iron Hand flush on the mouth. The blow sent the Comanche back, knocking down three men behind him; they all ended asprawl. Iron Hand was hastily raised to his feet. His lips were a ruin and seven front teeth were broken. He spat them on the ground.

"Tie him! Beat him!"

The Comanches knew how to do that to perfection. No rawhide for them, just slender willow branches incapable of drawing blood with a single blow, but after two hours, after a thousand blows, McCabe's back was a bleeding mass. He was cut down, unconscious, and left to lie where he fell. Later that night, while the camp slept, a mangy dog came over to share his warmth.

To waken him in the morning, water was poured over his face, and he was driven to his feet like a lazy horse. He had wood to fetch for a dozen fires, and everyone wanted his services at once. He made many trips for water, and in a daze finished out the day, but they kept him working late into the night.

The children were a constant cancer, hitting him, running after him, pelting him with fresh horse manure. He was a man naked in body and, after the fifth day of this, naked in soul.

To live, that was his one thought. To survive and suffer in utter silence, for he was not allowed to speak to anyone. He tried and was beaten for his trouble. The children soon tired of pestering him. There is little pleasure in tormenting someone who cannot fight back. He found some relief there, but his work was heavy and constant, and he ate off the ground from the scraps thrown to the dogs. He even fought them for the bones with meat still clinging to them.

He thought of Gary often, and of Jane. This helped him to keep going. Then he stopped thinking of them altogether. There was no escape for him, he knew, for he was watched constantly by braves who never relaxed their vigil. Occasionally he saw Iron Hand with his bland face and toothless smile, but Iron Hand merely glanced at him and went on his way, leaving McCabe with the feeling that he did not really exist at all.

The camp moved unexpectedly on the tenth day, and McCabe carried his load the same as the horses. They walked for two days, then stopped by a creek. McCabe judged that they were another thirty miles south now, thirty miles farther to go if he could break away.

He began to make plans, working carefully so as to establish a routine. Nothing lulled a man like routine. He hoped the guards would grow lax, even for a few minutes. But they did not. The guards were changed every day, and Iron Hand seemed to know McCabe's thoughts. His work was changed, breaking the routine, destroying his hopes, his plans.

The thought came slowly to McCabe, as bitter thoughts do, but it was there—the realization that he would never get away. He would die here.

Chapter Sixteen

Senator Clifton Tremain took the first train West after receiving Colonel Frazer's wire, and he had sufficient influence with the chairman of the board to have the engineer break a few records. An Army detail met him at the railhead and quickly carried him to Fort Elliot. He arrived thirteen hours before Lieutenant Jim Gary, who took his time, rested the horses, and left Sergeant Goldman with the impression that he didn't care whether or not he got to Fort Elliot.

Gary checked in with the O. D., then went to his quarters, took a leisurely bath, changed his clothes, and carefully shaved. Only then did he report to Colonel Frazer, who waited impatiently in his office.

The orderly closed the door, and Frazer waved him into a chair. "Senator Tremain has been asking me how we are coming along with our prisoner recovery. I told him well. And I hope you substantiate that, Lieutenant Gary."

"We've recovered two prisoners, sir. Janice Tremain and a boy in his early teens. Unfortunately the boy killed a female member of the camp and was hanged."

Frazer dropped his cigar. "He was *what?*"

"Hanged, sir. A fit of frenzy, I'm afraid, but by the time they cooled down, he was dead. Actually, he had it coming, and I don't think they were really sorry about their part in it."

Colonel Frazer sat down weakly and wiped a shaking hand

across his face. "In the name of heaven do you calmly sit there and tell me that after all this time you have recovered only two prisoners, and that one was killed? What have you been doing out there, Gary? Picking flowers?"

"No, sir. We've been quite busy, sir."

"The officer of the day reports to me that several wagons came back from Sand Creek. He's checking on the particulars."

"I believe they're discouraged, sir," Gary said. "May I ask why I was returned to the post?"

"Why, because Senator Tremain wants to talk to you. What did you think?" Frazer shook his head as though he were dealing with an idiot and did not want to lose his patience. "This evening the senator is giving a party for the officers and their wives in honor of his niece's return." He glanced at his watch. "That will give you exactly two hours and fourteen minutes to have your written report finished and on my desk. That will be all, Gary."

"Yes, sir."

He went outside, and on the porch he pursed his lips for a silent whistle. If Frazer was now shocked, Gary could only imagine what he would feel when the report reached his desk. The score: two captives returned, one now deceased. Iron Hand antagonized. His brother, Stone Calf, killed. Guthrie McCabe missing, assuredly a prisoner of the Comanches, possibly dead. General morale of the civilians, very low. Six percent returning to Fort Elliot. Possibility of that growing to twenty-five percent most likely. Future prospects of recovery, very slight. Total abandonment suggested.

With the report on Frazer's desk, Gary walked to the officers' mess, now gaily lighted and brightly decorated for the dance. The musicians were there, tuning their small band, and two orderlies scattered soap chips over the floor.

One man stood alone, pleasantly featured, somewhere in his early sixties. He appeared to be waiting for Gary, for he took his arm as soon as he stepped inside.

"You are Gary, aren't you? Good! I'm Clifton Tremain." He guided Gary to the punch bowl, speaking quite confidentially. Tremain was a likable man, soft-spoken, friendly. "I've been wanting to meet you, Lieutenant. And please try this punch. I understand that mixed among the neuter fruit juices there swirls two quarts of the sutler's best whiskey." He laughed and dippered a glassful for Gary.

He offered a silent toast, then drank some of the punch. A frown momentarily made a furrowed field of his forehead. "Ah, I may be mistaken there, Mister Gary. Perhaps it's closer to three quarts and not the sutler's best. Does that taste like horse liniment to you? No matter. I'm glad you came early. We have some matters to discuss."

"Exactly what, sir?"

"There's a matter of a reward, Mister Gary. Janice is my brother's daughter. Surely you did not expect to go unrewar. . . ." He stopped talking abruptly as Gary's expression froze slightly. "Of course! That was damned stupid of me, Gary. You'll have to forgive me. I'm so used to dealing with favor-seekers and putting my hand on my bankroll when a favor is done." He put his hand on Gary's shoulder and gave him a shake. "You're a gentleman. Forgive me for forgetting it."

"That's all right, sir."

"I wish everything else were all right." He steered Gary to some seats along the wall, where they could talk quietly and in private. "Janice has said very little to me about her captivity. I thought perhaps, since you delivered her, she confided more in you. Understand me, Gary. I want to help her."

"*She* must understand that, Senator. If you give her a

little more time, perhaps. . . ."

"No, no, I'm not making myself clear. Gary, the people who live here, the officers and their wives, they understand what it is to be a prisoner of the Comanches. Now Janice is returned safely but has remained silent about her years as a prisoner. That can be worse than the truth at times. The wives on this post talk, Gary, and you know how that goes. They operate on the theory that, if you have nothing to hide, you'll speak. So Janice must be guilty of . . . of anything you want to imagine. I'm giving this dance in her honor, Gary. I thought it would be a fitting homecoming. Perhaps I was wrong. Oh, I'm sure the attendance will be what it should be. Frazer doesn't want to offend me, and his officers don't want to offend him. But I'm afraid there are more ways than one to hurt someone. I don't want Janice to be hurt."

"Yes, sir. I understand. Senator, I know the officers on this post, and I don't think it will be like that at all."

"Do you know their wives? Or how any woman squeezes a man? Just let a husband cross his wife the wrong way, and the food gets bad, and his life can become pretty miserable." He frowned. "Politics is better than this, Gary, believe me. At least, you know what to expect there, and past experience has taught you all the dirty tricks."

"Senator, I can assure you. . . ."

"I'm too old a man to be assured any more," Tremain said. "Frankly, I believe in what I pay for, and I'm willing to insult you again by offering you a handsome remuneration to see that Janice is not deserted."

Color stained Gary's cheeks, and he got up slowly. "Senator, it could be that I fully intended to do just that, because I wanted to, or for my own reasons. But now you've changed all that. Whatever I do now will be spoiled . . . spoiled because you've put a price on it."

"I haven't yet," Tremain said. "I thought I'd let you do that."

"Do we really have anything more to say to each other, sir?"

"No. I guess not," Tremain said. "Gary, was she an Indian's . . . well, were there any children anywhere?"

"Good night, sir," Gary said stiffly, and left the hall. He let the first coolness of night fan away his anger, and then he walked slowly toward the infirmary. Guests were always billeted there. He could not hate Tremain, who was nagged by the same fears as other men. He could not blame him because he, too, had wished that she were different. He was a prudish man who wanted all women pure.

Gary felt slightly ashamed because he had blamed Tremain. He felt as Tremain did, so he had no right to be indignant, no right to be righteous. He had condemned her himself. And this bothered him.

Janice answered the door and was surprised to see him. Stepping aside, she invited him in and closed the door. Gone was the cast-off Indian dress. She wore a pale rose frock with a tight waist and collar and a puff of ruffles around her wrists. Her hair had been brushed to a shine. She wore a ribbon in it, which made her seem young and frightfully innocent.

"I was told that Uncle Clifton had sent for you," Janice said. "It seems that someone is always sending for someone, or doing something that someone else doesn't want. Won't you sit down?"

"Thank you."

"Smoke, if you like." She found a saucer for the cigar ashes and took the chair across from him. "This is the first time I've ever seen you without dirt on your face, and you're quite handsome. What happened to your head?"

"I fell up a tree."

She smiled. "I see. Mind my own business."

"No, it isn't like that. Really, it's not worth explaining." He put a match to his cigar and blew smoke toward the ceiling. "The party tonight was a stupid idea. Your uncle ought to have taken you home, but I guess he's human and has got to try to make up for the lost years."

"I'm glad you came to see me, Jim. Glad, because you know about me, which saves a lot of painful explanation. That's a very selfish reason, isn't it? But I think you understand."

"Made any plans?"

"No, and I don't want to. Do you have the time?"

He took out his pocket watch and consulted it. "A quarter to eight."

"I suppose it would be inconsiderate to keep them waiting, wouldn't it?" She took her wrap from the bed and draped it over her shoulders. "Will you walk with me, Jim?"

"Yes, it would be a pleasure." He opened the door for her and closed it after them. She waited at the base of the steps, and he offered her his arm. Together they crossed the dark parade, listening to the music grow louder. The dance had already begun. At the doorway Janice paused, took a deep breath, and stepped inside, her hand resting lightly on Gary's arm.

Whether by design or chance, the music ended and couples stood about on the floor, politely clapping, all eyes turned to Janice Tremain. These Army functions were not new to Gary, and normally a few men would have approached and asked her to dance. At least, the single men would have, and there were nine, not counting himself, at Fort Elliot. Yet they remained in their clannish knot at the punch bowl, and by their stillness drew attention to her. Gary expected the married men to mind their wives, but he expected something different from the bachelors.

The music began again, and there was that awful moment when she just stood there, trying to keep her composure from breaking, while the genteel of Fort Elliot moved in their own exclusive circle. The anger returned to Gary, but he kept it from his voice when he spoke.

"Will you do me the honor? I dance most awkwardly, though."

She put a bright, superficial smile on her face, leaving the hurt unerased from her eyes. "I think that is a lie," she said, and lifted her arms.

He was not as awkward as he claimed, and he danced carefully because it had been years since she had heard anything but chanting and he did not want her to trip, embarrass her further. She was a tense branch in his arms, but gradually she began to relax.

As they danced, she smiled at him again and said: "See? It was a lie. You dance well."

"Don't speak too soon. If I don't step on your feet, I'll trip on the hem of your dress. Did I tell you I took dancing lessons when I was nine? It's a fact. One lesson, and I was expelled forever."

The dance ended too quickly for both of them, and they stood undecided for a moment. Dancing, there had been an excuse for being together, but now that the dance had ended, Gary understood that no one would approach her, and he would have to dance with her again and again, which made her as much a leper as if no one had danced with her at all.

He led her to the punch bowl and handed her a glass. Senator Tremain eased over to them and helped himself. His face was stiffly set, and he spoke to Gary. "Everyone's thirst has vanished."

"I'm poisoning the water hole," Janice said softly.

"Nonsense!" Tremain said sharply, because it was true and he resented it. "Janice, I wanted this to be fun for you."

She looked at him oddly. "Fun? Uncle, how could it possibly be fun? And don't blame them. Blame me for being here."

"Now let's not talk like that," Tremain snapped. "Gary, what kind of friends do you have here? Frazer will hear of this rudeness, you can bet on it."

"Please," she said. "The solution is quite simple." She put her punch glass aside and looked around the room. The small talk faded as though they waited for her to speak.

"Don't do anything dumb," Jim Gary warned under his breath.

"I'll do what I have to do." She folded her hands together in front of her. "Ladies, and gentlemen." She put just the right inflection on the *gentlemen,* a light lifting of tone that was enough, for they knew what they were and scarcely needed the reminder. "I want to thank you for appearing here this evening. It was, in effect, a command performance, but my uncle meant well. Since I was released, since I returned here, I've said very little to any of you. Perhaps you think I've rejected your offers of friendship. I didn't mean to, and for my apparent rudeness I must apologize."

"Janice," Gary whispered, but she shook her head slightly, silencing him.

"All of you know that I was a prisoner of the Comanches. There may be one or two among you who know first-hand what that is like. To those who do not, I'll not keep you wondering any longer. After a year and a half I was taken for a wife by Stone Calf, who was a brother to Iron Hand. In his way, he was a good man who beat me only when I deserved it, and who killed his enemies quickly, with honor. I bore him no children, which I often regret. I think it would have made life more tolerable for me. Certainly it would have been more tolerable than my position here. Now enjoy yourselves! Jim, will you walk with me to my quarters?"

"Yes," he said. Then he looked across the room to the junior officers. "Calvin, Upston, and you, O'Flynn, I'll see you behind the rifle butts at dawn."

"Aw, Jim . . . ," one began, then closed his mouth.

He took Janice Tremain's arm and walked her outside. Shielded by the dark coolness of the porch, she stopped and leaned against an upright. The wind blew on her face, and she closed her eyes tightly. "That was hard, Jim. Harder to do than anything I've ever done."

"You were magnificent, Janice."

Senator Tremain stepped to the door, intending to come out, and Jim Gary motioned him back. He hesitated as though it was difficult to obey, then he turned and went back inside.

"I'm all right now," Janice said.

"Are you sure?"

She looked at him quickly, then she smiled, and he saw that her fear, her tension, had vanished. "Yes, I'm very sure. Everything will be all right now."

Chapter Seventeen

Colonel Frazer was in a towering rage. He paced back and forth in his office and occasionally glared at the four officers standing poker-stiff, their eyes locked front and center. Lieutenant Gary had a swollen upper lip and one eye was discolored and puffed. The three other officers bore more vivid marks, and Lieutenant O'Flynn's breath bubbled through the smashed cartilage of his nose.

"Utterly disgraceful!" Frazer roared. "Fighting!" He wheeled about and faced Gary. "What do you intend to do, Mister Gary? Trounce every bachelor on the post?"

"Yes, sir. There's Muldoon, Riggs, Cunningham, Shea, Parkinson, and Dunlop left, sir."

Frazer shook his finger inches from Gary's nose. "If I hear of you even going near the rifle butts again, I'll have you court-martialed! Now clear out of here. And have the contract surgeon take a look at you."

They saluted and did an about-face, Academy-perfect.

"Not you, Gary! The rest of you may go." When the door had closed, Frazer gave Gary the order to about-face again, but left him standing, at attention. "Mister Gary, with unbelieving eyes I read your report, not once, but five times. You have failed miserably, sir! Miserably."

"Yes, sir. I believe McCabe warned you of that possibility. . . ."

152

"Damn McCabe! I don't want to hear his name mentioned!" He sat down behind his desk and drummed his fingers. "Gary, do you understand that I have but little time left? You act as though I were going to be in the Army for another ten years, that I have the time to smooth out your incompetent mistakes."

"No, sir."

"I send you on a routine task, difficult to be sure but not impossible, and you bungle it. Gary, you're not putting your heart into this duty, and I'll so note it on your record. That captaincy is flying out the window, or don't you care about that?"

"Yes, sir." He licked his lips. "Colonel, I think it's a mistake to go further with this. I noted that in my report and. . . ."

"I read the damned thing! Get it through your head that we cannot abandon this. Why, Washington would make a shambles of the Army. Where do you think our appropriations come from? Heaven? Taxpayers have spoken, Gary, and now we jump. I've talked to Senator Tremain about this, and he endorses my view completely. Now I want an accurate appraisal of our possibilities. We have no choice but to continue."

Gary thought of changing that a little, for it was Frazer who wouldn't accept the choice of passing this on to his successor and not making brigadier on retirement. But a junior officer has to keep his mouth closed. Gary was in enough trouble as it was.

"Well, sir, I think a peaceful negotiation with Iron Hand is now out of the question. Besides, the civilians are ready to drop this and go. . . ."

Frazer waved his hands. "I'm not concerned now with what they want or what's good for them. They set the wheels in motion, and now it's too late for them to change their minds."

"We just run over them, eh, sir?"

"If it has to be done," Frazer answered. "So, discount the possibility of my dropping this. I won't have the last notation on my record read that I failed to complete an assignment or have my successor finish it for me. No, Mister Gary, I believe this calls for a punitive expedition."

"I beg your pardon, sir?"

"A hundred men," Frazer said. "Yes, that ought to be enough. We'll have to be careful, though, in order not to violate the terms of the treaty."

"An armed movement would. . . ."

"Unarmed, except for pistols and sabers," Frazer said. "Does this not pique your fancy, Mister Gary? You can make your base at Sand Creek with the civilians and make your sallies from there. If I read the treaty correctly . . . and I assure you that I do . . . I am within my rights to take troops into Iron Hand's country on matters involving the government. Now, McCabe is a government scout, and he is being held prisoner or, at worst, has been killed. Either way, it's no great loss to Texas but a blessing to me because this puts Iron Hand in direct treaty violation. Naturally the entire area will have to be combed, and all white prisoners taken. It will be easy to say that they will have to be brought here for identification, and, of course, they will be given over to rightful relatives, and we can appease Iron Hand and his sub-chiefs later with an extra beef ration."

For a moment Lieutenant Gary was too appalled to speak. Finally he said: "And what if the Comanches resist?"

"It will be part of your duty to see that there is no trouble."

"Mine, sir?"

"Of course. You'll command the detail, Mister Gary. At this moment I consider you most expendable. I'll give you Shea and Riggs. Their careers are as yet unestablished, and disgrace is less important to men of twenty-three than of sixty. Provided, of course, you bobble this badly. Succeed and you're a captain."

"Colonel, I could resign my commission."

"We all can, but we never do."

"Yes," Gary said, "you've got a point there. When am I expected to depart with this expedition, sir?"

Frazer paused. "With rations to draw, stock to select, men to pick . . . I believe a week or ten days would be reasonable."

"Very good, sir. I expect the Sand Creek camp will be vacant by then anyway."

"What's that?"

"Before I left, sir, I gave orders for them to vacate the camp if I didn't return within a specified time. There is no need for them to remain there, with myself and McCabe gone."

"That was quite a responsibility to assume," Frazer said. "However, it's just as well, the way it's working out. That will be all, Mister Gary. I'd get busy in the morning, if I were you. Shea and Riggs will be notified."

Gary saluted, and left the office. This development was too bold for him to accept entirely or think about clearly. Frazer was well within his technical rights, but Gary could not help feeling like a lawyer plotting to free a guilty client on some loophole in the law. He was getting to think like Guthrie McCabe. Another ten years of this and he'd be like him or Frazer. All for me and to hell with the next man.

He went to his quarters and found Senator Tremain waiting outside. "The door was open," Gary said.

"A matter of principle," Tremain said, and followed him inside. Gary put a match to the pair of lamps, then offered Tremain a chair. "A miserable night, wasn't it, Gary?"

"Yes, it was."

"I suppose it took a desperate courage to do what she did. My thought right now is the aftermath. Of course, I'll have to take her East with me, and there'll be reporters and newspaper accounts."

"How's that going to affect your political career, sir?" Gary asked this because he knew it was Tremain's worry. Actually he did not care if it were ruined.

"It's full of ups and downs, anyway." He looked at Gary. "All right, this will be one of the downs." He paused and said: "Do you have anything to drink?"

"There's a bottle in the bureau drawer . . . among the shirts."

Tremain helped himself, drinking from the bottle. "Gary, I hate to keep coming back all the time for help, but it seems that you're the only man I can talk to."

"Talk's cheap," he said. "You want to sit down?"

"Thanks," Tremain said, and took the chair. "Gary, I want to do what's right. You understand that?"

"Yes. It seems to be a favorite cry of most people . . . to do what's right . . . but underneath it all I suspect it's a cover-up for an intent to do what they please, which isn't so right."

Tremain stared at him. "You speak what you think, don't you?"

"No," Gary said. "No, I wish I could. I cover up as much as the next man, and I always clear my conscience by telling myself that it was something I had to do. Now let's hear your story. Or would you like to have me tell it? How could it go now . . . ? Sure, I know. Back East, when you got the wire, you were overjoyed and rushed out here before you stopped to think about it. That was a generous thing to do, Senator, but it's like making a speech while you're drunk. You're liable to regret it later. But once you got out here and saw Janice, you realized that you'd bought yourself a problem, a tainted

156

woman. Now, with anyone else you'd have pressed a check into her hand and backed away until the air cleared, but she was kin, and word would get around that you'd dumped her. That would be worse yet, because we may not do what's right, but we sure as hell won't tell anyone about it. So you're going to have to take her back and put up with her because you give odds that no man will marry her unless he's some no-good who doesn't care. Yes, sir, Senator, you've got a problem there."

For several minutes, Clifton Tremain merely stared at Gary. Then he said: "Lieutenant, you're insulting."

"Honest, but insulting. That's me."

Tremain remained angry, or maintained the pose, but it could not last long, for Gary had punctured the man's vanity, his aura of righteousness, and revealed for the moment the unpleasant truth. Tremain said: "I need another drink."

"Help yourself."

Afterward Tremain came back and sat down. "All right, Gary, suppose it's the truth. What do I do?"

"You could try doing what Janice did . . . standing up and spitting in their eye."

"No, no, I'm not built that way. I play angles, make deals, take the middle road. I've never been a man to commit myself on a personal or political issue. Call it a weakness, if you want, but I'm human. I want everyone to like me."

"Yep," Gary said. "You're no different from the rest of us."

"She needs a man, Gary. A husband."

"Maybe. If she does, she'll pick one."

"Can she?" Tremain shook his head. "There's nothing like a grass widow to tickle a man's fancy, but any further. . . ."

"And any further with that," Gary interrupted, "will only earn you a bust in the mouth."

"I beg your pardon?" Tremain frowned. "Did you threaten me?"

"No, I promised you something."

Tremain could not doubt his sincerity. He rubbed his hands together and tried to think of another approach. "Gary, you were gallant to my niece last night. And I believe it was above and beyond any consideration I might have offered you."

"It was."

"Don't say it like that," Tremain said. "Gary, can't you put that down to a man's concern?"

"Concern for whom, sir?"

"For her!" He wiped a hand across his mouth. "Gary, I'll give this to you with the hair on. I'm an influential man and not far from being rich. I have no relatives except Janice. One of these days I'll die, and everything will go to her and the man she marries. But I want him to be the right man, Gary. A good, gentle man who will never remind her that's she's been anything but a good woman."

"Get out of here," Jim Gary said.

He spoke so quietly that Tremain hardly seemed to hear him. "What did you say?"

"I said to get out."

"Well, you're horribly righteous, aren't you?"

Gary leaned forward quickly, so that he could reach the point of Tremain's jaw with his fist, and the force of the blow was enough to send man and chair against the wall. There was a dull melon thump of sound when Tremain's head hit the wall. He sat there, dazed, angry, and afraid.

"Lieutenant, you've just shot your military career to hell and gone."

Gary shrugged. "I figured that before I hit you. Get out anyway."

"Sure," Tremain said. He got up. Quickly he straightened his coat and tie and fingered his jaw gingerly. "You just threw away the chance of a lifetime."

"You really think so?" He opened the door and stood there. Tremain edged past him, and stopped on the boardwalk. He opened his mouth to speak, then closed it with a snap, and walked on, his heels striking hard, sending a rattle along the row of quarters.

Gary waited a moment longer, then closed the door by kicking it shut. He put the bottle away and stretched out on his bunk.

"That was a fool thing to do," he said softly. He had no right to hit Tremain, but he knew it would look right, seem right, even if it wasn't. Now Tremain would think he was an honorable, iron-bound man, loaded with principles. He had a bruised jaw to prove it, and Gary had nothing but disgust for himself.

He supposed that he ought to go over to the infirmary and talk to Janice Tremain, but he held himself back. There was no sense in talking with her just for the sake of talk. She needed a man who meant what he said, whose interest was genuine, who was there because she was a desirable woman. And Gary didn't feel that way. He wished he could, but he couldn't. She needed the kind of man who could ignore the looks and the talk that would forever follow her. Or perhaps a man big enough to lift her above this— lift her so high that no one would ever dare to speak of those five years.

And I'm not that kind of a man, Gary thought. He wanted to be, but wanting it wasn't enough. She needed a man like McCabe, who could be as hard toward the world as it was toward him. *That's not me,* Gary thought. *I'm jelly inside, and McCabe's gone.* He felt very sorry for Janice Tremain, and a little sorry for himself because his best effort had been only to hit her uncle on the jaw.

Chapter Eighteen

The Indian agent made a special trip from Fort Dodge to put his reluctant endorsement on Colonel Frazer's punitive expedition. The agent recognized the legal validity of Frazer's move but questioned the wisdom of his judgment. However, he affixed his signature to the document that made legal the movement of troops in Comanche country and took the first stage back to Dodge, as if, by leaving the fort, he could forget that this was happening or be blamed less for his part in it.

Lieutenant Gary worked his force into shape, carefully selecting men and mounts and seeing that all rations, forage, and equipment were ready. He worked slowly, carefully, as though in fear of making a mistake, while in reality he wanted to give the civilians at Sand Creek plenty of time to depart and return to Fort Elliot. By his figuring, they were already on the move, and so he asked Colonel Frazer for permission to quit the post four days early. This was a sound move, for Frazer interpreted it as eagerness and erased some of his harsher thoughts concerning his subordinate.

Lieutenant Gary and his command had fourteen miles behind them when the sunrise was full and a new heat began to grow over the land. Divided into three sections, Gary rode at the head of the column of twos, scouts out, flankers to the left and right, Lieutenants Shea and Riggs eating dust at the center and drag.

161

He held the march to regulations, saving men and horses, and camped that first night in the open. Some miles beyond—he did not know how many—the civilian wagons would be camping, and he considered that the meeting should appear like chance and rolled into his blankets.

Command kept him busy. He had a hundred things to check, for a good commander knows what goes on in his troop. Gary was the last to mount next morning, and he waved them southward, pushing across at the first dawn light with miles of emptiness ahead.

In the middle of the afternoon the scout reported dust to the left, and Gary altered course, making contact with the first wagon two hours later. He gave orders to camp, and, as soon as the squad fires were lighted and the picket lines established, he turned over the detail to Shea and walked across the five-hundred-yard interval to the first wagon, thinking it was Wringle's.

Sean Donovan met him, shook hands briefly, and said: "Jane's visitin' the Pardeen wagon, Lieutenant."

"Where's Wringle?"

"Sand Creek. He said he was going to stay, and I guess he meant it." Donovan reached into the wagon and brought out a jug. "I like a little snort at evenin' time. Join me?"

"Sure," Gary said, and laid it in the crook of his arm. He sighed and handed it back and wiped tears from his eyes. "That paint remover?"

"No, but it'll do the job. Where you goin' with the soldiers?"

"The colonel wants the job done," Gary said. He turned when he heard Jane's step. She ran to him, and he believed she would have kissed him if her father had not been there.

"Jim, I'm glad to see you. We left too early, didn't we?"

"No, you left just in time."

"Stay for supper," she invited.

"I should be with my men. Well, I guess it'll be all right."

"What kind of a job does the colonel want done?" Sean Donovan asked.

"He wants us to take all white captives from the Comanches . . . without force, if possible."

"Is it possible?" Jane asked.

Jim Gary shrugged. "Maybe, but likely it isn't. McCabe didn't come back?"

They both shook their heads. "Well, I didn't think he would," Gary said. "And this time it isn't because he doesn't want to. One of the main reasons I'm going along with Frazer is to see if I can find McCabe."

"Or where they buried him," Sean Donovan said.

"Jim, didn't you explain to the colonel that we're going home, that we've had enough?" Jane asked. "We've given up again, but this time it's for good. If any of our kin is alive, we don't want to know about it. We just want to forget now."

"Too late for that," Gary said. "He said that this will have to be finished to clean the record. I only follow orders, Jane. Some of them, like this one, I don't like, but I follow them just the same."

"You planning to take those you rescue back to Fort Elliot?" Sean asked.

"That's the order."

"He don't know what he's doing," Sean Donovan said. "He just don't know at all." He walked away, sadly shaking his head.

"Sit down," Jane said. "I have to make supper." She opened the chest that held her cooking pots, and then rummaged through the food chest. "Beans and hoe-cake and pork again. I'm getting pretty tired of that."

"When I get back," Gary said, "I'll take you to Tascosa

and buy you the best meal in town. Then we'll go to the opera house and see the show."

"I'll hold you to that," she said. He watched her make the batter for the cake, cut the pork into thick slices, and put the pot of beans on to boil. Without looking up from her work, she asked: "Did you see her at Fort Elliot, Jim?"

"Janice Tremain?"

"Is that her name? I didn't know it."

"Yes, I saw her," Gary said. "An uncle of hers came from back East to get her. Now he wishes he'd stayed home." He told her about the dance, and Jane Donovan watched him carefully as he talked "So she had it against her if she kept silent or spoke out," Gary said. "But I guess it helped her to speak."

"I think I would have kept silent," Jane said softly. "It's bad enough to know of the wrong in you, but I think it's worse when everyone else knows it, too."

"There's no wrong in you, Jane."

"Jim, there's wrong in all of us." She covered the pot of beans, and put the frying pan on to heat. "In the history books you can read about all the great things that have been done, all the wars that have been fought, and everything seems so logical and just and well-planned. Now I've been wondering how it actually was, if the sum total of the good came out of a mountain of mistakes and stupidity. What will they say about this, Jim? Will the flavor of it ever be truly captured, or is it just for us to know . . . the truth, that is?"

He shrugged. "I don't care to think about it. Call it laziness if you want." He got up. "I really should return to my men, but I'll be back for supper."

He walked slowly to the command post, a tent erected near the center of the compound. Lieutenant Shea was polishing his boots, when Gary sat down.

"Why do you do that?" Gary asked. "They'll get dusty in twenty minutes of walking."

"A cavalryman always rides," Shea said. "Listening to the civilian complaints?"

"No complaints," Gary said. "Shea, what do you think of this?"

The man looked up. "The expedition?" He shrugged. "One duty is as good as another. Why? Gary, you worry about the darnedest things." He put his boots down. "The trouble with you is that you're not a realist. It's simply that the colonel wants his gold star on his last report card. That's why we're here. For you, it could mean an up in rank, the beginning of something important to you. For me, I'll try to conduct myself gallantly and get mentioned in a dispatch, and my father will find out about it, and then I'll get a hundred dollars from him out of sheer pride. With that in my purse I can take leave, go to Tascosa, get drunk for a week, and forget the whole mess."

"Then you do care," Gary said.

"No, I don't care, and you'd better not, either." He waited a moment to see if Gary had anything to say, and, when he didn't, Shea picked up his boot and polish. "Jim, are you still sore at me? I mean, I'm not going to have to square off with you over that business at the dance the other night, am I?"

"I haven't given up the idea yet," Gary said. "Pete, what got into you the other night?"

"Nothing. What did you want us to do? Rush her like she was some . . . well, we talked it over and decided, that's all."

Gary let his anger show. "Why the holy attitude? Have you forgotten that time in Tascosa? I got you out the back door while Captain Lefever came through the front, looking for you."

"A different time and a different place," Shea said. "That

woman was what she was and didn't pretend to be different. Ah, why bother to explain?" He pointed his finger at Gary. "Janice Tremain slept with an Indian. All right, she says she was married, but not a marriage that a white man would recognize. You're an officer, Jim. What do you want to do, spend the rest of your life on back-yard posts and remain in grade? That's what would happen to a man who got mixed up with her. He'd be on the borderline, Jim. A most unfortunate man."

"Look out for yourself and to hell with her, is that it?"

Shea shook his head. "Jim, so she's a little smeared. What does that mean, that we should all wear the same paint?"

"You're a hypocrite."

"Sure. Did I ever deny it? And you'd better examine yourself, Jim. If you can honestly say you're clean, then we'll talk some more about it."

Gary returned to the civilian camp and ate with the Donovans, but his mood was one of depression. Jane noticed it and honored his long silences. He did not remain long, even when Sean and his son thoughtfully went to visit the Murdocks, leaving Gary and Jane alone. With a brief farewell, he returned to the cavalry camp and settled himself for the night.

When the sergeant came by, Gary left word that the troop would be fed and ready to ride by dawn. He meant to move on without delay, without saying anything to Jane Donovan or offering apologies for his briefness.

The trouble with me, Gary told himself, *is that I do 'most everything because I feel sorry for someone.* He decided that he would have to rid himself of that habit before it got him into something serious. He admitted that he had rescued Janice Tremain for that reason and almost ruined his military career by speaking critically of Frazer's decision, just because he knew that the civilians had had enough, and he was sorry for them. And now he was adding it up and silently crying in his beer because he felt sorry for himself.

This is one hell of a mess, Gary thought. Then he went to sleep.

By noon, they were deep in Iron Hand's country, and Jim Gary was not so naïve as to assume that they were unobserved. A hundred-man column raises considerable dust and noise regardless of the care exercised to do otherwise, so he assumed that browned runners were already scurrying ahead with the word that the Long Knives were marching.

That afternoon he found the first of the camps, deserted, of course, but a broad trail led away, and he followed it, giving up the idea of scouting out other, lesser camps. They were moving, lodges, women, and all, toward the main camp, under Iron Hand's wing, so he would meet them there, fell them if he had to with one bold stroke.

A very gallant thought, he knew, but hardly likely to turn out that way. Iron Hand would gird himself for war, and Gary wondered how he could prevent it. He knew he could not handle Iron Hand with a hundred men armed with pistols and sabers. Maybe that's what Frazer figured. He'd retire in a burst of glory, singing praises of the dead officers and men slaughtered by the war-like Comanches.

He did not expect Iron Hand to move his camp now. Likely he would deploy his braves and meet Gary somewhere between. Or he might leave only the women, children, and captives in the camp, tended by old men. That was a common trick. Gary could then have his unopposed way, but in trying to ride out he would find himself surrounded.

Iron Hand, in spite of his paint, was a soldier, a tactician. He had chosen for his campsite a depression of land surrounded by three prominent ridges, and Gary topped one of these late in the afternoon, drawing his column to a halt.

His hand motion brought Lieutenant Shea forward from the second section, and together they looked upon the camp. Women moved about, doing their never-ending work, and the children played, only closer to their lodges than usual, and here and there an old man crouched down with his blanket and solitary thoughts. The smoke from the lodge fires rose sluggishly in the still air, and the camp seemed normal to the casual eye. Only, Gary knew, that every brave of warring age was gone, probably in a position to attack them at the first hostile move.

"Now what?" Shea asked.

"Draw them in one line abreast," Gary said. "I want a line of mounted blue on the ridge. Pistols and sabers at the raised position, and I'll court-martial the first man who lowers them." Shea frowned, and Gary ignored this disapproval. He motioned toward the camp. "See those lodges on the fringes? They haven't been there very long. Iron Hand's camp is twice the size it was when I was last in it. All the sub-chiefs in fifty miles have moved in on him for protection."

"Protection from what? Pistols and sabers?" Shea nodded toward the hollow. "Before we get halfway down there, Iron Hand will cut us to ribbons." His eyes raised to the other ridges. "There's a Comanche with a rifle behind every depression."

"More like two," Gary said calmly. "Would you send Sergeants Davis and Ellsworth forward, please?"

"Yes, sir." Shea wheeled, and Gary waited there until the two enlisted men came forward. Shea and Riggs returned with them, but waited in the background, just within hearing distance.

"Gentlemen, I'm picking you to volunteer to go into that

camp with me. Select ten privates apiece and bring them along."

"Volunteers, sir?" Davis asked.

Gary looked at him and smiled thinly. "Davis, they're always volunteers, aren't they?"

"Yes, sir. . . . Come on, Ellsworth."

When they rode back to pick the men, Gary watched the line form, a very long line, properly dressed, each man with his weapons raised.

Shea could stand this no longer. He edged up and said: "Gary, you'll never get away with this."

"It is a gamble, isn't it?" Then the sergeants returned with the men, and Gary led them at a walk off the ridge.

Chapter Nineteen

Although the women and children did not scatter when Gary rode into the village, he saw that they were frightened, but not too frightened, for their men were nearby, waiting for some signal before attacking. Halting his detail before Iron Hand's lodge, Gary said: "Sergeant Ellsworth, take ten men and scour the village. Take into custody any white person, male or female, regardless of age. You take the remaining men and do the same, Davis."

"Yes, sir."

They formed their groups and turned to ride away, each starting at the far end of the village. Hardly had they begun to move when Ellsworth said—"Whoops."—and pointed to the south ridge.

Even in this moment of acute danger, Jim Gary thought it was an impressive sight, awesome. And if he lived, he would always remember vividly this moment when half a thousand half-naked men looked down on him with pointed rifles. His heart hammered and his face felt feverish, yet he enjoyed the moment immensely, for this was the moment a man always dreams of, when his courage is supremely tested and he finds himself strong.

"Hold up!" Gary said. He cupped his hands around his mouth. "With so many braves, is Iron Hand afraid to ride to meet me?"

He could not distinguish the leader, not until a lone Comanche detached himself from the others and came down the slope, the sun glinting from the polished hook that was his hand. Gary rode to meet him halfway, then stopped.

Iron Hand was painted for war, and he spoke curtly. "Does the enemy of Iron Hand wish to be destroyed?"

"Must we speak of war? I come to speak of peace."

"With soldiers?" He waved toward Gary's force. "There can be no peace."

"The white soldier chief wants the prisoners of the Comanches," Gary said. "The one called McCabe is the property of the white soldier chief."

"McCabe is mine. He works with the women and sleeps with the dogs. No one takes what is Iron Hand's."

"I mean to take him because those are my orders. But I want to take him in peace."

"No peace. You turn back or dic."

"Look to my hill, Iron Hand. How many of my soldiers will die?"

"Half," Iron Hand said.

"And the other half will enter your village and kill the women and children. Then you will have an empty victory, Iron Hand. In ten years there will be no more Comanches on this earth. Men will forget your name. The dust will cover the tracks you have made, and all will be dead."

"All white soldiers will die!"

"Yes, and the Comanches will die with them," Gary said. "Without women, the Comanches are dead, even if we cannot kill many today." He gave Iron Hand a moment to consider this before speaking again. "There will be no more beef issue from the white soldier chief. The Comanches will hunt like dogs for scraps to eat. That is what war will bring, if Iron Hand wants it. It is your choice, Iron Hand. Today is the day when all Comanches begin a slow death." He decided to give this one more push. "Which is more important to Iron Hand? Keeping the white slaves he has and dying forever? Or giving them up and living to old age?"

He was an intelligent man without grace, and he made that one final, disgusted motion with his hand, then threw his rifle into the dirt. From the Comanche line a wail went up, but it was over, and Gary spoke quietly to his sergeants.

"Get on with it now. We don't want to waste time here."

He waited with Iron Hand while the miserable, painful business was done. From the warriors, young white boys were taken, physically bound, for they fought wildly, and were escorted to the hill where the blue line waited. Women were herded together, some carrying their small children in their arms, the older ones following dutifully.

Comanche braves remained wooden-faced as their "wives" and children were gathered, and crying ran through the camp, for none seemed eager to be returned. Sergeant Davis found Guthrie McCabe and gave him a blanket with which to cover his nakedness, then brought him to where Gary waited, his expression impassive.

McCabe was thirty pounds lighter, bearded, dirty, and too stunned to be grateful. He kept scratching at the vermin that pestered him continually, and shifting his bare feet around in the dust as though he wanted to run and forced himself not to.

The prisoners were like cattle being driven, and they kept turning their heads and calling out to husbands and fathers, and so much emotion gripped Comanche and white alike that Gary grew fearful that Iron Hand might not be able to hold back his braves. Even when they were on the ridge with the soldiers, Jim Gary could hear the wailing. A ring of mounted men rode around them to keep them from breaking away.

Finally Gary had had enough. His business here was at a sickening end.

"Mount behind me," he told McCabe, then helped the man onto the horse. Quickly he rode up the flank of the ridge, organized his command, and began the march out.

Shea was in charge of the released prisoners, and the only way he could move them was to tie their hands together and put them on a long lead rope. Three miles of this proved that it wouldn't work, for they hung back and slowed the column. Shea then put loops of rope around their necks, so that hanging back meant choking. The men gave no trouble, but the women seemed to prefer strangulation to delivery. He had to tie a few to horses, forcing some of the soldiers to ride double.

In this fashion they began the night march, not stopping until midnight, when Gary ordered a camp made near a small creek. A close guard was placed around the rescued, and Gary thought this a strange thing. He could not accustom himself to the idea of such a sudden uprooting.

McCabe was given some clothes, spare shirts and pants, all ill-fitting. He borrowed soap and razor, and, when he appeared at Gary's fire, he was shaved and bathed. During the ride he had said nothing, and now the silent mood still clung to him.

"Help yourself to the coffee," Gary said, pouring him a cup.

McCabe hunkered down and drank. Then he said: "All the time they had me, I kept dreaming of a cup of coffee. Now that I'm able to drink it, I find it tastes like hell." He looked at Gary for a long moment. "You saved my life, Jim. I wouldn't have lasted through the coming winter."

"Well, don't thank me for it," Gary said. "The hand heal up?"

McCabe nodded. "I guess the Lord took a look at what was happening to the rest of me and felt pity. Gary, you saved my life."

"You're repeating yourself, Guthrie."

"I guess I am." He shook his head from side to side. "All my life I've tried not to owe anything to any man, but I sure owe you, Jim."

"You want to square it?"

"Sure," McCabe said.

"Then stand up."

"What?" He frowned. "What for, Jim?"

"So I can knock your block off," Gary said.

Guthrie McCabe's frown deepened. "Jim, you're not mad at me, are you? I didn't think you were. What is it, then?" He turned his head and looked at the lumped misery being driven back to the arms of their relatives. "You got a mad on against something too big to hit out at, is that it?" McCabe put his coffee cup aside and stood up. "All right, Jim. You go ahead and start pounding. I've got a few things to work off myself."

Gary sent his coffee cup flying and launched his attack against McCabe. Their meeting wrung a grunt from both of them, and they faced each other, eyes locked in the sockets, raining fists against flesh. When they parted, both men were bleeding, and the sound of the fight drew Shea and Riggs on the run. They stopped just outside the firelight and stared.

Riggs said: "For heaven's sake, sir! Back away! Back away!"

But there was no backing away in these men—no give at all. They hammered each other and wrestled, flinging each other down, twisting arms, striking out with their knees. They were like wild birds thrashing in the dust.

Riggs tried to pull them apart, and they turned on him with a raw resentment and beat him to the ground with devastating suddenness. Shea pulled the dazed and bleeding Riggs to safety.

Unable to stand, Gary and McCabe rested on their knees, still throwing punches; then McCabe could take no more of it, and he fell on his face. Jim Gary stared at him for a moment, then weakly lay across him, his breathing strained and painful sounding.

Almost timidly Shea stepped up to him. "Sir? Are you all right, sir?"

Sergeant Ellsworth, whose seventeen Army years had taught him much, stepped up to the fire. "Leave them alone, sir. They're all right."

Shea was indignant. "What do you mean, all right? They've beat each other to a pulp!"

"Yes, sir. But they're all right, Lieutenant."

"This is damned ridiculous," Shea said, and walked away.

The sergeant tried to help Riggs, but was shaken off. Riggs looked at McCabe and Gary. "They ought to be locked up for their own good."

"Yes, sir," Ellsworth said, and waited until Riggs left. Then he took a bucket of water and carried it over to Gary, setting it within reach. He, too, went back to his own fire and waited.

Gary found the bucket and washed his face, flinching when he touched the raw and bleeding areas. Finally he gained his feet and threw some of the water over McCabe, who groaned and stirred.

When he could sit up, Gary threw McCabe a towel he had soaked in the water, and McCabe washed his face.

"Good fight, huh, Jim?"

"Yes," Gary said. "The best I've had."

"How do you feel?"

"Fine. You?"

"Never better," McCabe said. He looked at Gary and grinned, and blood ran down his chin from his smashed lips. "Feel like taking this?" He held out his hand.

Gary took it, and they shook solemnly. Then McCabe eased himself erect, taking care to protect his bruises. "That coffee will taste like coffee now, Jim."

"Good thing we didn't kick the pot over." Gary rummaged around and found the cups. He knocked the dirt out of them, wiped them on his tattered shirttail, then filled both of them.

"Too bad Janice Tremain couldn't have licked somebody. Or even got licked. I can imagine her reception. It doesn't matter who wins, does it, Jim?"

"No. Who won this one?"

"I guess I passed out first," McCabe said, smiling. "But I don't care about that." He drank some of his coffee and burned his lips. "What we ought to have done, Jim, is to have roped off a section at Sand Creek and made all those civilians pound each other until all the anger and shame and resentment was gone. They'd have gone home then and there."

"Sure," Gary said. He studied the fire for a time. "I think I'll resign my commission anyway, Guthrie. This is as bad as Chivington's massacre, only we're not doing those women and children the favor of killing them off."

"Be a mess at Fort Elliot," McCabe agreed. "A mess I wish I was well out of." He sighed and drank some more coffee. "You been to Sand Creek lately?"

"No, why?"

He shrugged. "No reason, I guess, except that four days ago, nine bucks left Iron Hand's village and came back with hair."

Gary's attention sharpened. "You feel like riding, Guthrie?"

176

"I guess it won't kill me."

"Sergeant!" Gary waited until he came up. "Sergeant, saddle two horses. McCabe and I are leaving. And send Lieutenant Shea here on the double."

"Yes, sir. Sir, we don't have any remuda."

"Then have two light troopers ride double. Just bring McCabe a good horse."

"Yes, sir."

The two men waited in silence until Shea came over to the fire. He viewed both men with open suspicion. "You sent for me, sir?"

"You're in command, Shea. McCabe and I are going to ride to Sand Creek. Be on the move at dawn and make it twelve hours before your next camp. We'll pick you up around noon, day after tomorrow."

"Yes, sir."

McCabe and Gary were impatient. They walked to the picket line and talked in low voices while their mounts were being saddled. Gary was saying: "Wringle and his wife were staying at Sand Creek after the others left. I was recalled to Fort Elliot for nearly ten days, but I left orders for the civilians to vacate the creek camp. They did. I met them on the way to Iron Hand's village, and they told me that Wringle stayed on."

"That's not good," McCabe said. "Man, being alone out here is just asking for it unless you know what you're doing, and Wringle didn't know anything." He looked toward the horses. "Can't you move any faster over there?"

"Yes, sir. Just be a minute."

"Guthrie, you were there in the village. What did you see?"

"Not much. They kept me working all the time, but I heard talk. Iron Hand's braves brought back hair because

177

there was dancing in Stone Calf's lodge."

Their horses were ready, and both men mounted, turning out of the camp immediately. They rode for an hour without speaking, then dismounted to walk the horses. They had a long way to go and had to spare the mounts.

"I'll give you odds Wringle's dead," McCabe said.

"You'll get no takers."

"You've got to see him, huh? I mean, this will go in your report, won't it?"

"You know what I'll have to do," Gary said. "Do you think I like the implications? Nobody wants another war with the Comanches, but, if it's started, what can you do about it?"

"I know what I'd do."

"Yeah, but you're not Army," Gary said. "I am."

Chapter Twenty

No morbid sense drove Gary into making an all-night ride of it, just a clinical detachment, a positive suspicion that the Wringles were dead. There was a slim off chance that he was wrong in his guess, but he did not believe so. Still he had to go to Sand Creek and check for himself, and perhaps bury them, if there was anything left to bury.

He came into the grove just after dawn, and stopped, trying to find some sign of life. The civilians had left their untidy scars on the land, blackened circles where their cook fires had been, and outhouse pits, and rubbish heaps. Wringle had started to build on the other side of the grove, and Gary rode there, McCabe trailing a few paces behind.

Wringle's wagon, when they came upon it, had been burned for the iron-work it contained, and the two walls were a tumble of logs, also fire-charred.

"Hold up," McCabe said, and got down off the horse. He walked forward and from beneath a pile of rubble lifted the hem of Mrs. Wringle's dress. McCabe then kicked and tore at the rubble until she was uncovered. Her death had been heroic and merciful. A war axe had cleaved her skull from behind as she fought to aid her husband.

McCabe turned as Gary came up. "Wringle must be around somewhere, Jim. Take a look over there, where he was building. A man usually defends first what he prizes."

Gary walked over to the burned structure, not caring whether he found Wringle or not. He had seen enough to prove that the Comanches had broken their treaty, that a new war had begun, and that a lot of men on both sides would die before this was settled again. He wondered if this would ever be settled now, for the second treaty would mean even less than the first. There would be more to remember, and more to forgive, and men, red and white, seemed to have a small tolerance for forgiveness.

He found Wringle, dead, vacant-eyed, the eyeballs rolled upward as though he were trying to inspect the crimson patch where his scalp lock had been. Gary turned away and walked back to where Guthrie McCabe waited.

"You going to put all this in your report, Jim?"

"I don't want to," Gary said. "See if you can find a couple of shovels. We'll bury them."

McCabe found one shovel and a spade. He gave the shovel to Gary so his digging would be easier, and Gary looked curiously at him for a moment, but said nothing about this. They worked for three hours, barely pausing, and then they wrapped both bodies in a blanket and buried them together. At last the mound of earth was tamped, and McCabe threw his spade aside.

"I'll find his axe and cut something for a marker."

"No," Gary said. "We'll take the horses and run them over the grave until it's trampled flat."

McCabe frowned, yet his eyes contained a speculative hope. "Jim, what are you thinking of?"

"Another Indian war," Gary said. "This isn't going in my report, Guthrie." He waved his hand. "Yeah, I know, the Army and all that, but this is something I've got to do. Stone Calf's sons were only avenging their father, and that was my fault. You were right. I should have left Janice Tremain alone. As it turned out, we'd have picked her up anyway without all this."

"No, I wasn't right," McCabe said softly. "Just thought I was right. A lot of things have changed, Jim. I lived in hell, and I'm not the same man as before." He sat down on the mound and looked up at him. "Jim, if nothing is done about this, nothing said, the Comanches will get bold and kill others. You want that on your conscience?"

"It will be up to me to see that it doesn't happen. Guthrie, I'll be going back to Iron Hand with a lot of questions. I'll hold back his beef ration and dog him and worry him half to death over this, but I won't be able to prove anything. I'm going to put the fear into him so this won't happen again." He put his shovel aside and sat down beside McCabe. "This isn't easy for me. All my life I've lived as right as I could, done what's proper, studied the rules, and believed in them. But I've never done much good, except maybe this, what I'm doing now. There won't be any war. Peace is here, and it's going to stay that way. Wringle and his wife bought and paid for it, and I wouldn't sell them short."

Guthrie McCabe laughed softly. "For a minute there I thought your do-gooder morals were going to get the best of you, Jim."

"No, I've learned to bend them." He looked at McCabe. "You sure didn't make much money out of this, did you?"

McCabe threw back his head and laughed. "I've never come out any shorter in my life. But I'm not crying about it, Jim. Funny, that. Somehow I no longer feel that I have to apologize for my intentions." He tapped Gary on the arm. "You figure you can look the colonel in the eye and lie to him? You've never done it before."

"I'll do it. Lying isn't so hard, once you make up your mind to it."

"You're learning," McCabe said, and stood up. "We going to stay here?"

"No. I guess we're finished."

They threw the tools into the nearby rubble, then mounted and turned out, cutting toward the column's calculated position. After a time, Gary said: "Well, one thing, the Miles woman will have built up a big yearning for you, Guthrie."

"Yeah, but I've lost mine for her. That damned house was full of drafts anyway, and the roof leaked like a sieve when it rained." He shot Gary a wry glance. "Tascosa will look good to me now. Real good."

"One thing bothers me," Gary said frankly. "I like you, McCabe, but I can't make up my mind whether it's because you're less of a bastard than when we started, or if I'm more of one."

They rested for two hours at midday, when the heat was highest, then pushed on slowly, calculating time and speed to meet the column and yet conserve their animals. Because of this, Gary arrived three hours late, well after dark, guided the last few miles by the squad fires.

A trooper took their horses, and both men went to Lieutenant Shea's fire at the head of the camp. He was sitting on a folding camp stool, filling in his daily report. He rose quickly when Gary and McCabe stepped into the firelight. Both men were tired, dirty, and not inclined to talk, but this did not stop Shea.

"Was everything all right at Sand Creek, sir?"

"Everything was fine."

"The Wringles were all right?"

Gary frowned. "Mister Shea, the Wringles were not there. Obviously they thought better of it and returned to Fort Elliot. Now where's the coffee? We haven't had a meal or a decent sit-down since leaving you."

"Sergeant Davis has been holding some food, sir. Third fire over."

"Thank you," Gary said, and walked over with McCabe.

"Jim," McCabe said softly, "we forgot to trample the grave."

"I know it, but I'm not going back to do it." Davis started to get up as they approached, but Gary waved him back. "What is it, Sergeant? Beef and beans?"

"Yes, sir. I saved a pot, figuring you'd come in before midnight." He handed a plate to each of them, and they hunkered down to eat. Davis waited a moment, then said: "Mister McCabe, you speak Comanche. I wish you'd talk to the prisoners. They're giving us a devil of a time, sir. All the time trying to escape and go back."

"It's up to Gary," McCabe said. "I'm a civilian."

"We'll go over after we eat," Gary said, and wiped his plate clean before accepting a second helping. After he finished his coffee, he patted his pockets for a smoke, but found none. Sergeant Davis offered them his own brand, and, after taking a light, they passed through the camp to the outskirts where the white returnees were being held under guard.

"Seems a shame that they have to be prisoners, now that they're rescued," Gary said. He pointed to a woman in her early twenties. "Ask her what her name is, McCabe."

He did, then translated. "Shy Deer, or so she says. I think she speaks English."

"Do you speak English?" Gary asked her.

"Yes," she said. "I was eight when the Comanches took me." Three small children stood half hidden behind her. They stared at the two men with walnut-colored eyes. "Where do you take us?"

"To the fort," Gary said. "Your family is there."

183

She shook her head. "My family is dead. I remember."

McCabe glanced at Gary. "What are you going to do about that, Jim? You take her from one place where she had a home and turn her loose at Fort Elliot?"

"Do I have a choice?" He drew on his cigar. "Tell all of them to behave themselves. I can only take them to their rightful families who wait at Fort Elliot."

McCabe told them, and they moaned and wailed, and some of the young men struggled against the ropes that bound them. Gary turned away and started back to Shea's camp. McCabe walked beside him.

"Who's going to sort through these people when we get to Elliot, Jim? Or do you take them in with ropes around their necks and put them on the block like cattle?"

"Colonel Frazer will have to take that responsibility."

"If they never got there . . . ?"

Gary cut him off sharply. "Then another officer would round them up! Guthrie, when I had to kill that man, you told me why you hung back and watched the whole thing through your field glasses. This is the same thing. It's do it now and do it as clean as you can and then try and forget what you've done."

"Well, you've toughened up some," McCabe said. "But are you tough enough to forget it?"

"I don't know," Gary said. "I wish I did."

The return march to Fort Elliot was a trial to Jim Gary. The white captives slowed them down by every means, singing and chanting continually to wear on the troopers' nerves and make the horses nervous, and never letting up at night so anyone could sleep. The young men staged mock riots among themselves, butting heads and kicking, forcing the guard to be doubled and keeping the troopers on their feet when they should have been in their blankets.

Gary was vastly relieved to see Fort Elliot in the distance, and still more relieved when the officer of the day and a five-man detail rode out to meet him.

"You're late, Gary," the officer said, drawing up. "But that's no matter. The colonel wants you to report to him. Take your command onto the post. We'll take charge of the rescued group." He studied them, a frown building on his forehead. "Why are they bound and under guard?"

"To keep them from running away," Gary said. "Unless you want them to scatter, I suggest you keep them under strong guard."

"We'll attend to it," the officer said. "Report to Colonel Frazer immediately, Gary."

"Oh, sure," Gary said, and rode on.

There was the business of dismissing his men and seeing that the animals were tended. Afterward, he and McCabe walked to headquarters and found Frazer impatiently pacing up and down his office.

"When I request an officer's presence, I mean before he tends to his private toilet," Frazer said. "Sit down. McCabe, you can wait outside."

"This is good enough," McCabe said, and took a chair. Frazer showed his displeasure but decided not to press the matter.

"Report, Mister Gary."

"Forty-seven adult whites recovered, sir, male and female. About nineteen children of mixed blood."

"By George, you carried it off!" Frazer was jubilant.

"We sure did," McCabe said dryly. "You'll be a big hero with the Washington politicians, Colonel."

"McCabe, I'll thank you to keep your mouth shut," Frazer said. He raised his voice. "Orderly! Bring in the pay voucher!" A moment later a private brought in the book, and Frazer signed a sheet and tore it out. "Take this to the paymaster and get off the post, McCabe. I told you once that I'd take great pleasure in throwing you off, and now I'm doing it. If you're not gone by evening, I'll have the officer of the day eject you bodily."

McCabe was studying the voucher. When he looked at Frazer, he did so with anger in his eyes. "What the hell is this? Three weeks' pay?"

"You'll find that correct, sir," Frazer said. "And quite legal. You don't think the Army is going to pay you for time spent under some squaw's blanket, do you?" He laughed heartily. "You're bested, McCabe. Taken at your own game. Now clear out of this office."

"Sure," McCabe said flatly. "See you outside, Jim." He let the door slam behind him, and Frazer went behind his desk, a smile wreathing his face.

"You don't know how much pleasure that gives me, Gary. And I take pleasure in telling you that you've done a good job. Within months now you'll hear word on your promotion."

"Yes, sir." Gary locked his teeth together to keep from telling Frazer what to do with the promotion. *Get out,* that was his thought, *get out before I open my mouth and blow my military career sky high.* "What will the disposition be of the returnees, sir?"

"Not your concern," Frazer said. "They wanted their kin back, and now they've got them. It'll straighten itself out. By George, the Army can't do everything for them." He smiled in a fatherly fashion at Jim Gary. "You've had rough duty, my boy. Consider yourself relieved for the next five days. Draw your pay and go into Tascosa. Have a good time."

"Yes, sir. That sounds like excellent advice. Will that be all, sir?"

"Yes. You're dismissed . . . Captain." He winked when he said it and forever stained the rank in Gary's mind. He felt as though he had been handed a dozen filthy postcards while in church. In his mind there had been an almost reverential feeling about the military service, a religious adherence to his duty, but it would never be that way again.

He stepped outside and found McCabe standing in the shade of the porch. Gary said: "I'm footloose for the next five days. Let's ride."

"I'd kind of like to see that Donovan girl first," McCabe said. "You feel like going out to the camp by the creek?"

"Sure," Gary said. "I've got to face them sometime."

Chapter Twenty-One

The civilian camp was in turmoil when Gary and McCabe arrived, for the white prisoners were being pawed over and argued over and given out to the people foolish enough to claim them. The group that Gary and McCabe had taken to Sand Creek stayed near their wagons, yet there was an atmosphere of a slave auction in the camp while white mothers were separated from their half-Indian children. The relatives did not want the half-breeds at all, just their own, while the captives wanted none of their relatives.

The Army was there, trying to establish order. But there is little order in emotion, and the camp was a boil of it, ready for lancing, and Jim Gary did not want to see the operation, being able to guess at the poison that would be released.

McCabe left him and went on to Jane Donovan's wagon while Gary observed the slave block tactics and let the sounds of crying and begging soak into him. He seemed to desire punishment for his part in this and to see it was punishment enough, for this was something he would carry in his mind for the rest of his life.

The Donovan wagon was parked near the creek, but the sounds still carried to it. Jane gave McCabe some coffee, examined the scar on his hand to make certain it had healed properly, then sat down on the dropped wagon tongue.

"I wonder how many of this bunch they'll hang," she said morosely.

"Jim's thinking that, you can bet on it."

"Where is he? Why didn't he come with you?"

McCabe shrugged. "I guess he's got his reasons. I only came to say good bye. Jim and I are going into Tascosa for a few days. Probably you'll be gone when he gets back."

"You sound like you're making a speech for him, Guthrie."

"Maybe I am without knowing it," he said. "Jane, right now he needs someone who understands without a lot of talk, but I don't think he'll come to you. You can see why not, can't you?"

"Yes, but he tried to do right."

McCabe shook his head. "That isn't good enough for men like Jim Gary." He smiled and handed his half-empty cup to her. "Too bad you're not going to stay, Jane. You'd be good for him."

"Would I? I've been asking myself that."

"The Tremain woman . . . is she still on the post? He'll want to know."

"She left with her uncle. California, I think. He's retiring after this term of office. Tell Jim. It's a drop of good news in an ocean of bad."

"I'll tell him."

He started to turn away, but she took his arm and held him back. "I have to know, Guthrie. Was he in love with her?"

This made him laugh. "No. He was full of gallantry, but he wasn't in love. That's something that Jim wouldn't pass out to the first pretty woman that came along."

"Thank you. That makes it easier."

He left her then and walked rapidly across the camp to the crowd gathered around the Army and their charges. Gary saw him coming and came to meet him.

189

"I'm sick enough," Gary said. "Let's go." He sided McCabe, and they reëntered the post. In the stable, saddling their horses, Gary came out with it. "Guthrie, I hope you said my good byes for me."

"No, I didn't. You damn' fool, you don't ever want to say good bye to a girl like that." He tightened the cinch and then stepped into the saddle. "She'll be here when you get back. I've got a feeling."

"I wish I had it." He mounted his horse. "Let's go see the paymaster."

The office was in one wing of the guardhouse near the main gate, and Gary drew his pay while McCabe settled for his paltry amount. The guard let them pass, and they turned to the Tascosa road, facing a full twenty-hour ride. They camped early and were in their blankets before full darkness settled, and before dawn they were moving on. Gary veered off the road and headed for Anson Miles's place. This brought a sharp look from McCabe.

"I don't have to go there, Jim."

"A man should always look at a thing he's wanted badly after he's decided he doesn't want it," Gary said. "It sort of removes all doubt."

"All right," McCabe said. "Have it your own way."

The multi-roomed mansion at last began to loom before them, larger and larger as they closed the distance. Passing into the front yard, both men sat their horses and waited for Miles's dog to come yap-snapping out of the barn, but he remained hidden. Gary rode up to the porch, leaned from the saddle, and knocked on the post, but no one came out. Both men then rode around the place and saw that all the shutters were nailed closed.

"What the hell goes on here?" McCabe asked wonderingly.

"Maybe there's an answer in town," Gary said, and turned in that direction.

They approached it in darkness, tied up before the saloon, and went inside. The hour was getting late, and only a few men stood at the bar. In a corner a dull poker game plodded along with bored players and low stakes.

"McCabe!" the bartender said, placing a bottle on the bar. "When did you get back?"

"Just now," McCabe said. He looked around the room once, then let his traveling glance stop at a corner table. A nudge drew Gary's attention, and he also looked. Anson Miles had his bottle, glass, and his thoughts. He acted as though he never cared to look up again.

"Let's go have a talk with him," McCabe suggested, taking bottle and glasses with him. They sat down at Miles's table, and it seemed that he would never glance up at them.

He spoke without raising his eyes. "Heard you come in, Guthrie. How are you, Lieutenant?"

"Tolerable," Gary said. "And you?"

"The same. I'm going to get drunk. You want to stay and see it?"

"What you want to do that for?" McCabe asked. "I never knew you to suck the bottle, Anson."

"The world looks better when I'm drunk," Miles said. Then he looked at McCabe. "You left her alone too long, Guthrie. Now we've both lost her."

"What are you talking about?"

"My little wife . . . that's who I'm talking about." He laughed. "I wanted a new windmill put up. A salesman came out from Kansas City. She rolled her eyes, and he smiled with them pretty white teeth he had, and the next day she up and ran off with him. That's why I'm getting drunk." He studied

191

McCabe for a moment, then smiled. "Why don't you get drunk, too?"

"No reason."

"You got a reason," Miles said.

"Then tell it to me."

"You ain't sheriff no more. Nope, they threw you out for going away like you did, Guthrie. Folks will stand for just so much, you know, and you always was one for bending a thing out of shape."

Jim Gary spoke up. "All this talk isn't getting us anywhere. What we need is another bottle, one apiece . . . hey, bartender."

"This boy's got a head on him," Miles said. "How come I never saw that before?"

"You were sober," Guthrie McCabe said.

The bottle was produced, and each man filled his glass. McCabe offered the toast, for they were gentlemen with a common intent. "Here's to all the beauty in the world. May a strong wind come up and blow the dust off it."

"Yes, sir," Miles said. Their glasses were immediately emptied.

McCabe said: "Hey, Jim, you forgot to send money to your sisters. Better put some of that in another pocket."

Gary shook his head. "I've already figured out how many bottles it'll buy."

"Now you've grown selfish," McCabe said. "A toast . . . to youthful ideals destroyed."

The bottles were upped, the glasses upped; three men sighed and wiped tears from their eyes. Miles's voice was getting thick because he had a head start on them, but McCabe and Gary quickly caught up with him.

Closing time was midnight on week nights, and the bartender turned out the back lamps before approaching their table. They reeled in their chairs, sang songs together, laughed over nothing, and cried for their own private reasons. The bartender was disgusted with them. He secretly hated drunks, having taken the Keely Cure once himself, and their maudlin behavior angered him. He saw the tears and nothing else, and he spoke roughly to them.

"Time to get out! Come on, let's go!"

They paid no attention to him, and, when he tried to take Gary's arm, the young man knocked him down. The bartender was more surprised than hurt, and, when he got up, he went out and down the street after the sheriff.

Lon Caswell had been a deputy under McCabe, and he could not help recalling all those times he had bent his will to McCabe's. He handled Miles gently, carrying him off to the jail, then coming back for Lieutenant Gary. McCabe was saved to the last, slapped around a little and handled roughly, but he was too drunk to care.

They shared the same cell, and, after locking the door, Caswell sat in his office, dozing until dawn. A buggy rattling down the street woke him, and he got up to see who it was. Then he saw that it was an Army ambulance instead, driven by a burly sergeant. A young woman shared the seat beside him, and the rig stopped in front of the jail.

Jane Donovan got down with the sergeant's help and came across the walk. "Are you the sheriff?"

"Yes'm."

"Then you're the one I want to see," she said, stepping into his office. "It occurs to me that you might have a gentleman here who had too much to drink. I've come to fetch him."

Caswell smiled. "I expect you mean Lieutenant Gary. Yes'm, he's sleeping it off now."

"Is there a fine?"

"No," Caswell said. "They had quite a crying jag on last night, Miss . . . ?"

"Donovan," she said. "Will it be all right to take Mister Gary back to the post now?"

"Sure . . . it just saves me county expense of feeding him."

Caswell went to the cell block to get Gary, and Sergeant Davis came inside to help him into the back of the ambulance. Gary could hardly walk. He did not open his eyes; rather he held them tightly shut as if afraid to open them. Caswell came to stand in the doorway, and Jane Donovan and the sergeant climbed into the rig. They U-turned in the street and left Tascosa without delay. Jane kept her hands clasped tightly together in her lap for a mile or so, then she said: "Perhaps I should have waited and let him come back by himself, Sergeant. But I had my fears that he wouldn't come back."

"Mister Gary's not one to give a thing up," Davis said. "He's Army, ma'am."

"Yes," she said. Then she looked at him, her eyes shining with seriousness, dedication. "We'll have to look after him for a while, Sergeant. You, when he's on duty, and me when he's off. We can't fail him. You understand?"

"Yes'm." Then he put his gloved hand on hers. The rough planes of his face broke into a smile. "Mister Gary's just too good a man to lose. And we sure won't lose him, ma'am. Don't you worry about it."

"My, I forgot about Guthrie McCabe! Turn about, Sergeant. Perhaps the sheriff will. . . ."

"No, no," Davis said, shaking his head. "Mister McCabe will sober up soon enough, and he and the sheriff will play a little game to see who gets the badge." He grinned. "Ma'am, there's nothing wrong with McCabe except maybe a headache. He never asks a man for a favor." Davis laughed. "I've known the man since I was transferred here. If someone steals his place, he just roots another one." Davis clucked to the team. "I give him sixty days, or until the colonel is gone. Then he'll come riding out to the fort with a smile, and a badge on his vest, and money jingling in his pockets. The McCabes in this world are hard to put down, ma'am. Be glad of it."

"Yes," she said softly. "Now, I think I am glad."

PART TWO

1880

Chapter Twenty-Two

There was a sense of futility and frustration in well-drilling for Ben Stagg. He just wasn't cut out for it, and it was difficult for a man approaching seventy to do well with new things. He was a man with the good run of his life behind him, and now he puttered away, trying to stay busy while waiting for his life to end.

Stagg was a small man, hardly more than five foot four, and in his prime he had never weighed more than a hundred and thirty-five pounds. Age had pared some of that weight away and put a stoop in his posture, so that now he seemed even smaller and lighter. His years stretched back to the legends, to the mountain men, the rendezvous, and Bent's Fort. They spanned more than six decades, and he had seen things change that he had not believed would ever change, and he still could hardly believe it. Stagg's eyes had seen the Indian nations at their strongest and the prairie black with buffalo. He had smelled the smoke of a thousand lodge fires in grand council, but these things were all gone now, except in his memory.

He was all that was left, for the Indians were all on reservations, and the buffalo were gone, and there were towns everywhere, and railroads cutting steel slices across the country. And now he was digging a well for a farmer who insisted on fencing a portion of dry Texas where the Apaches had once camped in their running raids into Mexico.

Ben Stagg could remember this country well, as it once had been. Without closing his eyes he could blot out the farmer's fence and his squat house and barn and see the rolling land where there wasn't a town or a railroad for eighty miles. He could see the things others could not see, for he had been more than sixty years in this country. It troubled him and made him lonely because there was no one to share these things with him.

The steam engine hammered out power, and the drilling rig thumped and poked into this impossible soil. Two Mexicans worked the rig; one fed wood to the firebox, while the other tended the drill cable. For two days now Stagg had been taking samples, raising mud and clay, and he guessed he had hit salt water and would have to abandon the hole.

Far out to the south there was a mounted man approaching. He was as yet only a bare speck, raising a little dust. Ben Stagg kept his attention on him, because a lone man riding across country interested him. It was to the south that the railroad cut across the prairie, and out there, about eighteen miles, was a water tower, a telegraph office, and a coal station. Normally the train did not let off passengers there, and it was the fact that the rider came from that direction that especially interested Stagg.

The rider slowly grew larger, and, although he was still too far away for identification, Ben Stagg made his judgment. The man was Army—you could tell by the way he rode, and, as the man drew closer, Stagg could make out the shine of brass. He was young, Stagg reasoned, because an old man lacked that elasticity and carried himself differently.

When the rider was near enough so that Stagg could see he had been right on all counts, he yelled at the Mexican boy to stop throwing wood on the fire, but the drill rig made so much noise the boy didn't hear. Stagg pitched a clod of dirt over that way, and, when the boy looked up, Stagg waved his arms, signaling to let the fire and the power die. The rig began slowing, the bit and cable were hauled up, and the boy at the boiler valved off a geyser of steam.

The soldier was close enough now so that the sudden roar of steam startled his horse and set him to pitching. Stagg watched the soldier maintain his seat with no apparent difficulty. When he had the horse under control, he came on up to the rig and dismounted.

"Would you be Ben Stagg?" he asked. He was an officer, a captain of cavalry, in his mid thirties, and pretty stern in the eye which made Stagg think that he'd come out of the Academy young. "My name is Jim Gary, stationed at Camp Verde."

"That's a far piece," Stagg said. He jerked his head toward a wagon and the camp. "Water barrel over there if you want to wash."

"That was a damned dusty eighteen miles," Gary said. He took off his gauntlets and, using them as a flail, pounded most of the dust off his uniform.

Stagg went with him to the wagon, and Gary stripped to the waist. He was a tall man, well put together, and he wore enough scars to convince Stagg that he had seen his share of trouble and had met it all face to face.

"You come from the tanks?" he asked.

Gary was flinging water over his head. He straightened up, dried off, and then said: "Yes. They told me in Tascosa that you were drilling in these parts. I've been looking for you for two weeks now, up and down the state."

"Hell, I ain't that hard to find," Stagg said. "You want me personal like, or do you speak for the Army?"

"I speak for the Army," Gary said, slipping into his shirt. "I'd like to have you hear me out before you give me a flat yes or no answer."

201

Ben Stagg peered at the sky and judged the amount of daylight left. Age and exposure to weather had etched a sea of minute wrinkles in his skin, and he had wattles under his chin, as though his bones had shrunk and left his skin stretched and loose. He wore baggy pants, a patched coat, and Indian moccasins. A four-day gray stubble was on his cheeks. His long hair fell loosely over the back of his neck.

"I'm tired of hearin' that drill thump," he said. He yelled at the Mexican boys. "Lobo, make a fire, *andale!*" He grinned at Jim Gary. "How does beef, pan gravy, and biscuits sound to you?"

"Best ever," Gary said.

"We'll sit in the shade of the wagon while Lobo cooks," Stagg said, going over and squatting down. "I'm plumb out of tobacco, or I'd offer it."

"Have a cigar," Gary said, probing his shirt pocket. Stagg declined a match. He'd rather chew. He bit off a piece of the cigar and put the rest away for later.

"Don't see much Army these days," Stagg said. He squinted and thought about this for a moment. "Last time I seen a troop of cavalry on the prairie was in . . . let's see now . . . 'Seventy-Four. That's some six years ago. . . . Camp Verde, you say? Didn't know there was Army there. Last I heard it was a Texas Ranger post."

"Well, it still is," Gary admitted. "There's only about twenty of us there, six officers and the rest enlisted men. Mister Stagg," he went on, "I hear stories about you now and then. They tell me you roamed up and down and across Texas two years before the Alamo. That a fact?"

"It be," Stagg said, nodding. "I was like the wind in those days, just runnin' free. I trapped, traded, and squaw-manned it for a while up in the 'Rapaho country. Their women is real pelt, boy, but it's too late for you to try it."

Jim Gary grinned. "They tell me you once knew by sight every Kiowa and Comanche buck from the Canadian to the Gulf. Is that just talk?"

"Fer a fact it ain't," Stagg said. "Things was some different fifty years ago. A white man west of the Missouri was some beaver, and he got along with Injuns. Why, I've ate guts and dried corn in every camp clean to the Mandans." He squinted at Gary. "Boy, you keep shovin' in chips, but I ain't got the hang of your game yet."

Gary laughed and drew deeply on his cigar. "Do you remember Guthrie McCabe? Sheriff of Oldham County?"

"Do I? By golly, he's a Texas Ranger now, ain't he? In with the big politicians." He pursed his lips. "Gary . . . Gary . . . I remember that name from some. . . ." He snapped his fingers. "By golly, you was the officer with McCabe when they brought back prisoners the Comanches had been holdin'. That was some five, six years ago."

"Six years this spring," Gary said. "The Army made some mistakes in those days, Mister Stagg. We're trying now not to make so many. As you might have heard, we managed to bring back a number at the end of a rope, kicking and fighting all the way. We turned them over to their kin and, it might interest you to know, not many of the young people are alive today. Four were hung for crimes. One died of disease . . . ." He studied the end of his cigar. "They were savages, Mister Stagg, most of them taken as small children and raised as Comanches. Within a year, when five were dead, the War Department took a different view of the whole matter. We moved into Camp Verde five years ago. The first year we found three young boys. Instead of immediately turning them over to the first people who claimed them, we confined them and began to teach them how to live like civilized people." He sighed and shook his head. "I don't have to tell

203

you what kind of a job that was."

"No, I know," Stagg said.

"Through questions we began to amass a tremendous amount of what seemed like unrelated information concerning Indians and their movements, and prisoners they had seen come and go. This is my duty, Mister Stagg, going through this information, straightening it out, trying to come up with a picture of what really happened, so that we can return the right people to the right relatives."

"You must have paper stacked three feet high," Stagg said.

"Several rooms full of it," Jim Gary admitted. "Of course, we have learned of other captives still being held. Or rather, they no longer wish to return. But we're compelled by law to find them, fetch them back, and unite them with relatives." He took a final puff on his cigar and shied it into the fire.

The coffee was ready, and the Mexican boy brought two cups.

"Major Adamson," Gary continued, "who died last year was in charge of compiling the case histories of the relatives, where they were attacked, or where the child ran off or was stolen. We are now in the process of bringing the relatives back here and trying to match up these people."

"You do that and it ain't goin' to turn out any better than before."

"Mister Stagg, those are our orders." Gary sighed and shook his head. "Now I'll come to your part. We've learned, talking to returned prisoners, of the possible location of many others scattered now, traded off to Arapahoes and Kiowas, living on the reservation somewhere . . . God knows where. We want to find these people, Mister Stagg. The Army needs you . . . the man who knows the Indians, their ways, and their customs. You can see that we'd get nowhere sending in the Army."

Stagg's jaw worked on his chew of tobacco, then he spat and said: "Captain, you understand that the women have half-Injun kids, and the boys have counted coup?" Gary nodded solemnly. "Yes, you've run into that, all right. Be best if we left these people alone. You know that."

"Mister Stagg, I don't have any choice. I'm a soldier, and I take orders. If I refuse to carry them out, I'd be relieved of duty. In addition to sacrificing my career, I'd accomplish nothing, because they'd send another man to take my place, and he'd be faced with the same thing. Right or wrong, this is something that must be done. You can refuse. That is your privilege. The pay is the same as for a contract surgeon, a hundred and eighteen dollars a month and quarters, with a dollar a day ration allowance for you, and another dollar for your horse when you're in the field. I'd like to take back your answer, Mister Stagg."

Stagg did not hesitate. "You think I'd refuse? Hey, Pancho! You want to go into the well-drillin' business? The whole caboodle is yours. Yeah, yours. You can have it."

He stood up and flung his hat into the air, whooped, and did a choppy, circular dance, bobbing his body up and down. He was an Indian calling to his sun and wind and sky gods, and he was a part of it all now, unfettered by the necessity of digging holes in the ground to make a living. The Mexicans stood together, talking rapidly in Spanish.

Ben Stagg stopped and came back to where Jim Gary waited. He sat down and said: "You know the most important words in a man's language, Captain? *I woke up.* Sleep is a long darkness, and many a man spends his days in sleep with his eyes wide open, doin' what he dislikes, livin' his life because he can't bring himself to end it." He laughed and slapped Gary's leg. "I'll see you in Camp Verde in three, four days. All right?"

"Yes, I think I'll be there then," Gary said. "I have to go to Pecos. The sheriff wired Verde that Llano Vale was there, and I want. . . ."

"Vale?" Stagg interrupted. He reared back, his eyes wide. "Have I got to work with him?" He puffed his cheeks and seemed to be fighting his temper. "Why, the man's wild! He's been kicked off every Army post where he's ever worked."

"Besides yourself, who knows more about Comanches?"

Stagg hemmed a bit, rolled his shoulders, then gave in to the point. "He's trouble, Captain. Don't say I didn't tell you."

"I know that, and it's part of my responsibility to handle him." He got up, pulled the pan of biscuits away from the fire before they burned, then motioned for the Mexican boy to come over. "Take care of your business," Gary said to him sternly, and he drank from the water barrel. "Do you have any idea when the southbound train comes through?" he asked Stagg. "I thought maybe I could have it flagged down at the tanks."

"When'd you get off?"

"Around noon."

"Be another in the mornin', then," Stagg said. "Stay the night . . . I'll enjoy the company. Don't have anybody to talk to 'cept my Mexican boys, and they're a clannish lot. Just want to sit together and jabber. I expect they do it because they know we're against 'em. Their skin's just naturally dark . . . they wear that little cross around their neck . . . and they talk a language we don't understand, so we just got to suppose they're talkin' about us. That's the way most people think, ain't it?"

"It's a shame that you have to be right," Gary said. "Since I've lived here, I've learned to read, write, and speak Spanish, but still I find myself listening now and then to catch the gist of what they're saying."

"Man's just never goin' to learn to trust man," Stagg said. "Now, you take Injuns. We ain't ever goin' to be satisfied with Injuns, until they're all gone. First thing people did was take one look at 'em, and they knew the Injuns had to go. They was half naked, wasn't they? That's immoral. They was lazy, and that wasn't right. They didn't own property, and that wasn't good sense. They didn't believe in the right God, and that was just somethin' we couldn't put up with." He shook his head sadly. "Captain, there ain't much in my life that I've seen that ain't made me some sad." He waved his arms and included all the land. "A man could stand out here on the prairie for ten years and be burned by the sun, soaked by rain, froze in the winter, and pestered by insects and snake bite, and all that really wouldn't be half as bad as the things other people would do to him in two months of town livin'. Now that's a fact, and you know it."

"Or as bad as the things I have to do," Jim Gary said. "But we still do them, don't we, Mister Stagg?"

"Call me Ben." He got up to dish out the food. He came back with two tin plates, then the Mexicans helped themselves. "You see what I mean? They always do that . . . eat after I've taken my share. Told 'em not to do that a hundred times now, but it's still the same. We really don't change much with all our tryin', do we?"

They ate, talked a bit more, and then Stagg turned in as soon as the sun was fully down, and darkness marched across the prairie. This was not Gary's accustomed hour for retiring, but he turned into his blankets so as not to offend Stagg or to remind him he was in many ways different from the average man.

The pre-dawn coldness woke them. Stagg got a fire going

and the coffee on. They cooked pancakes and bacon and drank strong coffee. Then Gary saddled his horse, mounted, and rode back toward the tanks to catch his train.

The telegrapher was brooming out his place when Gary rode up and swung off. "When's the southbound to Pecos due?" Gary asked.

After consulting his watch, the man said: "Two hours yet. You want I should flag her?"

"Yes," Gary told him, and went to the shady side to sit and wait.

He dozed until he heard the train whistle, then he got up and watched as it slowed and came to a stop. The conductor and brakie both came forward to see why in the devil they'd been flagged. Gary saw the telegrapher point to him and wag his head. A cattle car was opened, a ramp was set up, and Gary's horse secured in a makeshift stall. He went to the rear and climbed aboard the caboose, and the train pulled away from the tanks.

The conductor asked for Gary's name, unit, and destination. He wrote all this down, then he made a show of looking at his watch. "That stop will throw us ten minutes late," he said.

"How long have you been railroading?" Gary asked pleasantly.

"Twenty-eight years," the conductor said. He was a thin, testy-mannered man with a waterfall mustache and thick glasses.

"And you've never run late before?"

"Of course, I have," the conductor snapped.

"Then why don't you shut up about it?" Gary suggested. He stared at the man and watched his face color deeply. Then the conductor turned and walked to the other end of the car and left Gary to himself all the way to Pecos.

The train pulled in after dark. Gary got down and got his horse. He rode into town where he tied up in front of the sheriff's office, which the city marshal shared. Gary stepped inside, letting his eyes adjust to the glare of the hanging lights. A man sat at the desk, paring his nails, and he relaxed when he saw the uniform.

"I'm Jim Gary. You sent me a wire."

"The sheriff did. I'm Radison, city marshal. Did you come for Llano Vale?"

"Is he still locked up?"

"Turned him loose two hours ago. He's down the street, going on another toot. I'll have to lock him up again tonight, after he passes out." The man grunted. "I don't want to try it while he can move."

"If you'll just point in the general direction of the saloon. . . ."

"On the main street about a block and a half down. Stay on this side. I think I'd better come along." He unkinked himself from the chair and shifted his pistol to the front of his hip.

They walked down the street together, and the marshal followed Gary into the saloon. There was a spirited crowd at the bar, and Gary saw the reason. Llano Vale was being encouraged to lift a full beer barrel off the floor and set it on the bar. He was a huge man, long in the arms and broad across the back, and the years had sapped none of his bear strength. He grunted, heaved, and hoisted the barrel up and over onto the bar.

There was wild cheering, and drinks were pushed his way. Jim Gary eased his way through, moving men aside without offending them. When he stood at Llano Vale's elbow, he said: "Mister Vale, I'm Captain Gary. I'd like to talk to you."

Vale was emptying a pitcher of beer, and, without looking

around, he put it down and said: "Well, I don't want to talk to you." Then he suddenly made a tremendous sweeping motion with his arm, and the force flung Gary backward. He carried two others with him when he fell.

The room grew quiet, and Gary picked himself out of the sawdust and brushed it from his uniform. Vale was watching him now, a smile splitting his broad face. When Gary took a step toward him again, Vale said: "I'll hurt you if you keep on bothering me, boy."

Gary did not hesitate, and Vale suddenly kicked out, and, although it surprised Gary, he was ready. He ducked the swing, grabbed Vale's ankle, and hoisted, using all his strength to heave upward, as though he were throwing a heavy ball aloft. This force, added to the power of Vale's kick, tore Vale loose from the bar and up off the floor. He went into the air and came down flat on his back, his head rapping the brass footrail with a loud ring.

There was no hesitation in Gary. He jumped, landed with both knees in Vale's stomach, and went into a roll, clearing Vale and getting to his feet all in one motion. He turned around and saw that Vale was rolling over, holding one hand to his stomach. But he was getting up, and, when he was halfway there, Gary jumped for him. He jumped high, catching Vale around the neck with his legs, and he locked them into a scissors even as the two of them fell together. Vale rolled and flung Gary around, but Gary hung on, applying pressure. Vale's face turned crimson, and his eyes bulged. He clawed at Gary's legs, but he grew too weak to break the grip.

He hung on until he passed out, then Gary released him, and got up. "Give me something to throw on him," Gary said between quick breaths.

"Got some slop here," the bartender said.

"Hand me that, and you'll wear it," Gary said. "I want clean water."

He was handed a bucket, and he looked at it before throwing it into Llano Vale's face. The man coughed and sputtered, then opened his eyes and sat up, spreading his arms to hold himself steady. His eyes found Gary and looked at him a moment, then he grinned.

"I ain't been put down in near thirty years," he said. He held up his hand. Gary took it and hoisted him to his feet. "We'll talk now, boy," Vale said, and went over to a table. After Gary had sat down and taken off his hat and gloves, he offered Vale a cigar, and lighted one for himself.

"You're heading for another toot," Gary said. "Would you like to work for me, or go back to jail?"

"Jail now and then is better than some work," Vale said. He brushed his wet hair and pawed water from his mustache. "What would I be doing?"

"Work for the Army. Searching out white people among the Comanches."

"Ah," Vale said, leaning back in his chair. "You're from that outfit at Verde. Heard about you. Heard you set up a school there." He shook his head. "White or not, once the Injun gets ground in, all the schooling in the world won't change it."

"Well, we're trying," Gary said. "Do you want the job?"

Vale puckered his forehead. "Who else you got?"

"Ben Stagg."

Vale made a disgusted noise. "Why, that old windbag, what do you expect out of him?"

"The same as I'd expect out of you . . . a thorough job. Mister Vale, either that reputation of yours is true, or it's a lie. Which is it?"

"How do I know what you've heard?"

211

"I deal in facts, not rumors," Gary said. "I understand that you know the Comanches better than any white man, that you used to take Quanah Parker hunting when he was a boy. I understand that few living men know Texas as you do. The rest I put down as so much talk."

Llano Vale laughed softly. "You got the facts straight, boy. How long is this job good for?"

"I'm in my fifth year and nowhere near done."

"How's the pay?"

"Reasonable," Gary said and told him. "I'd like to go back to Camp Verde in the morning. I'd like to have you come with me, Mister Vale."

"You're a polite cuss, aren't you?" Then he laughed and rubbed his neck. "Kind of the iron fist in the velvet glove. Do I have to work with Stagg?"

"If you're told to. But it may not be often."

"He and I don't get along. Never did."

"Learn," Gary suggested. "Well?"

"I'd like to know more about it," Vale said, hedging a little.

"I'll tell you on the way."

"Well, I like an early start."

"Is sunup early enough?"

"Better I meet you at Verde," Vale said evasively. "Got some personal things to attend to."

"Suit yourself," Gary said, and left him.

Chapter Twenty-Three

Camp Verde was situated on the south shore of an unnamed fork of the Guadalupe, and, as military posts went on the frontier, it was not without its comforts. Nestled in rolling hills, timber was plentiful. The post was constructed of log and adobe, and there were shade trees and an excellent well. The camp had originally been built without a palisade, but the Army had constructed one around the returned-prisoner compound, and this enclosed barracks, hospital, school building, and housing for a military detachment. The rest of the post was gravel walkways and precisely placed single-story buildings with calcimined rocks bordering the parade ground. The stable area, sutler's stores, and farrier yard were behind the enlisted quarters.

Captain Gary rode the train to the fifty-mile water stop where he got off and had his horse taken from the cattle car. Camp Verde lay eleven miles to the west, and there was a good road leading from the tanks. Gary mounted and turned west, believing he could make the post just after retreat.

He was barely an hour out of the station when the weather turned cloudy, and he dismounted and put on his poncho, stepping into the saddle again as the first rain fell. These showers came on suddenly and often. He did not understand the making of weather, but the frequency of rain kept the land green during the summer and the creeks up.

It quit raining before he reached the post. The sentry admitted him, and he rode on to headquarters and dismounted there. Lieutenant Jess Flanders came out, his manner highly agitated. "My God, Gary, I'm glad to see you!" He took Gary by the arm and drew him inside. The office was quiet, for the clerks had gone to evening mess.

Gary peeled off his gauntlets and tossed them on the desk. "I hope my wife is as anxious," he said, smiling. "Where's Captain Weldon? At mess?"

Flanders shook his head. "Dead. I've been in command for nine days." He flung out his hands in an appeal. "I didn't know what to do."

Gary opened the door to Weldon's office and stepped in. He lighted the lamp and motioned Flanders to come in. Then he got a bottle out of Weldon's bottom drawer—the bottle had kept Weldon from ever advancing past the rank of captain. He poured Flanders a drink.

"What did Weldon die of?"

"A knife," Flanders said, and he tossed off the drink. He shuddered and made a face. Then he doubled his fist and stabbed at himself in the stomach. "Right here, in the brisket. I've got the man locked up. You may remember him, the tow-headed boy we found in the Arapaho camp."

"Yes . . . been here about four months now."

"And not a damned bit of progress," Flanders said. "Not one damned word of English have I been able to get out of him, but I'll swear he understands it as well as you or I. You watch his eyes . . . they're quick and intelligent. He understands perfectly. Too bad he'll hang now. I had hopes for him."

"You reported this to department?" Gary asked.

"Reports! My God! There are some telegrams on your desk. Been lying there for days now." He looked at Gary who was calmly lighting a cigar. "Shall I get them, sir?"

"An excellent move, Mister Flanders."

Gary sat down behind Weldon's desk and adjusted the lamp. The man had been an untidy sort and had left a litter of paperwork on his desk. Flanders came in from the adjoining office and handed Gary the telegrams. He opened them, sorted them as to date, and read the first one.

Captain James Gary
Camp Verde, Texas
 Lt. Flanders report at hand—will await your report before advising.
          T. Caswell
          Brig. Gen.

The second message was longer:

Major James Gary
 My pleasure to advise your promotion now eight days old as of the third instant. They also serve those who stand and wait—warmest regards to your wife and children.
        Tremain Caswell

Gary handed this to Flanders who smiled and said: "I'll have this posted in an hour, sir."

"It's not that important," Gary told him and read the third message. "But this is. . . ." He handed this one to Flanders. "Have Sergeant Geer and a detail of five mounted men ready to escort the ambulance off the post in an hour. General Caswell will arrive in Fredericksburg on the morning train. See that suitable quarters are ready. We'll have a parade ground inspection tomorrow evening." He rubbed his unshaven cheeks. "The general doesn't understand why no further report was made. Mister Flanders, you really ought to open official mail. I hope you remember this. The next time this happens I'll make a note of it in your record."

"I've just never faced this situation before, sir. I'm sorry that I disappointed you."

Gary smiled. "Mister Flanders, no second lieutenant with ten months of service really disappoints me."

He got up and slapped Flanders on the shoulder. "I'm going to my quarters, bathe, shave, and spend an hour with my family. I'd like to see all officers here at eight o'clock. That includes contract surgeons and supply personnel."

"Yes, sir." Flanders clicked his heels and saluted as Gary went out. This made Gary smile, because he could remember himself being like that some twelve years ago, when his second lieutenant's rank had seemed a crushing responsibility.

His quarters, a rambling adobe set back from the walk, were not far from the headquarters building, and, as he turned along the walk, he could see his wife, Jane, by the front gate. The two girls were with her, dancing up and down and clapping their hands. Day was retreating into darkness, and the shadows were deepening. A few lights went on around the post.

Gary stopped at his gate and said: "I heard down the line a ways that you were short a man around here." He pointed to the girls, five and three, and winked. "Say, I hope you two aren't engaged or anything. A fella could have a lot of fun making up his mind." The two little girls put their hands over their mouths and giggled, and, when he opened the gate, they rushed to him and climbed his legs as though he were a tree. He lifted them high on his shoulders, kissed his wife, and they went into the house.

Inside he put the girls down and hung up his belt and pistol. His wife watched him, smiling, and he fended off the girls and shooed them into the parlor. He put his arms around his wife and said: "I suppose I missed supper?" She shook her head. "Give me fifteen minutes to bathe and shave," he told her.

"All right, but the girls are going to bed early tonight," she said. She was still a firm-bodied woman, although nearing thirty, with cool gray eyes and nice lips.

"Oh?" His voice rose slightly in surprise.

"Yes, they've played too hard today."

"Oh." His voice fell.

"And you must be tired from so much traveling," she said, keeping the smile in her eyes.

"I'm never that tired," he said, and kissed her again, holding her long this time. When he let her go, she drew back and took a deep breath.

"Well!" she said, brushing a hand across her cheek. "I guess you're not." She gave him a little push. "Get your bath."

They had a screened back porch where he took his bath. It was completely dark now. He filled the tub, and his wife brought him clean clothes. He bathed, letting the soap and water ease his muscles. After he had dried and dressed, he went into the kitchen to shave. The girls were seated at the table. They liked to watch this manly ritual, and he put a dab of lather on the tips of their noses.

"Mother says you've played hard today," Gary said.

Emily who was the older said: "We caught polliwogs at the creek."

"An interesting pastime. I did it myself as a boy."

"Were you always a soldier, Papa?"

Gary razored a cheek clean and wiped lather and whiskers

off the blade, using a piece of newspaper. "Sometimes, when I'm tired, it does seem like it."

"Mama wouldn't let us go to Captain Weldon's funeral. It was a grand affair. That's what the surgeon said."

Gary looked at her and kept back his smile. "Funerals are no place for little girls to be. Try to remain children as long as you can. It's always too short a time as it is."

He finished shaving, wiped his face on a towel, then took the lather dabs off their noses. "There. Not a whisker in sight."

Jane was putting the food on the table. This was a happy time for Gary, for he believed in talk at the table. He also believed in some hand slapping when the girls got out of line. Afterward he took them to the parlor, held them on his lap, and told them a story, while his wife washed the dishes. Gary was full of stories of far-off places, but many times he was hard put to remember them. The girls always did and wanted to hear them over.

He stayed with them for some time, then got them into their night clothes, and into bed. He gave them a kiss, and they hugged him. Then he went to the kitchen where Jane was finishing up.

"I've asked the officers to be in my office at eight. It's nearly that now." He kissed the back of her neck and watched goosebumps form on her bare arms. "Still gets you, doesn't it?"

"Oh, you're just so bad, Jim Gary."

"Want me to change?"

"Good heavens, what a thought! Will you be long?"

"No more than an hour," he said, and left the house.

Lieutenant Flanders was in the office, putting chairs around for the men. The two surgeons came in. Both were elderly men with the rank of first lieutenant and a miserable pay that made Gary wonder why they remained in military employ. Then the two quartermaster officers entered, one with a brevet major's rank and a first lieutenant's pay. Theirs was a branch where promotion came slowly. If a man was a stickler for duty and distinguished himself with his bookkeeping, he could expect to retire with the exalted rank of captain.

When they were seated, Gary went behind Weldon's desk and took his place. "It seems, gentlemen, that we've had a spot of trouble." He looked at each man for comment, but they remained silent.

"I also trust that your grief over Captain Weldon's death has not been overburdening." He turned his glance to the quartermaster major. "I seem to have inherited a command, and, in case you haven't heard, I've been promoted to major."

The two surgeons had been studying their fingertips. They looked up as one, and the quartermaster major's mouth settled into deep grimness.

"I trust that you understand," Gary went on, "that now that I'm in command we will no longer putter along in our duty. It seems to me that we all ought to face the facts. Major Adamson and I conducted this . . . this last outpost for outcasts together for nearly four years. When he died, Department decided to strengthen the command by addition of you gentlemen. They looked around, wrote to commanders far and wide, and got rid of the men they were stuck with and sent them here. Captain Weldon, frozen forever in grade because of drunken behavior and failure to discharge his duty, was placed in command because of his seniority."

Gary turned his head and looked directly at Lieutenant Flanders. "A new lieutenant, last in his class, the man they had to commission but no one wanted." He looked at the two surgeons. "Never once have I deluded myself that you were good doctors. Perhaps you once were, but each time your contract came up for renewal, it has meant a change of station. That can indicate only a dissatisfaction on the part of your commander."

The quartermaster major was watching Gary now. It was his turn and that of the second lieutenant sitting beside him, peering at Gary through thick glasses. "Major Halliday, you loathe this duty. You plod through it. Drag through it. I have learned to expect little from you except excuses and delays. If it weren't for Mister Beeman doing half your work, I'd have it in your record that you were incompetent."

"Telling us off isn't doing any good," Halliday said, color high in his plump cheeks. "I hate this duty, and I make no bones about it. Teaching these savages is a waste of time." He looked at the others. "They'd all tell you that if they had the guts."

"Your opinion has no weight at all with me," Gary said. "It never has." He placed his hands flat on the desk and spoke softly. "But I can promise you this, gentlemen, we are going to get cracking around here, beginning at reveille. We will learn to love our duty, and you will perform it flawlessly, because I will be breathing down your damned necks. If one man steps out of line, I'll have him transferred to duty so distasteful that this will seem like a post in Washington. . . . I have four boys who, after eleven years of captivity, have been completely rehabilitated. That, to me, is a victory. We will enlarge on that, gentlemen. Indeed, we will."

"What are you going to do with that young buck that murdered Weldon?" one of the surgeons asked.

"I can see in your face that you think he should be hung. If you think that, why didn't you hang him? Weldon was dead, and I was away. Who would have stopped you?"

Lieutenant Flanders cleared his throat and said: "I'm

afraid, sir, I'm responsible for that." He hesitated a moment. "Matter of fact, sir, Major Halliday has placed charges against me."

Gary's eyebrows went up. "Oh? What are they?"

"Refusal to heed the command of a superior officer, sir. And pointing a pistol at Major Halliday, sir." He twiddled his fingers nervously and glanced at Halliday. "Sir," he went on, "the gist of the whole thing is that Captain Weldon had a snoot full and decided to give one of the boys in the compound a thrashing. As it happened, he picked on this boy, the one they call Teddy. He gave him quite a mauling, sir. You know that Weldon was a bit of a bruiser. Anyway, by the time the corporal of the guard got the sergeant, and the sergeant got Major Halliday out of his bed, the boy Teddy had stabbed Weldon in the stomach. We don't know where the knife came from. Weldon staggered out, falling just outside the gate. The boy was immediately placed in the guardhouse by my order. Weldon was taken to the dispensary, and he died a little after dawn. It's all in my report, sir. I haven't presented it yet . . . I thought I'd wait until morning, this being the major's first night home in nearly three weeks."

"Very considerate," Gary said. "Now tell me about your pointing the pistol . . . ?"

"Yes, sir. Major Halliday wanted to have the prisoner brought out the next morning after Captain Weldon died, tried, and hung. I thought that was ill-advised, sir, and refused to unlock the guardhouse. I had the only key on my person. Major Halliday tried to make a rapid advance toward me. I confused this as an attempt to take the key by force, drew my pistol, and ordered him clear of the compound. Since that time I've moved my bedding and slept there . . . until you returned, sir."

Gary considered this, then touched each of them with his

eyes. "Does anyone want to contradict this statement? No? Mister Flanders, please bring me the charges Major Halliday filed against you."

He sat there, brows puckered, while Flanders went to another office and returned, laying the papers on Gary's desk. After reading them, Gary tore them up and dropped them in the waste basket.

This brought the major halfway to his feet.

"Do you want to say something?" Gary asked.

Halliday sagged back. "No, but this matter isn't ended."

"All right. General Caswell will be here before evening mess tomorrow. I'll schedule a hearing for you. But bear in mind that there are others who can talk to the general."

"I . . . I think the matter best be dropped," Halliday said softly, and rubbed his forehead with his fingers.

"Thank you . . . a wise decision," Gary said. "Gentlemen, I will do my best to get to the bottom of this matter, including the quality of medical attention Captain Weldon received after his wound. He was not a popular man, and neither of you healers of the sick bore him any good will. I recall last winter when Weldon had to have a carbuncle lanced. This was performed with a dull knife and no means to ease his suffering." He smiled thinly at the surgeons. "If I find that you played checkers while he expired. . . ."

"That's a hell of a thing to say," one of them snapped. "It really is. Damned uncalled for!"

Gary's patience ended. "In five minutes I can get your service records from the file, listing every station, every commander you ever served. How many of these commanders, if I wrote them, would give you a decent recommendation? Uncalled for? Do you insist on that?" He banged his hand down on the desk and stood up. "Understand something clearly, gentlemen. We are on this post because I knocked on doors and begged generals to give these boys and these girls, turned savage by years of captivity, a chance to adjust. I also wrote countless letters asking for more officers, men who in addition to their military duty could teach them to read and write again the language they had forgotten. Unfortunately there were generals who thought this was a waste of time, and who still think that, so I have been sent men who have barely managed to hang onto their careers. Gentlemen, I accept you on those terms, and I guarantee you this. You will complete this tour of duty with pride and exceptional records, or you'll leave the Army in a manner you deserve. You are dismissed. Mister Flanders and Mister Beeman, please remain."

Mister Beeman, the bookish quartermaster lieutenant, looked around as though to ask just what it was he had done, but he remained while the others filed out.

"Please close the door, Mister Flanders," Gary said, and, when that was done, he motioned them into chairs.

He looked at Beeman who sat there as though he expected the axe to fall and drop his head right in his lap. "Mister Beeman, I've been observing you carefully for a year now, and I want to thank you for presenting immaculate records."

"I . . . I'm pretty good with figures, sir."

"Yes. You are also a good English teacher. And you have patience, Mister Beeman. It's rare in so young a man."

"Well, sir, it's because of my eyes. I had a difficult time in school, sir, and I remember how it was to be yelled at and cracked with a ruler. It kind of sets a man against those things, sir."

"Since I'm now short an officer, I'm taking you out of quartermaster and putting you in command of a company," Gary said. There was no change in his expression as Beeman drew in his breath sharply. "I believe you will work out fine in that capacity. Please be good enough to bring any problems you might face to me before they get out of hand."

"Yes, sir."

"Mister Flanders, you will continue to command your company but will move into headquarters and occupy my old office as post adjutant."

"Sir . . . my. . . ."

"Do you stutter, Mister Flanders?"

"No, sir. Only I have no seniority, sir."

"That's true, but as adjutant you will have authority. I'm convinced you'll use it wisely." He got up and shook hands with each man. "Convey my best to your wives. Has that boy of yours cut a tooth yet, Beeman?"

"Well, the way he cries sometimes, I think he's working on it, sir."

"Good night, gentlemen." Gary answered their salute, and, after they went out, he returned to his quarters where he found his wife mending his socks.

"The way you go through these things," she said, "I can hardly keep up with you."

He smiled and sat down across from her. He lit a cigar. "A fine way to talk to a major." Her glance shot up. "Eight days old," he added.

"Jim, that's wonderful! I'm so happy for you."

"It means I may retire a lieutenant colonel yet," he said. "Not that the rank is really important, but the pay goes up." He dropped ash carefully in a dish. "I made a few changes tonight. Beeman has been given Weldon's company, and Flanders moved to post adjutant."

"Oh, good heavens!" Jane Gary said, putting down her mending. "Jim, I have to live with these women. Why, Missus Halliday will have a fit. She never liked it when Weldon was given command. Oh, dear. I suppose you reminded Doctor McCaslin and Doctor Rynder that they were quacks and just a step above snake-oil salesmen?"

"Something like that," Gary admitted. "What are you fret-
ting about? You're not thick with them."

"A military post is a small place," she said, and she sighed
and took off her gold-rimmed glasses. "I saw Sergeant Geer's
detail leave, and his wife came over and said that General
Caswell is coming tomorrow. Isn't that rather unusual?"

Gary shrugged. "He wants to look into Weldon's death
and see just what we're doing. There are more than a few who
think this post is a waste of time and money, but I don't think
they'll close it. The word has gotten around that this is a
pretty good dumping ground for officers no one wants. I'm
going to have to ask Caswell for a couple more, or he'll think
I'm sick. Want to bet they're real pips?"

She shook her head and got up, stretching. Then she
yawned, and he laughed.

"What's so funny?" she asked.

"You faked that."

"I did not!"

"I can tell," he said, butting out his cigar. He stood up and
put his arms around her, running his hands down to the
roundness of her bottom. "I always said, give me an impatient woman and. . . ."

"Oh, that's terrible," she said, slipping out of his arms.
But he could see the color in her cheeks, and the smile lifting
the corners of her lips. She started counting on her fingers.

"What are you doing?"

"Counting on my fingers."

"What for?"

She stopped. "Do you want to increase the size of the
family?"

He smiled. "I have nothing against it." He came over and
tickled her cheek with his mustache, and it made her quiver.

"Why don't you go and turn back the covers, and I'll lock the doors and put out the lights."

"Now who's eager?" She started to turn, then stopped. "Sergeant Geer's wife's cat had kittens, and Emily wants one. What do you think?"

He scratched his head. "You're asking me now?"

"I was supposed to earlier, but I forgot."

"You shouldn't have things on your mind," Gary said.

She made a face and started down the hall. She looked into the girls' room, gently closed the door, and went on to the back bedroom.

Gary went to the front porch and stood a moment, looking around the post. It was dark and quiet, and only the sentries, walking around the walled compound in measured steps, gave him a hint that anyone beside himself occupied it. Then he turned and went inside, locked the door, blew out the lights, and made his way back through the dark hall.

Chapter Twenty-Four

General Tremain Caswell arrived in the ambulance. He was so tall that he had to ride humped over slightly to keep from knocking his head on the roof. Sergeant Geer and escort brought him on the post, and the trumpeter sounded "Flourishes" and "The General." Gary met him at headquarters as soon as he climbed down. They exchanged salutes, shook hands, and went inside where Caswell stripped off his gloves, unfrogged his saber, and took off his belt. Then he drank the whiskey Gary handed him.

He sighed and kinked himself into a chair designed for a man six inches shorter. Caswell was near sixty, but only his gray hair indicated his years. He was slender as a rod, a tough man with a tough reputation and a bull voice that could peel the gold thread off a major's shoulder straps.

"It isn't like you, Jim, to be tardy with a report," Caswell said. "Before I raise my voice, I'd like to hear your explanation."

"General, I didn't return to the post until late yesterday. I'd been off post for nearly three weeks."

He explained the whole situation to Caswell, keeping it factual, and letting the general make any judgment he wanted. Caswell had another whiskey and listened carefully.

When Gary was through, Caswell said: "You are not certain, then, where the boy, Teddy, got the knife?"

"No, sir. None of the returned prisoners is allowed weapons, General. I strongly suspect that the knife was in the possession of Captain Weldon when he entered the compound. It is also a possibility that he attacked the boy with the knife and, in the scuffle, was stabbed himself."

"What is the boy's story?"

"He hasn't spoken a word since he's been taken, sir." Gary took a deep breath. "General, I don't want to see this boy tried and hung on the evidence now accumulated. To get to the truth may take a great deal of time, sir . . . a month, or six months, or even a year. General, actually we don't know that Teddy stabbed Captain Weldon. There were no witnesses at all."

Caswell studied Gary from beneath the thicket of his brows. "You want to save the boy, don't you?"

"Yes, sir." Gary got out his watch and looked at it. "Sir, there's time to take you about the post, if you're not too tired."

"I'd like to see what you've done," Caswell said.

Gary went to the door and spoke to the orderly. "Give Mister Flanders my compliments and have him join us in an inspection. Ask Sergeant Geer to join us, too."

They went to the porch to wait, and Flanders hurried up, saluted quickly, and stood at attention until the general gave him at ease. Sergeant-Major Geer hustled across the parade ground, hands hastily finishing the buttoning of his blouse.

Caswell made his appraisal of the buildings, the grounds, the stable and farrier yard, then they walked toward the compound. The sentry opened the gate. The compound was laid out in a square with all the buildings built against the walls. A young civilian was crossing the parade ground, books under his arm, and he drew Caswell's attention.

"I didn't know you employed civilians, Major."

"That's Tom Smalling, sir. We're trying now to locate his parents. . . . Oh, Tom! Will you come here a moment?" The young man turned to see who was calling, then smiled, and came over quickly. He was somewhere in his late teens, tall and straight and brown as a nut. "Tom, I want you to meet General Caswell."

"It's a pleasure, General." He shook hands. "I'm sorry, but I'm late for a class. Will you excuse me, sir?" He bowed, turned, and trotted away.

Gary said: "When he was four and half years old, he was taken by a Comanche raiding party somewhere along the North Washita. We have not been able to pin down the exact location, but Sergeant Huckmyer took a detail there, dug around for a few weeks, and found some rusty wagon parts, which makes us feel reasonably sure that it was near the fork."

"Is all this necessary, Major?"

"Yes, sir, as you will see. Without going into more detail, sir, we managed to trace his life from his capture to when he turned himself in to us. That was three years ago, sir."

"Turned himself in?" Caswell said. "That is a figure of speech, isn't it?"

"No, sir," Gary said. "General, we've had no success at all in bringing them back, tied hand and foot against their will. The Indians, after keeping a captive a few years, gradually give him more freedom and finally accept him into the tribe as a brave. Then he is free to come and go as he pleases. Actually, sir, there are no prisoners among the Indians on the reservation. I have felt that our chief duty is to record them, their whereabouts, and see that they are well fed, clothed, and generally left alone. Sir, I have details constantly on the reservations, talking to these people, trying to gather information, urging them to come back. Tom and the other three who live here come and go. They do good work for us, General, because they are an example. Now and then a man will surrender himself. This indicates to us that he is willing to work with us. We can't teach a man who is fighting us, sir."

"And this boy, Teddy?"

"He was taken by Captain Weldon's patrol, sir. Weldon wouldn't release him, because he disagreed with me on the method of rehabilitation, and he meant to use Teddy as an example. General, you simply cannot force learning or anything else on a man when his mind's against it."

Caswell nodded. "How many do you have here now, Jim?"

"Six, sir, not counting the four who have been with us for some time."

"No women?"

Gary shook his head. "No, sir. They all have children now, and they just don't want to come back. To be very honest, sir, I had an experience once when McCabe and I brought back the first captives, and I've never forgotten it. There was a young woman, quite lovely. She'd been taken by an important brave. I managed to rescue her and returned her to the post. She was of good birth and had relatives of some influence, but the strain was there, sir, even though she had no children." He shook his head. "I've not urged the women, but we've compiled records of where they are and who they are, as complete case histories as possible." He touched General Caswell lightly on the arm, steering him across the parade to another gate. "Would you like to see the camp area we have established for the civilians, sir?"

Sergeant Geer dashed ahead and opened the gate, and they passed out of the compound. On a level bed of pasture sheltered by good trees a camp had been erected with stone fireplaces for cooking and rubbish pits with metal covers. There was a central bathhouse near the river and farther on a cluster of outhouses.

"We've located the families of four of the returned captives, sir," Gary said. "They've been notified, and they should be here in two to three weeks. These facilities should accommodate them nicely. I don't want them cluttering the post or being in the compound."

Caswell smiled. "I trust, Major, that all this has been accomplished without ruining your budget?"

"Yes, sir. Local labor and materials."

Caswell turned, and they walked around the outside perimeter of the compound. Lieutenant Flanders and Sergeant Geer followed at a respectful distance, out of earshot in case the general wanted to talk confidentially.

"I suppose I might as well tell you," Caswell said, "that most of the brass consider this a complete waste of time and effort. The whole thing would have gone under two years ago if you hadn't had good friends in high places."

"High places? Friends?" Gary laughed. "I, sir?"

"What's this display of innocence?"

"Sir, I don't understand what you're talking about," Gary said. He was baffled and a bit alarmed because the general seemed to be leading up to something, and it might not be good.

Caswell said: "Jim, I have never known you to lie or evade. Are you telling me that you don't know Senator Jason Ivers?"

"I've never heard of him, sir. Is he a Texas man?"

"Iowa," Caswell said. "Jim, let me set you straight on something. Senator Ivers, who is chairman of the Military Appropriations Committee, has backed you to the limit. He has increased your appropriation year after year, and, through me, he has kept the other brass off your back. Now you tell me you don't know this man?"

"No, sir. I've never heard his name before."

"He keeps very close watch on everything you do, and, unless I miss my guess, he'll see that you're jumped on the promotion list to lieutenant colonel. This summer the senator plans to come here for a visit."

"Well, sir, I'd certainly be glad to meet him." Gary shook his head in genuine confusion. "But I give you my word, sir, that never once have I gone over anyone's head. . . ."

"Of course. I know that." Caswell laughed and slapped Gary on the arm. "Shall we get back? I wouldn't want to miss retreat and a full field inspection."

The general was Gary's guest for dinner, and Jane set a groaning table. Afterward, Caswell and Gary retired to the parlor for cigars, while Jane and Sergeant Geer's wife, who came over to help her, cleared the table and washed the dishes.

Lieutenants Beeman and Flanders showed up at the appointed hour and joined the two men. The fact that the other officers were not present brought a question to Caswell's mind, but he did not voice it, for he believed that a commander should run his own post without interference.

A knock at the door interrupted their talk. It was Tom Smalling, and he stepped in, quickly apologizing for the intrusion. He was offered a chair, and he sat straight, knees together. "Jim," he said, "when I took Teddy's supper to him, he spoke to me."

Gary slowly removed the cigar from his mouth. "Well, what do you know about that."

"I thought I'd better tell you. He wants to know when he's going to be killed."

After a moment's thought Gary said: "Tom, I'm going to give you a note to the sergeant of the guard. He'll unlock the cell for you, and I want you to bring Teddy here."

"Without a guard, Jim?"

"Yes."

"What if he runs? I might not be able to stop him."

"Tell him that there is a new commander who does not curse or drink. Tell him I want to talk to him."

Tremain Caswell cleared his throat. "Jim, isn't this a big step to take?"

"Yes, sir, but Teddy has taken a bigger one. He spoke, and that's something he hasn't done before." He looked at Tom Smalling. "Did he speak in Arapaho or English?"

"English, Jim."

"You bring him here," Gary said, and got up to write the note. He gave this to Tom Smalling who left at once.

When Gary sat down again, Caswell said: "Jim, if you were unhappy with Weldon or any of the others, you could have come to me."

"You know I don't do things like that, sir. Besides, you sent me men I needed. Getting a drunk as commander was something I hadn't bargained for, but it was something I had to make the best of." He studied his cigar tip and said: "I'm going to ask you for three more officers, sir, and another company of enlisted men. And, sir, you would be doing me a great favor if you selected junior officers with good records who want to remain on frontier duty and can't find an assignment."

"You're asking for picked men, Jim."

"Yes, sir, because I have a special kind of a job here. I need intelligence and dedication and understanding. I can't use misfits, problem cases, drunks, and malcontents, sir."

Caswell watched Gary for a minute, then laughed. "For a moment there, you were almost telling a general what to do. But you're right. I'll do my best, Jim." He stubbed out his cigar. "Let me ask you something. Why do Tom Smalling and the other three men wear civilian clothes? Wouldn't it be simpler to issue blues?"

"I've considered it, General, and decided against it. Some of these boys fought the Army when MacKenzie put down the Comanche trouble once and for all. I just believe that I get better results in not dressing them in the uniforms of their enemy. They may be white-skinned, sir, but. . . ."

"Yes, I know what you're going to say."

There was a step on the porch and a knock, and Lieutenant Flanders went to the door. Tom Smalling came in with Teddy, a rather short, stocky boy, fifteen or sixteen years old. He had dark brown hair, blue eyes, and a profusion of freckles.

"Mister Flanders, will you get Teddy a chair? Thank you." To General Caswell, he said: "Teddy has not spoken English, but he's a bright boy and attends school, and he understands everything that is said to him. You may stand or sit, Teddy, whichever suits you."

The boy stood a moment, then sat down in the chair facing Gary and General Caswell.

"This is General Caswell, Teddy," Gary said. "He came here to talk to me about the death of Captain Weldon." He glanced at Beeman. "Go into the kitchen and have Missus Gary get you a cup of coffee for Teddy. And have her tell the children that it is all right for them to play in the parlor."

"Sir?"

"Are you hard of hearing, Mister Beeman?"

"Indeed not, sir." He hurried out.

Gary looked at Teddy a moment and said: "You know me, Teddy. I don't lie, and I'll not be lied to. In the weeks that I was gone, I know that Captain Weldon drank whiskey. When he got drunk, he did strange things." As he leaned forward to speak more confidentially, his two daughters came into the room and stood with their hands behind them, watching Teddy.

"Come here, Emily and Marie. This is Teddy. Show him your manners, then go play in the corner. You can look at the stereopticon, if you don't disturb us with your giggles."

After the girls had curtsied and smiled at Teddy, they dashed for the bookcase and battled for a chair by the table lamp. Gary watched Teddy carefully. The boy said: "My sister dead. She small when she die. Many years ago. She get sick. Die." He looked from one to the other. "When I die?"

"Did you kill the captain, Teddy?"

"He drunk. We fight. He fall on knife. Get up. Run outside. Fall again."

"Your knife?" Gary asked.

Teddy shook his head. "He bring knife. Cut my hair." He reached back of his neck and took a handful of his shoulder-length hair.

General Caswell said: "I think that's the truth, if I ever heard it, Jim."

"Yes, he wouldn't lie to me," Gary said. "His honor wouldn't permit it, because he knows I wouldn't lie to him. You may go, Teddy, as soon as you finish your coffee. Mister Flanders, inform the sergeant of the guard that Teddy is to be given free access to the compound and the post. He may come and go as he pleases."

"Off the post, sir?" Flanders asked.

"Certainly. If he wants to go back to the reservation, he can do so. If he wants to stay here, he can do that." He looked at the boy. "Do you remember your last name?"

"Not now. Long time. Forget now."

"And your sister's name was . . . ?"

"Too long. Forgot now." He stood up. "You good man. I stay now. Go school. But no cut hair."

"You can wear your hair the way you want to," Gary said. "Come and see me when you feel like it, Teddy."

The boy went out, but Tom Smalling hung back long enough to say: "Jim, I don't know how to say thanks and mean it enough."

"We may save that boy, Tom. Good night."

"Good night, sir." He closed the door gently.

Caswell cleared his throat. "You knew that he had a sister. Pretty smart of you."

"General, this is all like the pieces of a gigantic puzzle that are dumped onto the table . . . you begin to sort it out, piece by piece. Finally parts of a picture emerge. Information comes to us from many sources, and we put it down on paper, study it, and try to match it up with what we already have.

"I first heard of Teddy about two and a half years ago. He was taken by the Indians over near where Paris now stands. That area was wilderness then, the nearest neighbor sixty miles as the crow flies. His first year was spent with the Arapahoes, then he was taken by Comanches one night when they went on a horse-hunting raid. Five years with them, and he was sold to the Kiowas. He grew up with them, became a man with them, and went on the reservation with them."

He made a motion with his hand. "This information came a piece at a time. Someone had seen such a boy, in such a place, at such a time. Finally you get the whole thing and can say with surety that his name is Teddy, and that his people came from Indiana, and that he must be about sixteen years old. There were two sisters. One died. The other lived. We haven't found her yet." He sighed and took the wrapper from a fresh cigar. "But we will. And we'll find Teddy's other relatives when he wants us to. But not until."

Jane came and stood in the archway. "May I put our daughters to bed now?"

"They were angels," Gary said, smiling. "Take after their mother, of course."

"That's pure blarney," she said, and crossed the room to take the girls by the hand. "Come along now."

"We want to look at the pictures," Emily said.

"Now we don't want to let the general hear us cry, do we?"

"I'm not going to cry," Emily stated.

"You will if I have to smack you on the bottom to make you mind," Jane said. "Come on." She shooed them out of the room ahead of her. "I hope this homey scene didn't embarrass you, General."

"With four of my own, I seriously doubt it," Caswell said, smiling broadly. When she had gone out, he looked at Jim Gary. "You said something just before your wife came in that interests me. You said that you do not notify relatives until the boys are ready and want you to."

"Yes, sir. We can accomplish nothing by forcing the captives to return to their people. With the others some years back, it ended in disaster for all concerned. Here, they learn the things they should know. We try to help them become what they would have become if they had never been captured. In plain English, sir, we try to take all the Indian out of them. Then, when they know they can get along, they want to go back, knowing they'll be accepted. But it takes time, sir. A lot of time."

"I'm going to have to furnish a report on Weldon, Jim. Are you going to tell me I'm going to hand his widow additional grief? He had a wife in the East, you know. Drunk on duty and attacking the boy . . . that's not going to look very good over my signature."

"General, may I speak my mind?"

"I wish you would."

"There's no question in my mind, sir. Take Teddy. He didn't want to be captured by the Indians. Almost everything that happened to him was something evil thrust on him. I know how Indians treated prisoners. The first few years were living hell for him, and it is a miracle he survived it. They made him fight the dogs for scraps, ran him naked while they rode their ponies, and he never knew the comfort of a blanket until he was big enough to fight for one. None of this was Teddy's doing or his fault. Now, Captain Weldon had some pretty marvelous opportunities in his life, and, compared with Teddy's, they were all miracles of largess. But he played it away, wasted it, sucked it dry, discarded it, and took his comfort in the bottle. The last act he performed on this earth was to molest a boy who most certainly did not deserve it. No, General, I'd put it right down there in black and white. I'd want people to read it, and maybe some commander somewhere will learn that justice is more important than covering the regimental dirt for the good of the service."

General Tremain Caswell digested this. He looked at Carl Beeman and said: "Do you agree, Mister Beeman?"

"W-w-well, sir, I do. I do exactly. I may sometimes have difficulty doing my duty properly, sir, but the Captain Weldons have never made it any easier."

"That's very well put, Carl," Flanders said, then realized that he had spoken without invitation. But he was wading in now and intended to get thoroughly wet. "General, if I may offer an opinion, I would like to say that I cursed this duty when I came here. But teaching my small classes has taught me many things . . . one being that I really had no notion of what genuine misfortune was, but to these boys it was a part of their day-to-day living. We were all disappointed when Captain Weldon arrived with enough seniority to assume command. He was not suited for the duty, sir. Perhaps there was little duty left for which he *was* suited."

"That's a strong way to talk about a dead man," Caswell said, reminding Flanders just how far out of line he was getting. He softened this by smiling. "Gentlemen," he added, "I bow to your wishes. We will stick to the facts and hope that they hurt others only a mercifully short time."

Chapter Twenty-Five

Every military commander operated on a budget, a restricted amount of money predicated on his mission and the number of men in his command, and this budget could not be exceeded without sound reason. As second in command, Jim Gary had been responsible for such matters and had managed to come to the end of each fiscal year with a surplus, which, of course, he promptly spent on necessities for the command. He knew from experience that reporting a surplus would have meant an immediate trimming of the budget. Once Weldon had taken command, Gary had continued to manage these affairs. With the days going into June, and a surplus existing, he had hired Llano Vale and Ben Stagg, an expenditure noted by General Caswell when he examined the records, a routine part of his visit.

They were in Gary's office. The weather was sweltering, building up for a brief rain. The windows were open, and flies were thick on the screen, buzzing about, made nervous by the weather prospect.

Caswell was working his way through a half-smoked cigar. He had a brandy nearby, and now and then he sipped it. A sheaf of papers lay in his lap.

"Why is it, Jim," he asked, "that every year you give me a budget proposal that I have to fight for? Can't you give me a figure I can lay before old Iron Pants and have him smile and sign it?"

240

"Has that ever happened, sir?"

"No, but it's something to look forward to." He drew on his cigar and let smoke dribble past his lips. "This is quite a jump up, you know. Jim, I like to do things the easy way as well as any other man. May I wire Senator Ivers and urge him to advance the date of his visit to this post? He is planning for the fall, but, with the families arriving so soon, I believe that it would be better for him to observe the whole thing during a period of activity. The man has tremendous power over military money matters. He could double your budget or cut you off without a cent in a matter of hours. A message over his initials to the right generals would do the trick. If I presented this with Ivers's prior approval. . . ."

Gary smiled. "General, that's hardly the chain of command, is it?"

"It's military politics," Caswell admitted. "Do I have your permission, Jim?"

"Of course, General. And thank you for the courtesy of asking."

"Fine. I'll avail myself of the services of your telegrapher." He snuffed out his cigar, finished his brandy, and left the office.

Gary got up and went to a row of wooden filing cabinets and, after sorting through a few, placed four folders on his desk. They were thick manila binders and written on the covers were the names of Tom Smalling, Huck Thomas, James Amory, and Arny Erickson. Leafing through one of the folders, Gary could not help thinking that probably no finer chronicle of a boy's misery had ever been compiled. From a hundred sources, a thousand scraps of information, these files had been painstakingly assembled, covering the time of capture by hostiles to the day the captive arrived at Camp Verde. Then another series of records began. His

progress at the hands of his teachers and every step in his recovery to the white man's idea of a civilized state were put
down. Each folder contained another section dealing with the
prisoner's parents or other relatives; copies of all correspon-
dence to them and the letters received from them were included.

It was to Gary's way of thinking as important to prepare
the relatives as it was to prepare the returned captives. When
the relatives arrived, they would not be permitted to take
their son and go away. They would have to remain a while,
meeting their son each day, talking together, learning to
know and understand each other. This was something Jim
Gary insisted on because in his mind, startlingly clear, was
the tragedy he had been instrumental in triggering six years
before. Of course, he had not been blamed. No one had been
blamed, yet he could not shake the responsibility for it. He
had gone into the Comanche country for prisoners, and he
had brought some back, and he had immediately dumped
them in the laps of relatives who were not ready for this repa-
triation.

There were nights when he woke up sweating, thinking of
Mrs. McCandless, who had been driven feeble-minded by
the loss of her son and then killed at the hands of the white
boy who saw her only with an Indian's eyes, a demon that had
to be destroyed. And the boy, that lost soul, hung that night
on an upended wagon tongue by men who understood him as
little as he had understood Mrs. McCandless's vacant mind-
edness, had died an Indian.

This was a recurring horror in Gary's mind, and he could
not put it down even now, long after it had happened. Gary
supposed that he was not to be allowed to forget any of this.
He considered it his destiny to be here at Camp Verde, to
make certain that these things did not happen again.

★ ★ ★ ★ ★

Teddy, now that he was no longer confined, spent part of the morning walking around the compound, then he left it and stood outside the gate, looking at the officers' row and the walk with the white-painted stones. The married enlisted men had quarters to the east of the parade. There the women hung clothes on lines to dry, and children played noisily. He watched for a moment, then saw Gary's daughters come out on their front lawn with dolls and spread a blanket beneath the shade tree, and he felt compelled to go over, walking slowly, ready to run the moment someone yelled at him.

No one did, although several soldiers walked across the parade ground. Teddy stood in the shade and watched the girls with their dolls and a cradle and several small blankets. They played for several minutes before they noticed him standing there.

Jane Gary stepped to the door and opened her mouth to speak, then saw him, and went back inside. A moment later she came out with a tray and a pitcher of lemonade and four glasses. Teddy started to leave but stopped when she said: "You don't have to go, Teddy. Come, have some lemonade with us."

Her tone more than anything else made him stay. It had been a friendly voice, casual, without suspicion. She poured the lemonade, and she handed him a glass.

"What this?" he asked.

"Something to drink. Cool. You'll like it."

He sniffed it, dipped his finger in it, tasted it, then drank and made a face. "Not good," he said, handing her the glass.

"It just needs more sugar," she said, adding it and stirring it in.

He sipped it again and smiled. "Good." He sat down on the grass, still smiling.

"Teddy, aren't you supposed to be in school?"

"No go today."

She frowned slightly. "Teddy, you're supposed to be in Mister Flanders's class."

"He do nothing but count. One, two, three. I no go today." He shrugged. "No go tomorrow maybe. Me free now."

"We are not entirely free," she said patiently. "Teddy, we must all do certain things. You must go to school." This wasn't reaching him, and she knew it. She decided to try something else. "If you don't go to school, you won't be allowed to come here any more. Do you understand?"

He looked at her, his expression serious. Then he looked at Emily and put his hand gently on her hair. "I go school now," he said. He drank the rest of his lemonade, handed her the glass, and walked rapidly back to the compound.

Mister Flanders was teaching mathematics. He had his advanced students working on fractions. He looked up when Teddy opened the door and sat down at his desk. Flanders's first impulse was to say something sharp, but he knew that wouldn't do. They were little children in adult bodies, and he had to put back into their lives that which they had missed.

Now that Teddy had agreed to talk, Flanders imagined his work would be considerably simpler, and he spent an hour with him, seeing that he wrote his numbers correctly on the blackboard. Gary had been right; the boy had a fine mind. He wrote a neat hand, now that he wanted to work instead of sit there and listen with a sullen expression on his face.

Near noon the bugler blew mess call, and Flanders dismissed the class and put away the chalk and erasers. He walked across to the officers' mess, a small building added onto the west end of the kitchen.

Brevet Major Halliday sat at the head of the table. Flanders had never known him to be late for a meal. McCaslin and Rynder came in and sat down, then Lieutenant Beeman entered, hung up his hat, and sat across from Flanders.

Halliday looked at them a moment, and said: "I trust that you scholars have been drumming wisdom into the little savage minds." His glance touched Beeman, then Flanders. "You two certainly know how to shine Gary's boots, don't you? Yes, sir . . . no, sir . . . certainly, sir . . . you're right, sir . . . absolutely, sir . . . you make me sick."

Carl Beeman said: "Then I suggest you leave the table before you vomit, sir."

"What did you say to me?" Halliday's voice contained fury.

"I suggested, sir, as a matter of hygiene, that you leave the table if you feel the need to regurgitate. Certainly Doctor McCaslin will bear me out. Won't you, Doctor?"

"That's god-damned impertinence!" Halliday roared.

Lieutenant Flanders said: "I thought Mister Beeman's suggestion was full of merit, sir. You can never tell who has a delicate stomach, now can you, sir?"

"So-o-o, you put in your oar, do you, Mister Flanders?"

"I'm sorry, sir, but that's a naval expression, and I'm not familiar with it. Would you be so kind as to expl. . . ."

"Damn you, don't toy with me!" Halliday bellowed.

"Toy, sir?" Beeman asked. "Mister Flanders is quite proper, sir. I don't believe he'd ever do that. May I ask why you've been shouting, sir?"

"You smart whelps, I'll put you on report for this!"

Beeman looked at Dr. McCaslin. "Don't you think you'd better prescribe a powder for the major, sir? Excitement in this weather can. . . ."

"All right, that's enough," McCaslin said quietly.

Halliday turned his head. "McCaslin, when I need a

quack's advice, I'll be in dire trouble . . . and I'm a long way from that. Do not encourage these smart whelps who chose to flout a superior officer."

"I wasn't. . . ."

"I *know* what you were doing," Halliday interrupted. He glared at Beeman and Flanders. "You're at attention, both of you!" They sat straight, backs slightly arched, chins tucked in. Halliday threw down his napkin and walked behind them, pacing up and down. "I believe you gentlemen have let your new duties color your thinking, but I will correct that. Both of you will report to my quarters after evening mess. We will see if we can't file some of the smart edge off those tongues."

"I trust we'll be digging in the major's rock garden," Beeman said.

"Don't talk at attention!" Halliday shouted.

The mess door opened, and, as soon as Flanders saw General Caswell, he roared: "'Ten-shun!" Then he leaped to his feet so violently that he managed to ram an elbow deeply into Major Halliday's bread-dough belly. The major fell like a bundle of wet clothes and gasped for breath.

"At ease," General Caswell said, and he looked at Halliday. "Is that the position you assume when a general officer enters the room, George?"

Quickly Halliday got to his feet and snapped to attention.

Caswell smiled and said: "George, I've already given at ease. Go on with your meal, gentlemen."

"General, did you see what happened? Lieutenant Flanders struck me!"

Caswell stared at him. "For heaven's sake, George, you're being ridiculous." He turned his back on Halliday. "I'll be leaving in the morning, gentlemen, and it would give me great pleasure if I had the company of you and your wives for dinner this evening. At seven o'clock?"

They acknowledged the invitation together, and Caswell, nodding, left the room. George Halliday sat down. He pointed his knife at Beeman and Flanders. "Life is going to become increasingly difficult for you two. That's a promise!"

Dr. McCaslin looked at Dr. Rynder. "Do you want to say anything, Lew?"

"Yes, I believe I do," Rynder said, wiping his mouth and fluffing his mutton-chops. "I have always wanted to remark, Major, about your fat ass, and how comically it wiggles when you walk. You provide amusement for the entire post." He got up and pushed back his chair. "You certainly can ruin a halfway decent meal."

"Rynder, I've had my eye on you!"

"You're a jackass," Rynder said. "And in twenty-three years of contract surgery for the Army, I've seen my share of jackasses." He turned and walked out, slamming the door.

"If that man were a line officer, I'd challenge him," Halliday said. He looked at his stew, then pushed it away. "Who can eat this slop, anyway?" No one answered him, and he blew out a long breath. "God, I'd like to shed this assignment! My wife hates it here. I hate it here. I haven't had a command with a decent officer in it for fifteen years. Fifteen years!"

McCaslin got up, nodding to Flanders and Beeman to do the same. "Let's get out of here and let him cry." He took his hat, clapped it on his head, and stalked toward the dispensary.

Beeman said: "We're very sorry you're unhappy, sir."

It drove Halliday to wild anger, and he hurled the sugar bowl at Beeman who closed the screen door just in time. The bowl showered sugar through the screen and broke when it fell to the floor. The noise drew the mess sergeant.

He studied the spilled sugar and said: "That'll sure atrtact ants."

Quarters A, normally vacant, now housed the general. It was reserved for visiting dignitaries, and every post had one furnished, waiting, the focal point of social activity when great men entertained.

A detail from the mess hall spent most of the afternoon preparing the food, and another detail decorated the large parlor. Four men, musicians, got together and decided what they would play that evening. No one had said anything about dancing, but they knew from experience that music could soothe any general's humor and make the evening less likely to run on the rocks.

A good general—and Caswell was that—would extend an invitation to the sergeant-major and his wife, as well as to all senior sergeants on the post. By three o'clock this had been done. This invitation was not necessary, and regulations did not encourage it, but officers who had the respect of their men could carry off such an affair without lessening the discipline one whit.

The meal was a success, the placements just right, and the conversation remained general, so that no one felt shut out or was made conscious of his rank. When the ladies went to the parlor for their coffee, the men took their cigars to the large screened porch.

General Caswell took the chair he wanted. The others remained standing until he had made his selection. Then they sat down and waited for him to establish the tenor of the conversation.

He looked at Sergeant-Major Geer. "You've been on the reservations recently, Sergeant. Tell me, how are the Indians getting along?"

This was something he could have asked Gary and gotten an answer, probably the same answer as the one Geer would give him, but he wanted to get an enlisted man's viewpoint, which was often somewhat different from an officer's.

"Well, they've been licked, General, and they'll never forget that. Indians are funny that way. They just don't understand that people get whipped every day and come back. To them it's the finish. The end of something." He paused to light his cigar. "Of course, the buffalo are gone, and the railroads have cut up the land, and farmers have moved in everywhere with windmills and wells. I don't think they're getting along worth a good god damn, General."

Caswell laughed, and the others did, too, quietly. Caswell said: "Once in a while I hear talk about the possibility of the Indians breaking away from the reservation, going on a tear again. Is that possible?"

"No, sir, it ain't. Where would they go, General? The land's gone now, and land was everything to an Indian. He didn't own a square inch of it and didn't want to, but it was there for him to travel across or live on. Now it ain't."

"Then I can confidently say that Texas is safe from the Indians?"

"Yes, sir, only it's more the other way around. The Indians are safe from the Texans. Major Gary's taught me that, sir, and he's right. We always had less to fear from them than they had from us."

"That's an odd philosophy," Caswell said. He turned to Gary. "Would you like to expand on that, Jim?"

"Yes, sir. I suppose it's merely a way of looking at it, but time has taught me that all the Indian ever took from a white man was his life. He left everything else alone. But the white man wasn't content to kill the Indians, sir. He had to change their way of life, drive them from one place to another, destroy the buffalo, kill off the grass with the plow, and fence the land."

"Those things had to happen," Caswell said. "It's our way to form things to our image of what's proper. They call it civilization."

"Yes, sir, and I don't fight it. But I like to have it straight in my own mind."

If he intended to speak further, he had no chance, for the orderly came to the porch, saluted, and said to Gary: "Message, sir. And Mister Ben Stagg has just ridden onto the post, sir. He's put up his horse and is now at the mess."

"Tell him to wait for me at headquarters," Gary said. He ripped open the telegram and turned so that light fell over his shoulder. "Ah, the senator and his wife will arrive next Tuesday." He folded the paper and put it into his pocket. "General, would you see that my wife is entertained? I'll not be too long at headquarters."

"Did you say Ben Stagg?" Caswell asked. "Not *the* Ben Stagg?"

"Yes, sir, the original. I found him drilling a well for a farmer up in the Staked Plains country. I intend to expand, General, if I get my appropriation and, if I expand, I need Ben Stagg. . . . Now if you'll excuse me?" He nodded and left them.

He went to his office and there prepared a wire to Senator Ivers, stating that an ambulance and escort would be waiting to meet them when they got off at the tanks. He had just sent the orderly out with this when Ben Stagg came in.

Stagg grinned, shook hands, and sagged into a chair. "Don't want to seem to have taken my time, Cap. . . ." He bent forward and looked at Gary's oakleaves. "Say, you fellas go up fast, don't you? As I was sayin', I got delayed some in Mason. Llano Vale was there. Says you hired him. It was enough to make a man change his mind and go back."

"So why didn't you?"

Stagg shook his head. He wore a suit now, his hair had been cut, and his beard had been trimmed. "Figured since I was hired before Llano Vale, it was *his* place to go if anyone quit." He scratched his head. "He's got me some worried to tell the truth."

"Why?"

"Well, he was sober, that's why. Cold, stone sober. I couldn't believe it."

"Do you suppose you'd be ready to ride tomorrow?" Gary asked.

Stagg shrugged. "Tomorrow's as good a day as any. Got no horse, though. Rode here double with the mail orderly."

"I want to go to the reservation," Gary said. "You and I and a boy named Teddy. We'll catch the northbound at the tanks, and we'll be gone three or four days. Our first stop will be Fort Sill. All the Kiowas and Comanches are on the reservation in the Oklahoma Territory. If we don't have any luck, we'll try the agency headquarters at Fort Reno."

"What kind of luck are we lookin' to find, Major?"

"Women," Gary said solemnly. "Women and their children." He paused to light a cigar. "We've got to make the move, Ben. We can't go on, trying to return only the male captives."

"People bein' what they are, do you think folks'll take a girl back when she's got a passel of half-Injun kids?"

"Maybe they won't, but we have to offer them the opportunity. Ben, we haven't done that yet. And what says that a woman might not like to go it on her own?"

"She wouldn't get far, and you know it."

"I don't really know that," Gary said. "I only suppose that it's so. But times are changing, Ben. God, you know that better than any man. In your lifetime, all that you once saw has gone. We've got to try. And I don't mean just once, but try for a couple of years."

"I hear there's a general on the post. What does he think of this?"

"He doesn't know. War Department has always had an unspoken policy, Ben. We just never *find* any females. Somehow we can't trace them down. Well, it's a damned lie, because I've got two file drawers full of information. That's why you and I are going, Ben. I'm going to try to persuade one or two to come back and give it a try. To come back and let us help them."

Stagg studied him for a moment, then said: "Jim, I've done gone and finally figured you out. You know what your trouble is? You want to make everybody happy. You want everything to come out just right for everybody. I don't know what's drivin' you to do this, and I sure can't fault the notion, only I know it won't work. There's got to be hurt and cryin' and things that just don't come out even, no matter what you do."

"I brought a white woman back once," Gary said, "a lovely girl. She had a relative pretty well up in politics. In many ways, what happened to her when she got back was worse than what she had endured as an Indian's wife. I've never been able to forget that, or stop wondering just whatever happened to her since. She left for San Francisco, and I heard nothing more. But it's always been a hope of mine that somehow she lived it down."

"Who's this boy, Teddy?" Stagg asked.

"Captain Weldon brought him back on a length of rope," Gary said. "This is against policy, but Weldon was a man who didn't like failure and yet had little capacity for anything else. I think the boy will eventually come around, just as we will eventually find his parents or other relatives. Anyway, I want him to go back to the reservation with me and compare it in his own mind."

"And you hope some captive girl will see how it works and get her hopes up."

"Yes," Gary said. "Is that all wrong, Ben?"

"It might not turn out that way. But you've got to try, huh?"

"Yes, Ben, I'll just never give up trying."

Chapter Twenty-Six

The southern boundary of the Kiowa-Comanche reservation began at the Red River and ran north for seventy miles, bordered on the east by Beaver Creek and on the west by the North Fork of the Red and by old Camp Radzimininsky. To demonstrate to the Indians that even this land was not immune from the white man's progress, the railroad, running north from Wichita Falls, passed smack dab through the reservation with a stop at Fort Reno.

On the trip north, the conductor was not pleased with Teddy's riding in the coach with white people, but, because Jim Gary was there and Ben Stagg, he wisely refrained from making any comment. Several male passengers walked up and down the aisle a few times, giving Teddy a hard look, but they did not stop or say anything.

At Fort Reno the train stopped long enough for the three of them to get off. Reno was sort of a town grown up around the military post, but now there wasn't much military there, just a detachment of signalmen, a farrier sergeant and six men, and the sutler. They got horses from the livery stable for the ride to the agency which was thirty miles south. They rode the distance in seven hours.

The agent, Milo Lovering, was the nephew of a Minnesota politician and had received his appointment through that channel, even though he was not particularly qualified. His father had four sons who became lawyers, but Milo, who was the youngest, only became a schoolteacher, a disgrace the family could not bear. He was a small, twittery man, very nervous. When in this state he always fluffed his mustache with the tips of his fingers. Lovering did not understand military men, and he was uncertain around them. The moment he saw Major Gary approaching, he began to fluff his mustache. He took pride in keeping his office and records in order. His clerks considered him a martinet, but, when faced with Army officers, he was never sure that everything was all right.

Gary came in and introduced Ben Stagg. Lovering darted his hand out, gave Stagg's a fleeting touch, then pulled back as though he were in some danger.

"Mister Stagg is employed by the Army and will be accorded every courtesy extended to an officer," Gary said. "He'll remain at the agency a while, but he'll come and go as he sees fit."

"Yes, sir, I understand. But I'm sure you'll find everything in order. My, you've been promoted, Major."

"Mister Lovering, it's not Mister Stagg's purpose to find fault with your operation here. He is assisting me in the return of prisoners. We'll be here a few days. Would you see that quarters are provided?"

Lovering looked past them at Teddy. "Is he with you?"

"Yes."

This did not appeal to Milo Lovering. He felt such familiarity would undermine his authority with the Indians, and he knew how little he had to begin with. But he wasn't going to be written up in a report just for the pleasure of being contrary.

"The facilities are at your disposal," he said, snapping his fingers to summon a clerk. When the man came over, Lovering said to him: "Show these gentlemen to rooms."

They were billeted next to headquarters in a long building made up of eight small rooms that opened into a common hall. Gary had only a small traveling bag. Teddy and Ben Stagg had no baggage at all.

As a concession to the autumn heat, Gary changed from his dress uniform to summer pants, a shirt, and his forager cap. His pistol belt and accouterments he left in the room, and then he took Teddy across the small parade ground to the sutler's and bought him a clean shirt and pants. He understood an Indian's vanity about bright shirts, and he insisted that the boy take a bath before he could put the clothes on.

The sutler furnished the tub and water and a bar of strong soap, and Teddy reluctantly took the bath. Ben Stagg found them at the sutler's. Teddy was dressing, and he spoke a few words of Kiowa to the boy, praising him.

"Got us some horses," Stagg said to Gary, "and a couple day's rations. I guess we'll be goin' south."

"Yes," Gary said. "You're not armed, are you?" Stagg shook his head. "I want you to get the lay of the place, Ben. We're going to make two calls, then I'm going back and leave you on your own for a while. Just mosey around, talk, make friends, play on old times if you have to, learn all you can, and write it down so there's no mistakes made."

He bought some cigars from the sutler and put them in his shirt pocket. Then he went on. "The women are naturally reluctant to talk, to reveal anything about themselves that would permit us to . . . to help them. All information I have has been given to me by boys. Still, I believe it's enough. Our biggest job, Ben, is to beat down this sense of shame the women have."

"Uhn-uh," Stagg said. "The big job is gettin' people to stop talkin' when they move into a town."

★ ★ ★ ★ ★

The horses Stagg had selected were surplus cavalry mounts; nearly everything at the agency was surplus military property. It had been well used and was no longer needed, and was handed down to the agency—which made most commanders feel very generous and most agents resentful.

To new officers on their first assignment an Indian reservation was a surprise, and many never became adjusted to it. In their minds a reservation stood for an orderly community, logically planned and executed, while in reality the reservation was anything but that, generally seventy-five or eighty square miles that the public had rejected as being too poor, too lacking in water for commerce. The reservations were government acres set aside as the home of the transplanted Indian who was rarely allowed to remain in his habitual haunts.

Gary, riding south across this rocky, barren land, was thinking that many people probably supposed that moving the Indians would somehow cause them to lose their war-like ambitions. It was true that the shock of finding themselves is such a state of poverty kept their minds off revenge, raiding, and other things distasteful to white men.

The town of Fort Reno was not on reservation land. In fact, the agency itself was just outside the boundary. Entering the reservation without permission was risky for civilians, although there was a good deal of illegal trading with the Indians. Conditions for whiskey and bead trading were ideal. The Indians were reasonably confined, did not possess firearms, and they could not tell on the peddlers without telling on themselves and risking some punishment.

In Gary's mind, there was reason to suspect that agency personnel were playing their games with the Indians, shorting them on the beef rations, overcharging them at the agency store, and pocketing the profit. Yet he felt that he could not afford to look into the matter unless he increased the size of his command, thereby freeing an officer and detail to conduct the investigation.

All that day they rode southward through the Wachita Mountains, camping that night near a spring, with a good fire that would attract attention. Gary expected the Indian police to have a look sometime during the night, and they would come and go without a sound.

At dawn they were riding south again toward a camp on the west fork of Cache Creek where there was a sub-agency and a detachment of Indian police, as well as cattle pens and an agency store. Throughout the day they saw many small huts and patches of land where an Indian family, never accustomed to agriculture, was trying to scratch out a living.

In late afternoon they reached the place where the road topped a sharp rise and then dipped down. Several miles ahead they saw the agency store buildings crowded together beside the creek. Spread out along the creek and the swale of both banks, Indians huddled in their huts. Here dogs ran free, and smoke rose from the fires. As they approached the agency, they could see the stockpens crowded with cattle. The drovers crowded around the agency store, passing a jug back and forth, and pestering two old Indians who were trying to get inside to buy.

Gary swung off by the agency store, and Stagg tied the horses. The sub-agent came out, a harried man with unruly hair and thick glasses. He looked at Gary, waved, then trotted toward the cattle yard, a thick sheaf of papers in his hand.

This was, Gary knew, a very busy time, for tomorrow the monthly beef ration would be issued and everyone—Indians and agency people—was working overtime. But he had timed his arrival carefully and the rest of that day he and Stagg, followed closely by Teddy, walked around and observed the activity.

The civilian drovers, about thirty of them, were clannish, and they stayed close to the agency store or cattle pens. They liked to keep their eye on things since they had taken great pains to cheat the agency which in turn was going to cheat the Indians. The drovers had held the cattle away from water for over a day, and then, before driving them into the pens and scales, they had taken them to the river and let them drink half a barrel, adding a good deal to their weight that was good clean profit. The agents would weigh the steer before issue, after the scale had been "adjusted" to show a hundred pounds for every eighty on the platform. The agents would pocket this profit, and everyone would be happy but the Indians.

"Tomorrow the women will come," Gary said, speaking to Ben Stagg. "I figure it'll be better than riding our tails raw hunting them." He stripped the wrapper off a cigar and watched the drovers. "One of these days I'm going to declare war on them."

"Takes two crooks to make a deal," Stagg said. "The agents. . . ."

"Yes, I know. I'll do something about that, too."

"But not alone. Better bring a platoon."

"The first one I can spare," Gary said softly.

One of the drovers detached himself from the others and came over, batwing chaps swishing. He wore a canvas brush jacket, and, as he walked, it swung open long enough for Gary to see the pistol in the shoulder holster, clearly a violation of agency regulations. No firearms were allowed except in the hands of the police and the military.

"The name's Frank Skinner," he said as he came up. He was smiling, and his tone seemed friendly enough, but there was little friendliness in the man. His eyes had the cold stare of a naturally mean one. "I kind of got tired bein' stared at . . . ah. . . ." He made a show of studying Gary's rank. "Corporal? Sergeant?" he laughed. "I have a hard time gettin' it through my head about rank."

"I would suggest," Gary said, "that's not all you have a hard time getting through your head, Mister Skinner. Now that you've shown me your smart mouth, go back to your friends and tell them I'm not impressed."

Skinner's expression went slack, and he cuffed his hat to the back of his head. "Say, you're ready to fight, ain't you? I'd just like to point out there's no sense in makin' trouble for us. We're just earnin' a living."

"The manner in which you earn your living is going to be given my careful attention one of these days," Gary promised. "You might keep that in mind, and, when I'm through, you'll likely want to take up some other line of work."

Skinner grinned. "Major, you don't have enough soldiers to give me much trouble. Besides, if it wasn't me, then it would be someone else."

"Unfortunately that's true. Good day, Mister Skinner."

The man looked at Gary and rolled his tongue around in his cheek, then nodded, and went back. Ben Stagg, watching him, said: "A tough man runnin' a tough bunch, Jim. Maybe you should have hit him without warnin'. Warnin' only makes a man bolder."

"He can get too bold," Gary said. The heat and dust and stench from the cattle yard was like a woolly blanket over the camp, and Gary wiped his face with a handkerchief. "Skinner isn't hard to size up. He's a man who just can't turn down a dare, and I've dared him."

"It'll be a lively night tonight," Stagg commented. "All the bucks will be dancin,' and Skinner's crew will be lookin' for pelt, fifty cents a throw. They'll have plenty of takers, too."

This angered Gary, for it offended his stiff sense of morality. "Why do the women do it, Ben? God, have they no pride at all?"

"Pride's got nothin' to do with it. It's plain and simple . . . the fifty cents or the handful of trinkets." He sniffed the air. "The place has sure got a stink to it, ain't it? I've been in a hundred Injun camps, and none of 'em ever smelled like this. I tell you, Jim, it takes a white man to dirty a place."

There was, Gary had to admit, a certain truth in what Stagg said. He had known the Indians during the last ten years or so, but he had noticed that the normal actions of an Indian, immoral or savage by a white man's standard, seemed less so when compared with his actions after the white man had taught him his own immorality and genuine savagery.

That evening they went to a small mess building to eat. The sub-agent did not like to feed guests, Army or otherwise, and he started to make an issue of the point that Teddy was Indian and could not eat at the table. His patience drawn thin, Gary simply pushed the sub-agent in the corner, stared at him for a solid minute, then backed away and motioned for Teddy to sit down.

The sub-agent took his place. His expression was tight with anger. Finally he said: "Major, I'm going to write this in a report."

"Write what?" Gary asked pleasantly.

"That you intimidated me."

"Well," Gary said, "that wasn't very hard to do, was it? I just looked at you. If you want to do something important, restrict these cowboy drovers to the vicinity of the buildings tonight."

"Why, I couldn't do that," the man said. "They expect. . . ." He looked at Gary and let it drop. "I just couldn't do it."

"You're Mister Danniel, aren't you?" The man nodded. "I'm sure you've read the regulations thoroughly?" Again Danniel nodded. "Then I won't have to remind you that while Indian affairs come under one bureau, maintenance of order, discipline, and administrative integrity are the responsibility of the War Department, specifically the Army. Take a good look at my uniform, Mister Danniel. Could you possibly mistake it for that of a railroad conductor?"

The chill civility in Gary's voice was warning enough for Danniel. "No, sir," he said, and swallowed heavily.

"Perhaps you thought I was a cabman from some swank San Francisco hotel, a man who had mistakenly turned wrong off Market Street?"

"No, sir."

"Then what does it look like?"

Several of the cowboys had entered the mess. They stopped just inside the door and stood there. The cooks, holding platters of food, did not come forward and put them on the table, but stood listening, waiting for this to take the final turn.

Danniel looked around then said: "A major in the United States Army, sir."

"Then you might understand that I am your superior officer, Mister Danniel."

"Yes, sir."

"Then my question was not out of place, was it?"

"I . . . I've forgotten the question, Major."

"I'll rephrase it, then," Gary said. "I asked you why didn't you exert your authority and keep the drovers in the immediate vicinity of the buildings? To put it more specifically, Mister Danniel, I think it's high time the exploitation and monthly fornications cease. For a silver coin and some cheap beads these simple Indian women sell themselves to the cowboys. I want it stopped."

"Hold on there," Skinner spoke up. "You're askin' for trouble, Major."

"No, my friend, you've got trouble if you don't stay in camp tonight." He turned his head and looked at Danniel. "Will you issue the order to the police, or shall I?"

Danniel was a man badly pinched, and Skinner understood it. He said: "Bert, remember you got to live with us. This major will be gone tomorrow or the next day."

"Very true," Gary admitted. "And unless Mister Danniel complies, I'll wire Washington as soon as I return to post and have him relieved of duty. You understand what that means, Mister Danniel? Discharge from government service with a mark on your record. Hell, man, you couldn't carry the mail on a rainy day if that happened."

Danniel stared at Gary. "You wouldn't do that, would you, Major?"

"Don't try him," Ben Stagg advised.

Skinner looked at Danniel a long moment, then at Gary. "Major," he said, "did you ever see thirty drovers who were good and mad?"

"Yes. You'd better tell your men that Mister Danniel is calling for police reserves. There's a guardhouse on this reservation, and I'll bet it's lousy. There's one way for you to find out for sure."

Danniel started to get up, but Skinner put out his hand in a warning gesture. "Don't do it, Bert. He's putting one over on you. Hell, it's just him, the old man, and that Indian kid. We can handle this."

"Now, no trouble!" Danniel said. "Frank, for Christ's sake, what's the difference? There's next month. Can't you control your men?" He stepped away from the table and looked back at Gary. "I'll go along this time, but I can't guar-

263

antee anything. I have to bend the rules to fit the situation, just as you do."

He went out, slamming the screen door, and the cooks put the food on the table. Skinner sat down, his expression grim. He ate half his meal before speaking. Then he looked hard at Gary and said: "Be dark in another hour. Don't bet that you can keep me in camp tonight."

After they had eaten, Gary left the mess hall with Stagg and Teddy. They walked to the creek, waded across, and went up on a hillside three hundred yards beyond. There they stretched out, smoked, and waited for full darkness. When it had come, Gary snuffed out his smoke and said: "Stagg, keep an eye on the drovers around the camp. Teddy, you go along with him."

"And what'll you be up to?" Stagg asked.

"I thought I'd take Skinner up on his bet."

"That's what I thought," Stagg murmured. "Jim, I'd feel better if you had a pistol. Skinner ain't the kind who'd hesitate to take advantage of a man."

But argument would do Stagg no good at all, and he knew it. He got up, motioned for Teddy to follow, and went back across the creek to the agency buildings.

Gary left the knoll and started making his rounds of the Indian camps. He looked over four quickly, not wasting any time, then kept circulating until he found what he wanted, a woman by a fire, just sitting there, cooing softly to a small baby.

From his place twenty yards away Gary could see her clearly for the fire was still bright. She was young—about twenty, he supposed. She had light brown hair and a tan complexion. From the shape of her face, the angularity of it, he suspected that she was of German descent. There were a lot of Germans in Texas, a colony that had been hit hard and often by the Comanches.

Presently the woman got up and took the baby inside the hut. She was gone no more than five minutes, then she came back, and sat by the fire. She was alone, and Gary surmised that her man was at the council fire across the creek from the agency buildings. There'd be a lot of dancing there tonight, getting ready for the beef issue come dawn.

It seemed strange to Gary to be hunkered down in the shadows, watching the woman, knowing so much about her, and yet having never spoken to her. He knew she was in this part of the reservation because Tom Smalling had told him. Tom remembered when she had come to the reservation. Others had mentioned her, and she became part of a file, part of a record, another person Jim Gary wanted to save for a better life.

Finally he heard a step, then Frank Skinner came into the ring of firelight. He looked around him as though he suspected he might be followed. He grinned at the woman and said: "You wait for me? You like white man?" He squatted across the fire with his grin and desire in his eyes. "Don't you ever talk American? I ain't ever heard you say one word." He reached into his pocket and brought out two fifty-cent pieces and rubbed them together. "A dollar," he said. "Buy you a lot of pretty things." He tossed the money on the ground. "You want to . . . here? I'd just as soon. Your lodges are all lousy."

The woman didn't speak. She stood up and started to unlace her dress. Jim Gary straightened and said: "Skinner, some men are so stupid, they just can't learn at all."

With a start, Skinner flung back and snapped his pistol free of the holster. He stood waving it around, trying to locate the place where Gary stood. Without a sound, Gary shifted position until he quartered Skinner. "I'm over here," he said, tipping his head back and making his voice come from everywhere.

Skinner turned, his hand nervously fondling the gun. Gary bent and felt around for a rock, found one, hefted it, took aim, and threw, putting his strength behind it. The blow, aimed for Skinner's head, hit him on the cheekbone. The bone cracked, and he was knocked down, dropping his gun as he fell. The skin was split to the bone, exposing the fracture, and he rolled on the ground, clutching his face and saying—"Jesus . . . Jesus . . . Jesus."—over and over.

Gary calmly stepped into the firelight, picked up Skinner's pistol, and put it in the waistband of his own trousers. He found the young woman watching him intently, half afraid, not sure just what he intended to do.

Moving over to Skinner, he kicked the man's hands away from his face, and rolled him so that the firelight revealed the wound. Gary was slightly horrified at the damage the rock had done, but he let none of his sympathy show.

"Get up," he said.

Skinner shook his head, but he staggered to his feet, moaning with the pain.

"Get back to the agency," Gary said. "Someone will take care of you. Tomorrow the police can take you to the agency guardhouse." He gave the man a shove, and Skinner wailed and staggered back the way he had come.

Gary threw some more wood on the fire, making it burn brightly. He could see the young woman clearly, and her eyes never left his face.

"Do you know your name?" he asked. She opened her mouth to speak, and he said: "Don't give me your Comanche name. Give me your Christian name."

She closed her mouth, and he waited a moment. "Don't you know it?"

"I know it," she said, and the sound of her voice surprised him, for it was clear and soft, although a bit unsteady, as if she had not used English for a long time.

"Do you want to tell it to me, or shall I tell you?"

She shook her head. "I'm not going back. That's what you want me to do, isn't it?" She waited for his answer, but it did not come. Then her glance dropped to the fifty-cent pieces. "Can I keep those?" she asked.

Chapter Twenty-Seven

Bert Danniel was greatly alarmed when Skinner staggered to the agency office where he banged on the door and then collapsed. Skinner's friends, suddenly angry, threatened Danniel for allowing this to happen. Danniel could do nothing but take Skinner inside and bathe his face and make him comfortable until morning, when policemen would haul him to the agency headquarters where a doctor was in attendance.

Ben Stagg watched for Gary and met him as he approached the agency. "I'd lay low for a while," he suggested. "These cowboys have their dander up."

"What do you expect me to do, Ben? Hide?"

He walked on toward the buildings, Stagg beside him, and Teddy just behind. When he was fifty yards from the door, the cowboys saw him and left their camp by the cattle pens and moved over fast. Gary stopped on the agency steps and faced them.

"Mister Skinner lost his bet," he said calmly, "so why don't you go back to your camp and forget about it?"

They saw Skinner's .44 thrust into Gary's belt, and one young man said: "We don't like to be hoorawed, mister. We don't like it at all." They muttered their agreement, but Jim Gary stood there, looking at them, moving his eyes from man to man.

"It seems to me," he told them, "that some of you are just

eager to join Mister Skinner in the guardhouse. Well, step forward. There's room."

"You busted up his face," one man said, "and that's enough."

"I'll decide that," Gary said, turned, and went inside.

Stagg closed the door, and Danniel came out of one of the rooms carrying a pan of pink water and a soiled towel. He looked at Gary and said: "Everything was fine until you stuck your bill in."

"Do you really think so?" Gary stared at the man until he began to show nervousness. "Mister Danniel, this prostitution among the Indian women is going to stop. Have I made that clear enough?"

Danniel put the pan and towel down. "For God's sake, how can I stop it? If they want to sell their goods, what can I do?" He wiped a shaking hand across his mouth. "Do I have to be responsible for everything?"

"Yes, you do. If you can't handle it, then we'll have to make some changes. Mister Danniel, understand me. Prostitution is revolting and immoral. I do not approve of it in white communities, and I do not permit it in towns near military posts where I command."

"You're sure a stiff neck, aren't you?" Danniel stated. He laughed, and rolled a cigarette, striking a match alight on the sole of his shoe. "Skinner went to the white woman, didn't he?"

"Which makes it even more tragic."

"Hell, she wants to stay here. No one's keeping her. She's gone Indian, all the way."

"You can't be stupid enough to believe that," Gary said. "She wants to leave in the worst way, but she knows she can't face the people outside this reservation. You idiot, can you really believe she chooses this?" He blew out his breath between stretched lips. "In the morning Skinner will be escorted to agency headquarters and placed in the stockade. I'll sign the charges, if you won't."

Danniel nodded. "And if I don't sign them, I'm as good as out of a job."

"Such perception astounds me," Gary said, and went to his room.

The issue of beef was an affair that began early and was finished by noon or shortly after. It need not have taken that much time, but the Indians insisted on making a game of it. All the women stood to one side while the men assembled at the pens, and each one had his monthly allotment driven out, weighed—and there was always an argument about it—before it was turned free in the yard. Then with brave whoops the Indian would pursue the steer on horseback—if he was lucky enough to own a horse—kill it with lance or spear, and then ride off to chat and brag while his wife came forth and butchered the fallen animal.

Many of the Indians, too poor to own a horse, went through this mock hunt by chasing the steer on foot. A few got away much to the disgrace of the pursuing Indian, but most of them were slaughtered there in the yard, butchered by the women, and carried off to their lodges.

In all, it was a dirty business, made additionally so by the Indians' desire to hunt again, and somehow they managed to make the chasing of a steer akin to the pursuit of buffalo. It amazed Jim Gary, this desire to live in their dreams and the past. Many of the younger men had been born too late to hunt buffalo, and some had never seen one.

The butchering drew his attention, especially because it was done by the women. He and Stagg moved around, watching. Gary saw the German girl and three others that he knew positively were white. Once he had identified them, he asked Teddy to find out to whom they belonged. A woman was always an Indian's property, for he had paid for her in some way and owned her outright like a horse or a rifle.

Stagg followed his own trails that day, and Gary did not see him until shortly before evening mess. Milo Lovering, agent in charge, wired Gary to confirm Skinner's arrest. Lovering was sure that the Indian police had made a serious mistake. Gary wired back that no mistake had been made, and that, when he returned to agency headquarters, Frank Skinner had better be in the guardhouse under lock and key.

After evening mess, Gary and Teddy crossed the creek and perched on the knoll under the trees where they could see everything. Ben Stagg forded the creek and came up to them, flopping down on the grass.

"Got a line or two," he said, biting off a chew of tobacco. "One's the woman of Tall Elk." He waved his arm in a southerly direction. "Got a lodge eight or nine miles from here. Maybe you saw her . . . a tall woman, dark hair. She'd pass for an Indian all right, but she's white. A man can tell even from a distance." He looked at the boy. "Seen you lookin' kind of hard, Teddy. Still lookin' for your sister?"

The boy nodded. "She dead. I know. But still I look."

"How old was she, Teddy?" Gary asked.

He shrugged. "Three. Maybe two. Small. She fall from horse. I see this. Try to get down, go back. Comanche beat me. When I wake up, many miles away. Sister dead now."

"Teddy, do you think you can find that place again?" Gary asked.

"Long time ago. She dead now."

Gary took him by the arm. "Teddy, we never give up. We always keep looking, keep asking questions. Sometimes we're lucky. We were with Tom Smalling. It took us a long time to find out who he was. Will you help us, Teddy?"

The boy nodded. "I try."

"That's good, Teddy." He paused to light a cigar. "When Captain Weldon took you from your camp, he did a wrong thing. The reason I brought you along was to let you go back if you want to."

The boy studied him. "You no want me?"

"Yes, I want you to stay with me," Gary said, "but we have to do what is right, Teddy. You were brought to Verde without proper authority. If you want to come back to Verde, you must do so freely. Understand?"

"Yes. I go back now. Study now. Be good man now." He smiled. "Bad Weldon dead now. Everything all right now."

"Captain Weldon wasn't the only bad man or bad thing you'll run up against, Teddy. From now on, you've got to face trouble, not run away from it. Do you still want to go back?"

"I go back," Teddy said. "Go where you go, Gary."

When Gary returned to the headquarters of the agency, Milo Lovering made a mistake. He tried to argue Gary out of his decision, pleading that Skinner had a contract with the agency and couldn't keep the terms of it in the stockade. Gary listened to Lovering's argument, and, when the agent was finished, he laid out the terms of the agreement.

"First, Mister Lovering, it would not be very difficult for me to get a set of weights from Austin, bring them here, and check your scales. Naturally we would find them in error in the agent's favor, and, of course, I would have to conclude that you've been cheating the Indians and include that indictment in my report, which would lead to a search for new employment for yourself and a black mark on your record as an administrator. On the other hand, if you maintain strict control over the drovers, restrict their sexual activities on the reservation, and maintain a stern code of conduct enforced by the Indian police, I would find it inconvenient to check your scales and inventory your stores and generally go through your books with a magnifying glass to expose your past conduct. Don't you agree, Mister Lovering? Isn't my way sane, logical, practical? Isn't it more convenient to curtail the drovers' pleasures than to lose your own tidy profits of the past . . . and your job?"

"You're treating me as though I was a crook."

"Then you welcome an investigation? I have a young second lieutenant in my command who is looking for any means to distinguish himself, bring himself favorably to my attention. He would welcome a chance to audit. . . ."

"All right, all right," Lovering said. "The drovers will behave from now on."

"I'll check on that from time to time," Gary promised. "Any irregularity and. . . ."

"There won't be any," Lovering said. "When are you leaving?"

"Tonight."

"Thank God for small favors," Lovering said frankly. "Just what is it that makes you Army officers such a pain in the ass?" He shook his head. "You make a hell of a lot of fuss about a few rag-tag Indians, and a few years back you were fighting them. I just don't understand how a man can turn about like that."

"In the Academy," Jim Gary said, "it is called . . . honor, duty, and tradition. It is the thing that makes a man advance when advancing is madness, and it keeps him from retreating when retreat is the only salvation. Do you understand anything I'm saying, Lovering?"

"Yes, Major, but I'm just one man. I can't buck the

system." He waved his arms in a futile gesture. "Hell, I didn't start out this way! I don't like Skinner, and I wouldn't do business with him if I didn't have to. Only the honest ranchers won't sell to the reservation because Skinner and his bunch have thrown the scare into them. No, Major, I'm just plain afraid to stand alone."

"You wouldn't be alone, Lovering. Every soldier in my command would back you. I could bring in a federal marshal, if it came to that."

"I'd like to see the Indians get a better deal," Lovering admitted. "Not that I care for them, but they've had it bad for so long, it's time there was a change." He looked steadily at Gary. "If I could be sure you'd back me. . . ."

"Suppose I wrote a directive for you to comply with. Would that satisfy you?"

"You'd give me a company in case Skinner made trouble?"

"A platoon," Gary said, "but a good one."

"All right," Lovering said. "I'd rather get fired for cleaning house than for stealing." He offered his hand, and Gary took it.

"Expect the arrival of an officer, a sergeant, four corporals, and a platoon within fifteen days," Gary said. "I would advise you to go quietly about preparing buildings. They'll set up their own quarters and mess. Try to keep Skinner's men under control until the command arrives and, in the meantime, quietly contact the ranchers hereabouts for the purchase of cattle. Buy from men who won't sell you half a barrel of water in every belly." He turned to the door. "I'm leaving Ben Stagg here on business. He's to have a free hand and the use of the telegraph. Teddy is going back with me."

"I thought you brought him back here because you didn't want him."

Gary smiled. "Mister Lovering, we want them all."

Jim Gary and Teddy arrived at Camp Verde late. Only the sentry and the sergeant of the guard knew they were back on the post until after mess, when Lieutenant Flanders saw Gary leave his quarters and stride briskly to headquarters.

Ten minutes later Mr. Beeman was summoned. He made a smart entrance, was given at ease, and a chair to sit in. "Mister Beeman, how do you like company duty?" Gary asked.

"Excellent, sir. I'm getting on well, if I do say so myself."

"Are you and Huckmyer hitting it off all right?"

"Well, sir, we had words, but it's straightened out now, sir."

Gary kept from smiling. "I trust you were not too hard on the sergeant?"

Beeman's eyes widened behind his glasses. "Sir, it was the other way around. The sergeant was straightening me out on a point or two, sir. I think it's called breaking in a new lieutenant, sir."

"I'm familiar with the process," Gary said, recalling a sergeant in his own career who taught him how to officer a command. "Huckmyer is a sound man. You can rely on him in every instance. He's a soldier of many years' service, and, if you frankly ask his advice, he'll give it. You may take it, confide in him, discuss problems with him, and never have any fear that the officer-enlisted man relationship will be changed, or his respect weakened. It took me a long time to learn this, Mister Beeman, but enlisted men do not expect officers to be perfect. They only ask that they are not fools."

"I'll remember that advice, sir."

"Mister Beeman, have you been north to the reservation?"

"No, sir."

"Ah, it's just as well. It will give you a fresh approach." He offered Beeman a cigar, lit his own, and went on. "With Sergeant Huckmyer's assistance and guidance, I want you to select a platoon. Avoid the real hard drinkers, and men with a reputation for pelt hunting."

"Pelt hunting, sir?"

Gary smiled. "Chasers, Mister Beeman. Men who habitually consort with loose women. I'm going to put you on detached service for two months. The reservation will be your station. Do not take the train. Make an overland march of it. It'll do the civilians good to see an Army on the move again. When you arrive at the reservation, report to Mister Milo Lovering, agent in charge. Now this is very important, Mister Beeman. Do not regard him as a superior officer. Perhaps an equal, but you are in command of your platoon and responsible for its function. Clear?"

"Yes, sir."

"The reservation is in a pretty mess, with fraud evident at every point of the compass. This will be eliminated, Mister Beeman. Do not allow the agency to be cheated and do not allow agency people to cheat the Indians. I would suggest that you examine every pound of stores purchased by the agency. Make sure that when a pound is paid for, a pound is received. The agency has a contract for cattle with a drover named Frank Skinner. You'll recognize him because one side of his face is freshly scarred. This man has intimidated the other ranchers . . . the honest ones . . . so that they will not sell beef to the agency. This will be corrected. You and your men will be everywhere, Mister Beeman, poking into this and that, stopping trouble before it starts, and putting it down . . . if you have to . . . after it begins. You will do everything and anything necessary to clean up the situation. Is that clear?"

"Yes, sir, it is. I've never had so much responsibility before. Perhaps Mister Flanders . . . ?"

"Don't sell yourself short, Mister Beeman. Discover now what you are. I have confidence in you. Isn't that enough?"

"That's very flattering, sir. When do I start?"

"I suggest that you can put the platoon together and be off the post in twenty-four hours. If there are no further questions. . . ."

"None, sir. I'll report regularly by telegraph." He stood up, saluted, and executed a precise about-face.

Gary stopped him at the door. "Mister Beeman, it occurs to me that you're a very precise soldier. Carry this precision out on your assignment, for it's been my observation that civilians are always a little baffled by the military system. Soon after watching the military perform by the numbers and getting the job done, they begin to think they're up against some kind of a machine. I have seen a squad, immaculate, disciplined, unlimber carbines on command and sit their horses like statues, waiting for the command to fire, and I have seen that break the mob spirit of three hundred men and turn them away without firing a shot. Never be ashamed of spit and polish, Mister Beeman."

"Thank you, sir."

After Beeman has gone out, Mr. Flanders came in, a sheaf of papers in his hand. "A few messages for you, sir. A letter from the general. He left it before he caught his train. Another wire from Senator Ivers."

"Thank you, Mister Flanders." Gary opened the general's letter and read:

Dear Jim:

Thank you for your hospitality. I'm sorry I couldn't remain longer and enjoy your wife's cooking. I've been reflecting on your request for another

277

company and three officers. With Senator Ivers arriving, there is no doubt in my mind that your appropriation will be enlarged, so I am doing a little spade work, culling out the ones I know you won't want and suggesting a few that might like the assignment. I don't know whether or not you remember Captain Dan Conrad. He was with Mac-Kenzie during the worst of the fighting. A Comanche lance pierced his arm, and he lost it. Somehow he's hung on, and now he's at Ft. Smith, acting as provost marshal. Conrad is a good man, and, if you can accept his disability, he'll perform in a most satisfactory manner. He will ask for no special considerations, and I recommend him highly. Another man that comes to mind is Captain Ellis Spawn. He was with Crook in the 'Seventies when the general put down the Apache troubles in Arizona by treating them fairly. Spawn became a crusader for the Indian cause. It made him very unpopular with certain political powers, and he found himself frozen in rank. He's been serving at the Presidio in San Francisco for seven years. Spawn is a scholarly man, a good soldier, and it would please me if you would accept him. I could get him his long overdue majority. Let me know your reaction.

Tremain

Gary penned a reply, sealed the envelope, and put it in the outgoing mail basket. Then he read Ivers's message. It was rather formal, an expression of pleasure at being invited. Ivers planned to stay a month. He wanted to be able to make a complete report on his return to Washington. Ivers reaffirmed his arrival date and closed the note.

There was company business that needed attention: two troopers up for discipline, and a corporal who was just about to lose his stripes if he didn't straighten up. Mr. Flanders brought the men in one at a time. Gary heard both sides in each case then chewed them up and down, and returned them to duty with his final warning.

Llano Vale came onto the post. The sergeant of the guard reported this to Mr. Flanders, who relayed it to Gary a bare moment before Vale came into the office. He threw his hat down on a vacant chair, grinned around his cigar, and sat down.

"As you can see, I'm cold sober." He looked at Mr. Flanders. "What's the matter, sonny, ain't you seen a *man* before?"

Flanders was flustered. "Will that be all, Major?"

Gary nodded, and Flanders went back to his office. Vale held his grin. "Major, huh? Been kicked upstairs?"

"You took your time in getting here," Gary said.

"Well, I told you I had a few calls to make. Got to keep those poor widows happy, boy."

"You're going to make a few of them sad, Llano, because I'm putting you to work today." He got up and went to a file drawer and withdrew a thick sheaf of folders. "During the years of the Comanche troubles, they took a lot of children as prisoners. In all of my investigations I have not come across one instance where they took a full-grown male."

"They killed those. Women and children had a value," Llano Vale said. "What's the point?"

"Conversely, there was a good deal of raiding against the Comanches by organized white settlers and Texas Rangers. I have some records here that lead me to believe that Indian children were picked up on these raids. Some were abandoned by the Indians, and Rangers or settlers took them

279

along to keep them from dying. Now it strikes me that, if we're set on recovering white prisoners, then we ought to make an effort at recovering lost Indian children."

He handed Vale several folders. "You will find Captain McCabe, F Company, Texas Frontier Battalion, at Fort Concho. I suggest you catch a northbound at the tanks and take it to San Angelo. Captain McCabe will be advised by wire that you're coming and will offer all possible assistance. I want these stories . . . these leads . . . run down, Llano. Don't just look into the matter. Run them to the ground. Remember, I don't believe there is such a thing as a blind alley when you're looking for another human being. Ask questions and write down the answers. Report by telegraph."

"That's some order."

"You enjoy the reputation of knowing every old buffalo wallow in Texas. Now let's see how much you really know. Your memory goes back to the fall of the Alamo. This was your stomping ground. If any man can produce results, it will be you. After all, you can talk to a man today and remember his grandfather."

"You put a man on the spot, don't you?"

"Llano, I'm trying to do my job, because I've been ordered to and because I think it ought to be done right. In a few days I'm going to have the civilian camp outside the post filled with people who've come here to collect lost kin. I've got to be right when I tell them that a certain boy is theirs. I've got to be so right I can build a bridge across their lives to cover the years since the boy went one way and they went another. I've got to see that the parents really want the boy, and that the boy really wants the parents. So if I don't show too much sympathy for your problem, it is because I consider the problems of these people vastly more important."

"It ain't often I can find a man I like well enough to work

for him," Vale said. "But damn it, I like you. Couldn't figure it out for a time, but I've got it now. You've got integrity, Gary. Good, old, straight-laced integrity." He glanced at the stub of his cigar. It had gone out, so he clamped it between his teeth. "Where's that old liar, Stagg?" he asked.

"At the Indian reservation."

"Good. I'd hate to have to meet him."

"Jealous of him, huh?"

"*Me?*" He tipped his head back and laughed, an old lion roaring. "Why Stagg couldn't carry my pelts the best day of his life. I'd wrestle a bear, swim the Red in flood time, take on six Kiowa bucks, and still have the wind to whup him into a whine. There never was a camp so big it'd hold both of us. Notice how he stays in one part of the country. He's learned to keep away from me."

"It takes two to stay apart," Gary said, smiling. "Now wouldn't it be hell if you two ended up friends?"

"Never happen."

"How can you tell? There's only two old he-bears left. Be a shame if they had to claw one another to death, wouldn't it? Llano, there comes a time when an old renegade like you becomes the property of Texas, a living legend, a symbol."

"Blue and gray marchin' together in a parade?" Llano Vale shook his head, and his mane of hair stirred against his shoulders, and the fringe of his buckskins waved like tall grass in a wind. "By golly now, you do all the plottin' you want about your lost children, but you better not try and make peace between us two. I don't puff smoke with that man."

"Never?"

"Never," Vale said.

Chapter Twenty-Eight

The arrival of the civilians was, in Major Gary's mind, a thing of anticipation and of dread. He was glad to see them because it meant linking up his work of the past years. Yet he worried because he wondered if they were fully prepared to meet and accept the kin they had lost years before.

A military detail brought them to the post and saw that they were given quarters outside the confines of the post. On his porch at headquarters Jim Gary thought that these four wagons carried a very small measure of his efforts. There were only four families, and that averaged out less than one a year. And the work wasn't done yet.

He gave them several hours to get settled, several hours to get their suitcases and boxes inside and unpacked, and washed up. Then he left the post in the company of Lieutenant Flanders and made his calls.

He knocked at the first cabin, and a husky blond man answered the door. "I'm Major Gary. May I present Mister Flanders." Gary extended his hand. "You're Mister Erickson?"

"Ya, come in," the man said, speaking with a thick accent. In a fumbling manner he introduced his wife, a dumpling of a woman who kept bobbing her head, feeling ill at ease because this was a strange house. Erickson beckoned them to chairs. "I have no coffee on yet . . . ," he began.

"That's quite all right," Gary said. "We can only stay a moment. You had a pleasant journey?"

"Good, good," Erickson said. "When can we see the boy?"

"I thought you might like to invite him to your meal this evening," Gary said. "Mister Flanders will see that you can draw from the commissary stores anything you need."

The woman looked at her husband, then at Gary. "Must wait?"

"I think it would be a mistake to hurry now," Gary told her. "After all, we've really waited years, haven't we? A little longer won't hurt. Besides, the boy is your brother's son. Get to know each other. Make sure you make no mistake about wanting him."

"You are right," Erickson said. He offered his hand as Gary turned to the door. "He must like us, ya?"

"Yes," Gary said solemnly. "If he goes back with you, he goes because he wants to and for no other reason."

He and Flanders went to the next place. These people were the Amorys from Des Moines. They were tall and thin, dry-mannered, blunt, and they reminded Gary of cornstalks. Amory was not a sociable man, and he was not given to laughter. Lieutenant Flanders made a small joke, and Amory stared at him as though wondering what in the world he was talking about. This couple, too, were not the boy's own parents, but were now his closest relatives. They had four children of their own, all boys, all working the farm. Amory was concerned about the condition of young James Amory's health. It took a strong young man to farm, and, nephew or not, he had to earn his bread. Gary was not impressed with Amory, but he told himself not to sit in judgment of these people. They went on to the next place.

Mrs. Smalling was a surprise, a small, fluttery woman who had a teapot ready and cups set out. She insisted that they sit down and have a cup. Her husband had died in the spring, and she admitted having kept this from Gary because she was afraid he might not think her capable of managing a nearly grown boy with a Comanche background.

"The store was much too much for me after Albert passed to his reward," she said, smiling from behind her gold-rimmed glasses. "Mister Harbinson wanted to buy it, and his price was reasonable, so I sold it and opened up a small ladies' shop. I realize that it might not be the kind of work a young man would prefer, but I have to consider the possibility that you might think young Tom too much for me. I needed an income, Major. It would have been imprudent to have lived off my savings."

"Missus Smalling, you impress me," Gary said, genuinely pleased. "Tom will be over for supper. He has a fondness for peach pie. You may draw what supplies you need from the commissary and, if you need help, call on Mister Flanders or myself."

"You're a very good man, Major Gary. I knew by your letters."

"Good?" He smiled. " 'He that does good for good's sake seeks neither praise nor reward, though sure of both at last.' "

"William Penn," she said.

He took her hand, pressed the back of it against his lips, and went on to the last house.

The man who answered the door had the strong aroma of Irish whiskey about him. He needed a shave, his suspenders were dropped, and his underwear hadn't been changed for several weeks. Before Gary could introduce himself, the man said: "Where the hell's my kid?" He stepped outside and closed the door. "I figure to get the hell out of this country the day after tomorrow at the latest."

"Not if you expect to take your son back with you," Gary

said civilly. "We have our regulations, and we'll all abide by them. Figure on a month at least, Mister Thomas."

"Listen, I know the Army. Seven years in the Army . . . that's how much I put in. Lost my kid on the frontier. So don't tell me about the Army."

"I wouldn't try," Gary said. "At the same time, I'm sure you'll not try to tell me how to run my affairs. Your son will be over for supper. Draw what you want from the commissary." He started to turn away, then swung back. "When a man gets drunk on this post," he said, "he usually ends up in the stockade. No matter who he is."

"I can hold my booze," Thomas said. "I run a saloon . . . in case you're interested."

"I'm not interested," Gary told him, "but to set you straight, I know a good deal about you." He nodded curtly. "Good day, sir."

On the way back to headquarters Flanders kept a respectful silence. Presently Gary said: "Well, a man has to expect all kinds. We can't pick and choose everything, can we?"

"We can always hope the boy won't go back with him, sir."

"Then we'd have a nice report to write," Gary said. "It's going to be difficult for us to win, Mister Flanders. Very difficult, indeed."

"Now don't be nervous, Mama," Sven Erickson said, and patted his wife's hand. The cabin was full of baking and cooking odors, and Erickson kept pulling out his watch and looking at it. There was a knock on the door, and it surprised him so that he dropped the timepiece. It would have fallen to the floor had not the chain caught it.

He went to the door, opened it, and looked at Arny Erickson. Tears suddenly filled the man's eyes, and he clapped his arms around the boy and crushed him to him. Then he drew him inside and laughed and wiped his eyes. "Helga, see, so tall and straight like Lars."

"Ya, ya, the same hair and eyes." She blubbered and pressed her pudgy fingers to her mouth, but she brought him to the table and began heaping food on the plates. "Is so good to see you, Dag," she said. "So good."

He looked at her steadily, curiously. "You know my name? You remember it?"

"Ya, how could we forget your name?" Sven Erickson asked. "Why they call you Arny, Dag? Is not your name."

"I . . . I couldn't remember my name," the boy said. "It was such a long time. The soldiers called me Ornery, because I . . . well, I didn't behave myself too well. And it got shortened to Arny."

Mrs. Erickson was crying quietly, and her husband clucked in sympathy. "Please," he said, "the food will get cold. Please eat."

Dag Erickson stared at his plate and, in a voice slightly choked with emotion, said: "It was very good of you to come here for me. Really very good." Then he looked at them, and his tears shimmered in the lamplight. "It's been a long time since I've had anyone who really wanted me, Uncle Sven." He brushed his tears away and smiled. "I remember you now, you and Aunt Helga. I was about four years old, and you let me play on your kitchen floor. There was a dog with a litter of puppies. They were brown and soft. I remember it now."

Lieutenant Carl Beeman arrived at the reservation in the early evening, his detail of dusty, worn troopers weary in the saddles. Milo Lovering was very surprised to see them. He looked at them and said to Beeman: "My God, haven't you heard of the railroad?"

"There's nothing like riding to take off fifteen pounds of fat," Beeman said, stripping off his gloves. He began to flail dust from his clothing, and it set Lovering to coughing. "Sergeant Huckmyer, dismiss the men and turn them to billets. I'm sure Mister Lovering can provide mess facilities. Stable the horses. One guard will be sufficient."

"Oh, you don't need a guard around here," Lovering put in. "With the Indian police and all. . . . ."

"Permit me to command my own detail," Beeman said, hoping he sounded frosty enough. He took Lovering by the arm, and they went inside together. Beeman tipped up the hanging water gourd and drank deeply.

"Ah, that's delicious, Mister Lovering. Somehow a canteen soon turns water brackish, but a gourd always preserves a certain sweetness. I suppose it's because it's organic."

"Is this a botany lesson, Lieutenant?"

Beeman looked long at Lovering, and sized him up carefully, realizing that what he would do now would effect his relationship with this man hereafter. There was about Lovering an air of superiority and a challenge in his eyes that made Beeman suspect there were really only two kinds of men in Lovering's mind: the kind he could run all over and the kind who rode roughshod over him.

There was really nothing in Beeman's background to qualify him for dominating anyone, but he felt a strong bond with Jim Gary, who had put trust in him and given him responsibility, and Beeman knew that he would not let Gary down. *I couldn't,* he thought. *I'd kill myself before I'd report back to him that I had failed.*

Lovering was smiling as he lighted a cigar, and suddenly Beeman lashed out with his gloves, slapping Lovering's hand and sending the cigar spinning. The smile vanished, and Lovering bent to pick up the cigar, but Beeman ground it to shreds with his boot sole.

"When I'm talking to you," Beeman said, "do not occupy yourself with lighting a cigar or paring your nails or staring at the ceiling or doing anything else that will take your full and undivided attention from me. Is that clearly understood, Mister Lovering?" His stare through his glasses was intense.

Lovering nodded. Beeman put his hands behind his back and paced the small office, trying to recall the exact wording of the countless chewings superior officers had handed down to him.

"I've come here, Mister Lovering, not to conduct classes in basket weaving or to lead the Indians in prayers, but to clean up the stinking mess that's been made of the reservation management." He wheeled about and fixed Lovering with his eyes and was pleased to find that by pulling the brows down he managed a pretty cold stare. "I was informed by Major Gary that you were in a co-operative frame of mind. It seems that he was mistaken, and I'll have to draw his attention to this in my first dispatch."

"There was no mistake," Lovering said quickly. "I apologize if I seemed a little heavy-handed. You get that way after dealing with the Indians. Get so it's hard to speak civilly to anyone."

"I trust that in my case you'll make an effort?"

"Yes, sir. I certainly didn't. . . ." He let his words trail off and studied his knuckles. "But you're going to have to raise hell with someone besides me, Lieutenant."

"That's why I arrived well in advance of the beef issue," Beeman said. "We'll begin by posting notices that the agency will buy beef from independent ranchers. I will post these notices myself and see that the individual ranchers are called on. This fellow . . . ah . . . ?"

"Skinner."

"Yes, Skinner, the one who got in trouble with Major Gary will either come up to the mark with his beef or the agency will not buy from him, contract or no contract."

"Well, if it's going to be broken, you'll have to do it. Skinner and his men make sure no one else will sell to us. Others have tried it and have been beaten for it. And you won't scare him with that piddlin' detail you brought with you. He'll outnumber you nearly three to one."

"The Army," Beeman said, "is accustomed to being outnumbered."

"Well, it's your problem, but you won't be in town five minutes before someone is riding to Skinner's place with the word."

"Then I won't have to worry about finding him, will I?" Beeman said. "Now, if you'll show me to my quarters?"

Beeman had a good meal with his men, and his quarters were clean. He undressed, had a bath, and stretched out to catnap. He woke just before dawn thoroughly chilled. He got up, cursing himself for sleeping so soundly that he hadn't even pulled up the covers.

His intention was to find Huckmyer, but the sergeant knocked before Beeman could leave. "Orders, sir?"

"Have fresh mounts caught up. We're riding into town to hunt a little trouble," Beeman told him, and briefly explained the threat Frank Skinner held over the smaller, independent cattlemen. "I believe the first order of business is to bring Skinner out and get this settled."

"A fight, sir?"

"You were once a cowboy, Huckmyer. Do you think it can be settled without a fight?"

"Not by a damned good sight, sir."

"Very well," Beeman said, tugging on his boots. "Let us

go about this the right way. We'll be outnumbered. I think shooting would be a disaster. I'm open to suggestions, Sergeant."

Huckmyer pawed at his dense mustache. "Well, sir, I'd suggest we get ourselves some kind of an edge."

"Like what?"

He stared at the ceiling and twisted his mouth. "It brings to mind the time the Third Ohio was challenged by that New York outfit. Those Irishmen always did think they could lick anybody. We melted up some lead and made pieces about three-quarters of an inch around and three inches long and put them inside our gloves." He grinned. "I tell you, sir, you hit a man once, and it just plain rocked him to sleep." He let his grin fade. "I could have the farrier's forge fired up and the whole thing done by the time you was through with breakfast, sir."

"If you feel it's the thing to do," Beeman said. "Of course, I wouldn't want to know about it."

"Oh, hell, I understand that, sir." He turned to leave, but stopped. "If I have any left over, would you like to. . . ."

"Well, I don't see any harm in trying a thing once, Sergeant."

"That's what I thought, sir." He coughed into his hand and went out.

Beeman was finished with his shave and breakfast, and the horses had been picked and saddled. The detail was ready to mount when Huckmyer came to his quarters. He laid the two lead billies on the dresser and saluted. "Detail ready, sir."

"Thank you, Sergeant." Beeman picked them up and held them in his palm while he slipped on his gauntlets. Then he made a fist and the heavy leather was drum-tight.

"They keep the bones of the hand from givin', sir. Matter

of fact, you could hit a bull in the head without hurtin' your hand."

"Well, Sergeant, the world is full of little odds and ends of information, if a man only keeps an open mind. Isn't that a fact?"

"Sure is," Huckmyer said, and went out.

Beeman made a fist again and struck a fighting posture, then put out a hand and tested one of the boards of the wall. It gave slightly, and he cocked his fist once more and hit it, opening up a wide split. He looked to the fist that had done the work, and he smiled. "Oh," he said softly, "that's going to smart."

He went outside and mounted his troop and rode on into Fort Reno.

The printer made up the notices, and Beeman took them, ink still a bit damp. Sergeant Huckmyer and the four troopers were each given several, and they went about town, putting them up. Beeman and the others waited in front of the hotel.

Beeman figured he did not have long to wait, and, within an hour, Frank Skinner and twenty men rode into town. They swung off and tied up across the street, then stood there and looked over to the hotel. Several hundred people lined the walks, crowding each other to make sure they got a good view of everything. Beeman's soldiers came back from their poster hanging. They formed in a rank along the walk, keeping a decent interval but making a clearly drawn line.

Skinner's face was scabbed and healing, and it gave his face a twisted cast. Looking at Beeman, he said: "I'll tell you once, soldier . . . take those posters down!"

"They stay," Beeman said. "If you want a fight, Mister Skinner, then we'll make it."

Skinner looked around, measured again the strength of his

men, and laughed. "Two to one, anyway," he said. "Ain't that a little more'n you can chew, soldier?"

Without taking his eyes off Skinner, Beeman said: "Sergeant Huckmyer, advance the detail to the center of the street." He stepped off the porch and walk and took his place while the detail formed in a row alongside him. "Sergeant, you will see that every man has his holster flap secured." He took off his glasses and pocketed them.

There was a pause, then Huckmyer's voice came. "Secured, sir."

"Thank you, Sergeant. When this soirée commences, each man will continue the fight until these saddle tramps are stretched out in the street."

"Yeah, sir," Huckmyer said. "You just blow the whistle, Lieutenant."

Beeman had all the time watched Frank Skinner. "Any time Mister Skinner is ready, Sergeant."

"By God, don't think I'll back down!" Skinner roared, and ran toward Beeman. His men jumped the hitch rails and stormed into the street, yelling, whooping, and setting up a big commotion. Skinner reached Beeman first, and, in his eagerness, he missed with a looping swing. Beeman went under it, came up inside, and made a piston of his fist. He hit Skinner squarely between the eyes, and the blow stopped the man cold. He looked at Beeman for an instant, his eyes round and glazed, then he made a precise half turn and fell motionless in the dust.

The street was a-crawl with struggling men. A few of them wrestled, but most of them danced about, swinging, ducking, looking for openings. One of the soldiers went down, but he got right up again. The cowboys were beginning to drop and stay dropped. Beeman, turning, searching out another opponent, saw Huckmyer knock one man completely off his feet.

The man crashed to the street and did not stir.

Dust from the scuffling boots was getting so thick that it cut off the view from the sidewalk, and a fraternity of bold souls crowded out into the street for a closer look. Beeman took a blow over the eye that made his head ring. He hit his man twice, once in the body and once on the jaw. He saw him go down.

Someone jumped on Beeman's back, looping blows at him, and he hunched himself, threw the man over his shoulder, and leaped a-straddle of him. He hit him several times, hard, and, when the man grew still, Beeman got off him and looked around for some other infidel to slay.

He saw that the fighting had tapered off sharply. Only Huckmyer and Sergeant Geer were busy. In another moment Huckmyer downed his man and went to the sergeant's aid. But the cowboy made a dash for the walk, and the sergeant, remembering his orders, went after him. He caught him against the drugstore wall and hammered him senseless, then dragged him back to the street, and pitched him headlong among his friends.

The dust was beginning to settle, and Beeman put on his glasses and looked at his detail. They were a sorry sight, with torn uniforms, bleeding lips and faces. They were dirty from rolling in the street. But they stood, by God! They weaved, some of them, but they stood! It was a sight he believed he would always remember, his first clear-cut victory over any-thing.

Skinner and a few of his men were trying to sit up. Beeman said: "Sergeant, bring Mister Skinner here. Don't be ceremonial about it."

Huckmyer, a man who took orders seriously, had a private help him, and they dragged Skinner by the scruff of the neck and held him that way while Beeman had his say.

"Look around you, Mister Skinner. You've just had your ass whipped. And that can be repeated, if this lesson fails to soak in. Do you understand me?" Skinner glared but said nothing, and Beeman gave him a stern frown. "Sergeant Huckmyer, see if you can't get some kind of response from Mister Skinner."

The cowboys were getting up and stood scattered about without a leader. Their inclination was to get out of the street, but they couldn't bring themselves to run outright. So they stood there and watched Sergeant Huckmyer cuff Skinner across the face.

"Better speak sharp, mister," Huckmyer advised. "The lieutenant's got a mean streak in him."

Skinner nodded and said: "I heard you." He kept staring at Beeman. "The next time. . . ."

"Really? What next time?" Beeman laughed dryly. "You fool, the next time will be with a bullet. Now get your men out of town. Stay out of Army and Indian agency business."

"This isn't the end of it," Skinner said, shaking off Huckmyer's grip.

"Look around you," Beeman suggested. "Look at these people watching you, Mister Skinner. They found out something today. That you could be licked, and licked hard. This is the end of one brand telling another brand what to do. The Army put you down in the street today, Mister Skinner. Continue your ways and, by God, we'll put you out of the territory or in the ground."

Beeman stood there with his men around him, and Skinner tried to stare him down, then he suddenly turned, made a cut with his hand, and went to his horse, his men following him quickly. They mounted up and wheeled in the street, kicking up dust. It seemed for a moment that they meant to run down Beeman and his troops. But Beeman said:

"Unflap holsters." The thought in Skinner's mind vanished, and he turned with his men and rode rapidly down the street.

It was over, but Beeman had difficulty controlling the tremble in his voice. "Sergeant, take the detail to the stable yard and get cleaned up at the watering trough. We can't have the United States Army look like street brawlers."

This brought a ripple of laughter out of them, and the men left the scene. A man approached Beeman, notebook in hand. "Name's Cassidy. Run the local paper. I never thought I'd live to see the day when Skinner would leave town a whipped man."

"Did anyone here ever try?" He curbed his irritation. "I meant to fix no blame. Now, if you'll excuse me?"

"Do you spell your name, B-e-a. . . ."

"Two e's," Beeman said, nodding pleasantly before walking on down to the stable yard. His men were stripped to the waist and were cleaning up, and, when they saw him coming, one said: "Hey, here's Mister Beeman."

"Right in here, Mister Beeman. We saved a place for you."

"Let me take your cap and shirt, Mister Beeman."

Laughter from all of them.

Someone slapped him on the back, and someone else took his arm and clasped it briefly. Beeman hurriedly masked his emotion by splashing water over his face and sputtering.

Nothing could compare to this moment, not even his graduation from the Academy, or his marriage, or the birth of his first child. He supposed the followers of Cæsar knew this feeling. It must have sailed with Leif Erickson. It was a bond between men, equal men, proven men. He would always remember them, their names, this moment.

About the Author

Will Cook is the author a numerous outstanding Western novels as well as historical frontier fiction. He was born in Richmond, Indiana, but was raised by an aunt and uncle in Cambridge, Illinois. He joined the U. S. cavalry at the age of sixteen but was disillusioned because horses were being eliminated through mechanization. He transferred to the U. S. Army Air Force in which he served in the South Pacific during the Second World War. Cook turned to writing in 1951 and contributed a number of outstanding short stories to *Dime Western* and other pulp magazines as well as fiction for major smooth-paper magazines such as *The Saturday Evening Post*. It was in the *Post* that "Comanche Captives" was serialized. It was later filmed as *Two Rode Together* (Columbia, 1961) directed by John Ford and starring James Stewart and Richard Widmark. That serial has now been included, as was the author's intention, as an integral part of A SAGA OF TEXAS. Along with his steady productivity Cook maintained an enviable quality. His novels range widely in time and place, from the Illinois frontier of 1811 to southwest Texas in 1905, but each is peopled with credible and interesting characters whose interactions form the backbone of his narratives. Many of his novels deal with more or less traditional Western themes—range wars, reformed outlaws, cattle rustling, Indian fighting—but there are also exercises in historical realism such as THE RAIN TREE (Five Star Westerns, 1996). A common feature in all of Will Cook's fiction is the compassion he has for his characters who must be able to survive in a wild and violent land. His protagonists make mistakes, hurt people they care for, and sometimes succumb to ignoble impulses, but this all provides an added dimension to the artistry of his work.